WISPS OF GOLD

WISPS OF GOLD

Leah Lindeman

Lindeman Publishing House

For James

You not only love me, you respect me.
We are equals, lovers, partners in crime,
husband and wife till death do us part.

PROLOGUE

Dearest Rose, *May 3, 1871*

It's been six months since I last wrote to you. Much has changed...words fail me. I know my previous letter was vague and nondescript. Business affairs haven't given me much time for anything else. If my silence has caused you to wilt or to harbour a deep resentment toward your last living parent, I am sorry. I promise you, you will be happy with the surprise I have waiting for you once you arrive home.

I hope you haven't persisted in creating a little chaos and mischief at Angela College. Has your class yet seen Victoria's hub of established mining industry? I suggested the outing to Miss Craig some time ago because I don't believe girls should be cooped in stuffy classrooms all day. Of course, you'll conjure some nonsense to liven things up.

At the end of June when school is done, I will send a man to you with a sealed letter. By that letter, you'll know he'll be the one to bring you home. I pray you will be able to weather the hazards you will certainly face on the journey. God speed.

Your most loving father,

Harland Wood

She was not really bad at heart,
But only rather rude and wild;
She was an aggravating child.
Hilaire Belloc
Rebecca

Chapter 1

"Well, what did the letter contain?" A cream-white hand curled around the creaking pine door. The lightest of footsteps traversed the length of the square room—a hand upon a hard shoulder. "Rose?"

"Oh, Priscilla, forgive me. I was so…caught up with the contents."

"Which are?"

Rose thrust out the letter. "Here, you read it."

"I cannot. This is your father's letter to you."

"Read it." Rose shoved the piece of paper toward Priscilla's face. "No, wait!" She laid the letter in her lap and folded her hands.

"I'm not sure…"

Rose rolled her eyes. Mock regret dripped from her lips as she said, "It was very unladylike of me to hand it to you like so. If Miss Craig were present, she'd be very pleased to give me a lecture on proper handling of paper and such nonsense."

1

"It is not..."

"I know *you* don't think it's nonsense. Just let me do it again." She brusquely cleared her throat. "Miss White, would you be so kind as to peruse the contents of my letter?"

"I will even though your mockery is uncalled for."

"So long as you aren't a tattler." Rose settled as comfortably as she could in her worn chair, the slats' edges biting into her aching back.

Priscilla's baby blue eyes watered. Suddenly, she let out a giggle and said, "If your father only knew what kind of pranks you've pulled in the time it took for you to receive this letter!"

"Yes, I know I'm incredibly clever. Now keep reading."

As Priscilla returned the letter, her pale lips twisted into a pucker. "How odd!"

"How many times have you received a letter from your family in the last year?"

"About fifteen."

"This and the previous one were the only ones I ever received from my father in the last five years." Bitterness coated Rose's tongue.

"Rose, I'm sure he has...his reasons. Did you see he mentioned a surprise?" Priscilla's placating tone annoyed Rose a degree more than she already was.

"I don't know what to think. I'm tired of waiting and learning. I want to put on my bonnet and gloves and get out."

"Our outing to Victoria's parks is not yet another week."

"I know." Rose's chocolate eyes glimmered with wild glee.

"Oh, no, I won't be a part of this...scheme you're cooking up. What are you going to do? Run away?"

"Of course not. I haven't the means. However, I will slip in and out, just for the day."

"And miss all your classes?" Priscilla asked, flabbergasted.

"You call sewing, etiquette, and embroidering cushions classes? Those skills may suit many young ladies

2

back home on the continent, but not here! Why, what will we do when we're done finishing school?"

"I would like to marry."

"So would I! However, I'll need to learn a whole lot more if I want to be of any use to a husband in these parts. Think about it. What kind of men settle here?"

"Is this a trick question?" The lines of Priscilla's forehead knit together, the canopy heavy and unflattering. Her skin was as white as cream skimmed from the milk jug. Her baby cheeks had never grown lean.

"I will tell you. You either find a young man, eager for adventure and ready to dig for gold, or you find the old frump who's body is decaying on the spot and lives in riches because he happened to come across a rich vein a few years ago."

"So?"

Rose pushed herself off her chair and stomped. "My point exactly! The young man isn't going to want a frivolous young wife who only knows how to sew as you do, and I'm sure you don't want to marry a man who's thirty years your senior!"

"I see. My only fate is to marry the old frump. No handsome young man will ever want me according to you. Please excuse me." Priscilla smoothed her sea-foam skirts as she rose from the bed.

"Oh, Priscilla, I didn't mean…surely you don't think…"

"It's exactly what you meant. I've been your friend for five years. I know you better than anyone else does, even more than your father does, goodnight."

"Don't you dare drag…"

The door closed as quietly as it had been opened. The floorboards hardly murmured against Priscilla's weight.

She's right, and I know it.

Sighing, Rose plopped onto her bed, stomach first, and buried her face into the thin quilt. She wished she could roar at the walls, but the scandalous noise would travel through the floors until it reached the headmistress's ears. If the headmistress didn't hear it, the teachers would certainly give her a thrashing of hostile words.

God, how did I become like this?

Her windowpane was speckled with raindrops, sliding until they dropped and lost their melancholy form. Why did she feel the same? She was sliding away and away until she would break. And then what?

"Why be so sad when I can plan my escape?" Her full lips curved into a small smile.

Priscilla will come back. She always does.

The next morning, an hour before the students were to awaken, she slipped out of the covers and quickly dressed in her town attire. Being shabbily dressed in her school dress would just incite derision from any passerby in the street. Perhaps a well-meaning lawman would kindly escort her back to where she desperately didn't want to be.

She gently tugged on her black-laced gloves. Next, she placed her burgundy bonnet atop her pinned-up hair. No one would think she was a schoolgirl now.

"Whew…ready."

This was the first time she had ever attempted any sort of escape from this well-established school. The outside world, its tantalizing promises of adventure appearing as a mirage in her mind, beckoned to her as she quietly opened her door and tiptoed out. A couple maids were already awake dusting and sweeping floors.

Rose tried to stifle a giggle as she twirled down the wooden corridors past a few crouching backs. She rounded a corner and knocked into Lily, the assistant cook. Rose swung her right hand behind her back; for in her hand, she held her black pumps. She had taken them off from the beginning to aid her in her stealth.

"Oh, I'm so, so sorry ma'am. I…"

"Sh, no need to wake the girls. There is nothing for which to apologize."

"Pardon me for askin', but what are you doin' here at the school at this ungodly hour?"

Rose quipped as she walked backward down the hallway, "Well, I had to personally deliver a parcel to the headmistress intended for my daughter. Now if you'll excuse me."

As soon as she reached the end of the hall, the main entrance room was just a hand's stretch away.

"But ma'am, the headmistress ain't woken up yet. Why ain't your shoes on? Wait! Is that.... You little...Headmistress!" Lily hollered.

Rose, grinning, fiddled with putting on her pumps. Rustling and bustling noises from within the girls' dormitories intensified. Many of them started poking their heads out into the hallway. Once her pumps were on, she bounded down the steps two at a time, raced to jiggle the front door's handle, and burst out the front door.

The heavy glow of dawn warmed her face. Fuelled by the brisk wind, she propelled herself around the corner of the sleepy street and doubled over laughing. Even from this distance, she could hear the teachers shouting and demanding answers from the cowering Lily.

If only Priscilla could see me now. This is my best one yet!

Rose smoothed the faint wrinkles in her striped burgundy and black dress and strolled west toward the city and the beginning noises of industry. Angela College was situated in a respectable residential neighbourhood east of downtown Victoria and the Inner Harbour.

Five minutes into her walk, the whistles of a steamship rang in her ears. As she turned off Courtney Street and north onto Government Street, she could see bleary-eyed miners a couple blocks ahead lumbering into the Hudson Bay Company, the Royal Bank, and various other shops. Rose eyed a man coming out of the local grocers shop carrying an assortment of mining tools and canned food in a large crate. He swaggered toward the harbour. His eyes burned with a hunger for gold.

Rose had never before been in such invigorating company nor amongst such a large number, even when she had lived in her homeland of England. After her mother's death when she was three, her father, preferring to hole himself away in his country estate, had barely ventured into London again. He only visited the city when he had a pressing business matter to attend to, and that was not often. He had never invited her to go with him.

She donned her confidence and made sure that no bystander could ever believe she had a small amount of jitters strolling amongst strangers. She also made sure her footing was secure although the angular wooden porches and the mud-clumped roads from the previous day's rain proved the doing of this task to be quite a hassle. No matter the cost, she was determined no man would look down upon her and tell her to go running to her needle and thread.

As she passed the groups of men, their gazes locked upon her and her womanly figure. She returned their attentions by batting her eyelashes before coyly turning away to look at the goods in the shopkeepers' windows.

One grimy man with straggly hair in his forties elbowed his companion and crowed, "I'm going to have a mighty fine time here if all the women look like that."

An older gentleman clapped his hand upon Percy's outside cheek and swung Percy's head forward. "Shut up, Percy! We're here to find gold. Your excitement for…play time is irritating at best. Now look straight and focus."

As long as I stay away from…Percy—ugh, what a name!—I'll be all right.

After she passed a few more buildings, the door from the Hudson Bay Company, just a few paces ahead, swung open. A tinkling bell sounded. A man in his late twenties stepped out. His demeanour was quite different from most of the crass men she had seen parading around town. His wavy black hair, long enough to touch the tips of his ears, was exquisitely combed. It shone in the light of the rising sun. His black boots matched his hair although they were slightly speckled with mud. His clothes were coated with a fine cologne. She almost swooned as he passed her. As she stared at this handsome creature, he acknowledged her in return by tipping his hat and flashing a dapper smile. She stepped closer and closer, he, crossing the street and growing the distance between them…

Suddenly, a brunt force sent her tripping upon her skirts. She careened into one of the porch's posts. "What on earth…?" Her head snapped up to see who or what had happened.

"Sorry, I…" The man ground to a stop and looked her way. He outstretched his hand toward her in a placating manner and breathed out another "sorry" before racing toward the man who had caught her special attention. "Mr. Shaw, I don't think Sam meant to..."

A few middle-aged men gathered around her to help straighten her out.

"Thank you, oh, you are so kind. I…yes, that's my bonnet." Flustered, she beamed a charming smile to her aids just so that they would leave her be. "Excuse me. I must be getting on my way, good day."

They waved her off as she strode west toward the beach, clutching her skirts in a tight fist. A few curls fell loose from their perch atop her head. Her slipping hair style was no matter. She was too preoccupied with threatening tears blurring her vision. She excessively blinked to try to see what was in front of her.

She passed rows upon rows of newcomers' tents. As her welling tears subsided, she looked toward the water to see some men packing up their tents and provisions. A man, wearing nothing but long johns flapped open his tent and started shaving his scruffy beard.

She came to a quiet spot along the water, past the decks and incoming ships, past the miners' conversations and guffaws. She stepped to the water's edge to see her reflection. What a mess! Her bonnet, off to the side, was dragging down the bun of curls she had crafted. She quickly untied her bonnet, withdrew the pins from her hair, and shook out her raven tresses. As she finished setting her hair to rights and pinching her cheeks, a slow movement to her right caught her attention. Slightly bent at the waist, she turned her head to see a doe hesitantly moving to the water's edge. Closer and closer the doe edged while cautiously looking at Rose.

What are you doing here? This isn't fresh water.

Rose remained still, watching for those lips to touch the ocean and be revolted by the salt.

Instead, the doe drank and drank.

"Stop! Shoo! It's not fresh…." She looked back toward civilization to see if *anybody* could do something. She was too far for anyone to notice. She spun on her heel to chase it away; but the doe was gone!

She blinked a couple of times and looked for it in every direction.

I know I saw it. Why did it drink even though this water is its poison?

She peered at the water and saw, not her reflection, but the doe's. A blink—her reflection returned. Her hand trailed down the side of her face.

Why do I seek poison?

Returning to the centre of town, she kept a considerable distance between herself and the men's encampment. On this stroll, she took no notice of the shops or men but gazed into the dust swirling beneath her boots. All the industrial noises, which had so fascinated her before, blended into one harsh flow of grating. As she passed by an alley, a hand reached out and grabbed her sleeve. Another hand clamped upon her lips. She struggled to think a coherent thought. Whoever the man was, he was burly and smelled atrociously of some hard liquor.

"Hey there, little missy, I saw you out walkin' a little time before. You sure looked mighty fine in yare high state. I think I be likin' you better with your hair down long just like so. Now, now, no fightin' back." He dragged her to the end of the alley and pushed her against the wall. "Ah, now ya remember me. I knew you looked my way. That's right. I'm Percy, the fool who couldn't shut up about you." His free hand slid down her waist and started to pull up her skirts.

Rose's eyes roamed wildly, seeking for an escape. She tried to push against his repulsive body with no avail. She worked her mouth open enough to bite on any skin of his she could. A yelp escaped his lips. Suddenly, a fist boxed him in the ear. Percy fell to the side, his clothes all crumpled and dusty.

Rose inhaled and exhaled heavily while trying to right her skirts. Her fingers fumbled so much that the outer skirt was still exposing her undergarments.

"Here allow me." A man's hands reached for her holstered hemline.

"No, don't…" She cowered against the wall.

"Miss, I'm not going to hurt you. Please let me help."

She searched for her rescuer's face. All she saw was the little stubble along his jaw line as he bent down. A dark brown cowboy's hat hid all facial features.

His hands gently searched through the folds of her white petticoat. She looked down to see him trying to steer clear of any unintentional touching of her thigh. The hemline was now being let down. He held out his hand for her to take.

"Thank you. I'm sorry…"

"Sorry? Why are you apologizing? None of this was your fault. That man's got no right to even be living."

That voice…his build. Rose asked, "Have I ever made your acquaintance?"

He took one step closer, hands on his hips, his head cocked to the side. His eyes roved from the peeps of her boots up to her eyes. His eyes widened as his lips formed a silent *O*.

She put her hand to her forehead and said, "Ah! Now I remember! You sent me careening into one of the posts outside the Hudson Bay down the street. What kind of man are you?"

A frown replaced his guilt-ridden features. "Excuse me? I just saved your…dignity!"

"That's right, you did now. Earlier this morning, you didn't properly apologize for making me look like a fool."

"Oh, so it's not about any physical injuries. It's about your pride, miss…"

She crossed her arms. "You're no gentleman."

He smirked, "Maybe I'm not. What are you doing out of your fancy home anyway?"

"How dare…you…good day!" She stomped off until she reached the opening of the street. She realized she must look extremely dishevelled. She turned a half circle to her right then hesitated, boring her gaze into the wooden building. She slinked back to her rescuer. She cleared her throat and said, "Would you happen to have a looking glass or know where I could find one?"

"I do."

"Which?!"

"Well, I have a mind to let you buy your own, but since I'm a gentleman and since you probably have no money of your own…I have a looking glass."

As she rolled her eyes, a chortle escaped her throat. "You do?"

"Why are you so surprised?"

She looked down her nose at him. "Men don't strike me as the kind to look at themselves for long periods of time."

"What an insult! We all don't look half as bad as this man does." He jerked his thumb toward Percy. He bent to retrieve something from the inside of his boot. "Here, it's small. Don't take hours trying to find your whole face at one time."

"I just need five minutes!" She viewed her hair at different angles, trying to figure out where she would pin her hair. She started to pin a strand when a hand touched her arm. She jumped.

"I'm sorry." He retracted his hand. "I didn't mean to…. Don't. Your hair looks…good just the way it is."

Her hand holding the looking glass came down. She then turned it toward her dress to see whether any buttons had become undone and whether her skirts were fully covering her lower body. "Thank you. Why do *you* need to use a looking glass?"

He flipped out his razor. "I use it to shave."

"Well, in that case, I think you have more need of it than I do."

He slid it back into his boot.

"Why do you keep it in your boot?"

"Some of us enjoy the fact we look good. I like to keep it handy."

"Don't flatter yourself too much. You might be disappointed one day."

His arms crossed, he chuckled.

"Thank you again for…" She glanced toward the busy street, eager to be done with this awkward encounter, "good day."

"Wait, miss. I do want to apologize for having barrelled you into the post. I just…I…I didn't realize you were there until it was too late. Please forgive me for my…impertinence." He mock-bowed.

"Perhaps I will, perhaps not." Restored to her good spirits from the sarcastic banter with her rescuer, she strode out of the alley and into the street.

***

Hours later, she opened the ominous school's door. She hoped no one would catch her in the entrance. Unfortunately, a maid was just walking into the entrance when Rose slipped through.

The maid strode toward Rose. "Miss, you are wanted in the headmistress's office."

"I know. No need to escort me. I know the way."

"I'm sure you do." The maid eyed and followed her until she saw Rose open the door with the headmistress's bronze-tinted name plate.

Rose entered and cast a hesitant look upon the bent form of Miss Craig scribbling a lengthy word upon a pad of paper. She rolled her eyes as she took her *favourite* seat in the whole building.

"Don't roll your eyes at me, young miss. I know everything you do."

"I don't think…"

Miss Craig still didn't look up as she accused, "I know you're the one who put glue on one of the girl's seats last week causing her to ruin her perfectly good dress. This week, you barred a group of girls in their dormitory by placing a chair under the doorknob, making them miss their watercolours class. Perhaps, I'm not the only one who is privy to your secret pranks."

Rose put out a placating hand. "No one else…"

Miss Craig's head snapped up. "Leave Priscilla White out of your disgrace. She's a capable girl with a bright future ahead of her. She could go on to be a teacher, or answer the highest calling a woman can, motherhood. You, on the other hand…"

"I know the lectures."

Miss Craig breathed in through her nose. "Yes, you do. You are *the* regular visitor to this office. The term is almost over. I have no more time to give lectures on all subjects which annoy you."

Rose gave a sickeningly sweet smile. "Then why am I here?"

"To appeal to your moral compass."

Rose waved the appeal off. "My moral compass is broken."

"It can always be renewed. I ask you to take care, to think before you act. Your foolish mistakes may injure others, as well. The one thing you are blinded by will cut you deeply in the end."

"Why are you telling me this? You don't even like me."

Miss Craig replied swiftly, "Of course I do."

Rose crossed her arms, "Really? I find that impossible to believe. I've been your number one target since you arrived here."

"Do you know why? Let me explain myself. You remind me a lot of myself when I was a young girl. Headstrong, feisty, taking chances."

Rose asked nonchalantly, "What happened?"

Miss Craig's sky-blue eyes darkened to a tempestuous ocean blue. "Sorrow."

Rose was caught off guard by the sincerity with which Miss Craig released this sensitive and personal information. "I see."

"No, you don't see. I like these things about you. However, you walk a very fine line. Lose your balance, and you will plummet. Keep them in check." With a blank face, she looked down and started writing. "That is all."

Rose swallowed hard, "Miss Craig? I appreciate your honesty."

"That and the labour of love to this institution is all I have to give." Miss Craig's voice, far-sounding and hollow, haunted her all the way to her room. Rose had never seen the headmistress show an ounce of vulnerability.

She scraped her chair backward against the floor. She sat—the overwhelming silence resounded in her mind.

Sorrow. What kind of sorrow had made Miss Craig lose all the vigour she'd been given at birth? Sorrow. Rose had already experienced some sorrow. But were they really sorrows compared to *the* sorrow Miss Craig hinted at. What was it?

Rose looked around her room. There was no note. The bed had no creases. Priscilla had not come to reconcile.

What to do now?

She couldn't go to Priscilla. Priscilla had several roommates. What a sight it would be for those other girls to see her crawling back to the only person who could stand her presence and dare love her! No, she would wait. Angry with her father, estranged from Priscilla, there was only one thing she could do. Write a due paper upon the historical implications of Great Britain's end to slave trade.

It's my fault that this is the only thing I have to do with my time tonight. This is going to be a long week.

***

After a fitful night, Rose jerked her upper body from her comfortable mattress. Her dark amber eyes squinted in pain as they were met by the sun's morning glare. She closed her eyes and saw red. Slowly, she opened them once again to see dust motes dancing in the light.

Having dressed, washed her face, brushed her hair, and put on her shoes, she headed toward the dining room for breakfast. She stood in line with the other girls and swivelled her head from side to side looking for Priscilla. The line started to move forward and on to the buffet table where they were greeted with porridge and sugar on the side to sprinkle (all girls were allowed a teaspoon and no more). As she sat down, she spotted a crown of golden hair near the wall opposite her. Priscilla was sitting with seven other girls laughing and smiling in such a lady-like fashion.

Rose chose a seat amongst some younger girls who gawked over the newest shoes some girl's father had bought her. Rose sneaked a peek underneath the table.

Not bad, but it's not the latest fashion.

Although she prided herself on excelling with whatever small mathematics and sciences they were taught, she did appreciate a good sense of fashion.

She looked at Priscilla once more and found Priscilla looking back at her. Rose offered a tentative smile and waved, her hand slightly seen over the table's top. Priscilla merely turned her head and resumed her conversation with her other friends.

Throughout English, music, drawing, watercolour, and singing classes, Priscilla would not turn her head toward Rose.

The bond between the two friends weakened day by day.

At last, the day came for all the pupils to take a turn at Beacon Hill Park, south of the city. Rose had been feeling extremely cooped all week, especially since loneliness ate at her like a persistent disease. She took great pains to look perfect. The upper half of her hair was pinned in curls while she let the lower half flow to her waist. She gingerly put on her black-lace gloves and clutched her lace parasol at her side.

The hallway bell rang, signalling to the students they were expected downstairs promptly. The girls were divided into three groups. The younger were with one teacher, the middle-grade girls were with another, and the older ones were undertaken by Miss Craig.

The girls stood still until the doors to the outside world slowly opened before them. As they descended the outdoor stairs, at once a crescendo of giggles and hushed voices burst from the girls. Miss Craig, in one turn with a raised eyebrow and lips in a straight line, brought down the uprising in the girls' soaring hearts.

After a fifteen minute walk, they arrived at the Beacon Hill Park. Rose, bored with not talking to anyone, decided to "accidentally" bump into Priscilla. She weaved her way through little clumps of chatting girls, surprised to see Priscilla alone. Rose touched her arm.

Priscilla immediately spun and fiercely embraced her friend. "I'm sorry that I've been upset with you for so long. I realize grudges do not become me."

Rose breathed a sigh of relief. "I've missed you. I'm ashamed of the way I spoke to you last time. Sometimes I don't think before I speak."

Priscilla frowned.

"All right, maybe much more often than sometimes. I don't think you're petty. And..."

"Shall we continue walking while we discuss this? Everyone else is moving on."

"Yes."

The girls linked arms and trotted a little to catch up with the main group.

Rose reported, "I have a delicious story to tell you of my adventures in town."

Priscilla giggled. "I've missed your masterful storytelling."

"Well..." Rose told Priscilla of her topple after seeing the intriguing Mr. Shaw and then of her ordeal in the alley. Only her moments by the ocean did she keep to herself. Rose's trust was hard to come by, and she believed some thoughts, the truest ones, should be kept to oneself.

"Rose, your virtue—you could have lost..."

"I know. I cannot tell you how I wish I could have taken away my earlier parading around so that I wouldn't have come so close to losing something I hadn't realized I wanted to keep. He saved me, and I'm extremely grateful."

"Yes...that part must have been excruciatingly pleasant. I am indebted to him for saving you."

Rose shook her head. "Oh, I don't think I'll be seeing him again."

"And Mr. Shaw?"

"He might be a different story.... He was quite something—made me speechless!" Rose's cheeks turned pink at the thought.

"I would love to catch a glimpse of him!"

"Perhaps someday..."

On the right-hand side of their path was a line of trees. For a moment the line was broken by a small clearing, and that's when they saw him...with a lady upon his arm. His looks were impeccably groomed just as Rose remembered. As Rose stared with her mouth slightly open, Mr. Shaw looked her way. He made a double look, winked her way, and tipped his hat. Obviously, she had made an impression upon him just as he had upon her.

She smiled and waved. "Look! That's him!"

His companion tugged on his arm to grab his attention.

After flashing a wicked grin, he reluctantly turned his head toward his companion.

"That was Mr. Shaw," Rose cocked her head toward the other side of the trees.

"My, Rose, how exciting! He's viciously handsome. He seems to quite like you."

"You can't tell from a glance!"

Priscilla squeezed her arm. "We shall see."

***

The last two weeks of term were spent on preparing for examinations. To make sure she passed all the criteria so she could leave for good, Rose temporarily gave up any rambunctious pranks. Once exams were done and they were awarded appropriately, it was time to return to their homes.

Rose dragged her ornate trunk from the corner of her room and gently opened it. She grabbed her dresses from the closet in one armful and dropped them upon the bed. She was going home.

I don't even know what home is.

Knock, knock.

Rose called out, "Come in."

Priscilla entered. "I'm all packed. Would you like some help?"

"No, thank you. I'm trying to make the process as long as I can."

"I thought you couldn't wait to leave."

16

Rose slowly folded each dress, packed each shoe, padded each set of papers into her trunk until she was done.

Priscilla sat down. "I think you're done now, Rose."

"I do want to leave, but I don't want to see *him*. Tomorrow's the day when we leave this...place. I don't seem to have the heart to jest about it at present. So strange..."

"Rose, may I pray with you, for you?"

"Priscilla, I think not."

"You may think He's forgotten you, but I know He hasn't."

"How do you know?"

"Well, how can He forget when I talk to Him about you everyday?"

"You do have a point."

"Father, thank you for having brought Rose and me to the finality of our studies here at Angela College. We ask that You bring us safely to our homes, and that the bond of our friendship shall never fail. Amen."

"Amen," Rose whispered as she lay on her side on her bed. "Will I ever see you again?"

"I pray we will. If ever you're in Barkerville, that's where I'll be with my family. I'll see you tomorrow, goodnight."

"Goodnight."

As Rose exchanged her school dress for her nightgown, a few tears slipped down her cheeks and wet the pillow as she lay her head down.

God, I don't feel at home anywhere. I'm scared, and I hate to admit it.

The next morning, thunderclouds roiled overhead. The wind, strong and gusty, carried away the green leaves from their safe holds. As Rose looked out her window, a sudden onslaught of rain slapped her window and slid down the brick walls of Angela College. Not being able to stay in her room and watch the dreary show, she wandered the halls. The other girl's doors were slightly ajar, and Rose could hear some of the frantic responses to the storm within.

"What am I to do? My dress and hair will be ruined if I set one foot outside the school! I don't have an umbrella. And my trunks?"

"You won't have to carry your trunks," the companion to the ridiculous girl replied. "Your father's servants will take them out for you."

"I know that. But they'll get wet anyway! These are brand new trunks. Ugh!"

A smirk came to Rose's lips.

I'm a lot more level-headed than that.

Rose came to Priscilla's door and knocked. There was no answer. "Priscilla, I know you're in there." Still no answer. She turned the knob to find the room spotless and Priscilla's bed made. On it was a note. She started to open it when footsteps crossed the threshold.

"Prisci…Oh, hello." A short girl with straggly blond hair and freckles all over her face hesitated to come in. "I'm Ann."

"Oh, yes, you were Priscilla's roommate."

"Yes."

"Where is she?" Rose asked still holding the unread note.

"She left early."

"Why?"

"I don't know. It looked as if she were in a hurry. It also looked as if she'd been crying."

Rose barrelled out of the room and stomped to her own to read the letter alone. She sat hunched upon her bed as she read the rushed handwriting.

Dear Rose,

I'm so sorry to leave without saying goodbye. I'll inquire in town as to your father's whereabouts and write to you again, I promise.

Your dear friend,

Priscilla

Strange. Priscilla never writes sloppily. She is too diligent. Something must be wrong.

Rose reread the unusual letter. She crumpled it and threw it into her valise. As she paced, a heavy knock arrested her attention. "Yes?" She threw open the door to find a rugged mountaineer standing behind one of the maids. His hat hung low over his brow, and his boots were a clouded leather. A small trail of mud could be seen behind him.

The maid's nose crinkled as she said, "Miss, this…this man said that he was here— although I don't believe a word he says— to bring you back to your father. How could a well-meaning gentleman such as your father let you go off..."

"It's all right. I'll speak with him."

"But Miss..."

"Do you have a letter for me? From my father?" Rose directed the question to the stranger.

"Yes, miss. I do." He reached into his green grey coat and pulled out a slightly crinkled and browned envelope.

"Thank you." Rose picked it up with only her thumb and index finger careful not to touch his large, wet hand.

Dear Rose,

You cannot know how excited I am to see you come home soon. I'm sure the man standing in front of you is not what you expected, but he is able and the best at what he does. He will divulge to you the hardships you may face on your route. I pray you will be safe in his care.

Your loving father,

Harland Wood

"So, you are the man who is to bring me home alive or dead?"

"Yes, miss."

"Of course. Shall we?"

"Miss, have you gone mad?" the maid gasped.

"No, I believe my father has, excuse me." Rose walked toward the one wooden trunk and pointed to it. "This is the only thing I possess. I expect we can manage?"

"Yes miss."

"All right then, shall we?" She led the way downstairs. Without one backward glance, she stepped over the entrance threshold of the school and out into the rain, which had gone from tempest to drizzle over the last few minutes. Rose desperately wanted to turn her head around and find one familiar face. Yet she was too stubborn to admit that, perhaps, school could be more comforting at present than the unknown ahead.

The mountaineer stomped around her skirts as he hoisted the trunk into the back of the cart. He heaved one side of the trunk into the cart and then the other.

Thank goodness, I have nothing fragile.

"Miss?"

She cleared her throat. "Do we not have transportation with a covering?"

He shook his head. "Sorry, miss."

Although she had jested about another girl's folly earlier, the drops of rain were shards of ice, numbing her mind even more than it already was. "What's your name?"

"Joe, miss."

"Joe, let's leave before I change my mind."

Chapter 2

Believe me, my young friend, there is
nothing—absolutely nothing—half so much worth
doing as simply messing about in boats.
Kenneth Grahame

By the time Rose and Joe reached the Victoria Hotel
(the only hotel in town made of brick) Rose and her clothing
were drenched. She shivered. Her bones ached from the cold
minutes into the drive. The wind ripped through the air with a
fierceness she had not seen in a long time. The silence which
existed between Rose and Joe was calm, not awkward in the
least. Surely her father didn't expect her to converse with him,
save for knowing how to survive the journey. The rain
slapping against the wooden boards of the cart and the wooden
walkways in town sounded as the dull beating of a drum. The
way the dirt turned to mud in a matter of minutes—the
destruction a heavy rainfall could exact brought Rose to a
deeper understanding of how short her life just might be.
    "Whoa! Whoa! Easy." Joe let go of the reins and
placed them on the bottom of the cart. Joe went round to the
back and carried her trunk to the door of the hotel.
    Rose waited for him to lend her a hand, but when he
left the cart, she decided to jump out on her own. She gripped
her water-soaked habit and went down with a couple slips,
desperately trying to hold onto the edge of the cart. As her feet

hit the ground, mud engulfed the first couple inches of her boots. She slugged toward the hotel entrance, found beneath the farthest arch to the right, and tried to wipe the wet mud off her soles by scratching them down the edge of the wooden walkway. What a sodden mess she'd make going into the finest hotel in Victoria (although it could only boast six rooms)!

As soon as she opened the door, the warm glow from the inside beckoned her to enter. It was a beacon of comfort in the midst of darkness. Lunch was being served. The smell was so enticing that Rose was tempted to eat without changing into dry clothing. Joe came stomping in, shaking off whatever rain drops were dripping down his rain jacket. Many of the drops spattered onto Rose's face. The receptionist and Rose both cringed. They dared not say a word for fear Joe would unleash any fiery temper his mountain-bear figure seemed to possess.

Joe swayed his shoulders and, with leaden feet, approached the front desk. "We need two rooms, one for the lady and one for myself."

The receptionist licked his lips and fearfully raised his eyebrows. His oily hair glimmered in the dim light of the table lamp before him. "Which, uh, kind of rooms would you like?"

"Look at the young, miss. Do you know who her father is? He's Harland Wood."

"I'm sorry, sir, I don't know who he..."

"He's just about one of the richest men up in Cariboo territory. She gets one of your best. Give me whatever's available."

"Yes, sir." The receptionist handed Joe the room keys. Joe huffed, "Good."

"We'll get your bags, sir."

"Thank you," Rose interjected, hoping to save the man from further embarrassment and snivelling. "The accommodations I'm sure will be splendid. Joe, will you escort me to my rooms?"

He grunted in response.

Rose led the way up the stairs.

"Room six for the lady." The first half of the
receptionist's information was a shout which quickly faded to
a whisper once Joe turned to look at him with a scowl.

"Joe!" Rose reprimanded.

"Yes, miss." His voice was strained.

"Leave the poor man alone. How did you come into
the possession of so much money?"

"How do you mean?"

"Well, I'm sure you could not easily afford a room to
which you are now escorting me. You seem to be a simple
man with no need for extravagant pleasures."

"Your father is a generous man."

Hah, generous with money but not with affection.

"Yes, very."

Down the hall was the room marked six.

"Thank you, Joe." Rose turned the handle and stepped
into the room, decorated in the fashion of the day. Light cream
wallpaper graced the planes of the room. A poster queen-sized
bed stood against the wall farthest from the door. A sprig of
lavender spread its aroma from its place upon the pillow
spread. As she stepped around the perimeter of the room, two
men brought in her trunk, heaving small breaths of exertion.

"Right here, miss?"

"Yes, thank you. Here, for your troubles."

The lead porter, perhaps only a few years older than
she, tipped his hat as a slightly darker flush spread over his
already flushed cheeks. "It was no trouble, miss." The men
bowed out and closed the door.

Although she was famished, her exhaustion was
greater. She changed into a bright blue day dress and then fell
upon her bed. A few squeaks escaped. At last, her damp head
found comfort.

Realizing her hair needed a little drying, she sat up and
grabbed a folded towel near the wash basin. She then
proceeded to take her brush from her handbag and brush the
knots from her hair.

Trepidation rising, her hands searched for an empty
journal she had decided to write within. She had never felt the
need to have one; for Priscilla was always a willing ear to

listen to any of her tales. Now that she wouldn't see her friend for a long time, she decided she needed…another outlet of sorts, however inferior it may be.

I am lonely already….

She huffed, the querulous tones abrasive to her mind. About to tear out the page, another knock sounded on the door.

"Who is it?" Rose called out.

"Joe."

She slammed the infernal journal and opened the door. "Yes, Joe."

"Miss, I'll be going into town to get the last few supplies we'll be needin' on the trip."

Silence…Rose cleared her throat. "Very well, you may go."

"The kitchen staff is done with the lunch hour, but they'll be ready to serve you with whatever you need."

"Thank you, Joe." Sincere gratitude coated her reply.

Joe curtly nodded his head and left.

Surprisingly thoughtful! Perhaps he'll spring a few more surprises on me.

She traipsed down the steps with the grace of a dove. Upon entering the dining hall, she remarked many customers had left. A waiter marked her presence and hastened to seat her near the window. Once she had given her order, she allowed herself to relax her posture somewhat into the natural curvature of the chair. The rain had lessened into a light drizzle which tapped lightly at the window.

The doors to the kitchen swung wide open and out stepped the man who had saved her dignity in the alley almost a month before. Her mouth gaped open, and she quickly grabbed a small menu which had been left upon her table. She couldn't tell if he was upset by the way he had swung open the doors. She peeked a look above the corner of the menu. No, instead, he chuckled and was in a very hearty mood.

He quickly looked round the room and hesitated upon her hidden visage. A second later, his boots continued to cross the wood floor, and the front door *clacked* against its frame.

A little loud, isn't he? Well, I won't have to ever deal with his genteel brusqueness.

Joe was out all afternoon. She reclined upon her bed, intending to take a long nap. Who knew how long it would be before she could receive a good rest on a comfortable mattress once again.

Bang, bang, bang!

Goodness gracious, what a racket!

She stretched her arms over her head and quickly wiped her eyes before answering the door an inch open, her awakening face the only visible part of her. "Joe? What's going on?"

"Miss, it's time to go."

"Time to go...so soon? Isn't it late in the evening?"

"Miss, it's already seven in the morning."

"I slept all night?"

Joe nodded.

"And what about breakfast?"

"I've bought canned beans and salted..."

"Joe, I plan to have a good breakfast before I leave. We can leave the beans until later. Please."

"All right, miss. We should really get an early start. Oh, and..." From behind his back, he produced a bundle of brown material.

"What is this?"

"Your traveling clothes, miss."

"Thank you. I'll be down shortly." She closed the door and laid out the bundle to inspect—a pair of trousers and an overly large brown overcoat covered by a slick coating. As for a blouse, she grabbed one of her white ones from her traveling bag and resigned its fate to becoming forever sullied by all the dirt she was sure it was going to encounter on its journey. Rose was not looking forward to the cramped quarters she was sure to live in and fewer baths she would be able to take during the weeks ahead. Everything in its case and packed away, she marched downstairs, forcing herself to not be embarrassed by wearing men's clothes. She peeked out the window of the front door and saw that Joe had already packed their necessary belongings, except her trunk, into the wagon they would drive to the boat.

Joe returned and asked, "Miss, are you ready?"

"Yes, let's eat." Rose was thankful that only a handful of men were up and sipping some tea with a few biscuits on their plates. However, most of them arched their eyebrows at the sight of her, and many of their eyes glinted in mischief.

Rose and Joe were seated in a corner. Throughout breakfast, Rose savoured every little bite she took of the eggs, bacon, and fresh fruit. She would terribly miss these fine delights. What was the situation at home? Did her father still live in extravagance or had he hardened and settled for the more basic furnishings of life?

With a last look at the hotel, Rose turned toward the wagon and hoisted herself into it.

"Miss…here let me…"

"Joe, you cannot possibly be practical in our voyage and always try to remember what's usually expected of a gentleman. I know you weren't bred for such graces. I am determined to do my part. There will be very little to do in this next stage of my life except be useful. Understand?"

"Yes, miss."

I will not be weak.

"Lead the way, Joe."

And so started the journey, which slowly separated them from civilization and all that she had known for so much of her life.

It was a short drive to the paddle-wheeler. There it lay upon the waters of the Inner Harbour of Victoria as a fat cat lies upon its Persian rug. The *SS Lillooet* could boast of two levels with a small cabin at the top of the stern. Its charcoal coloured chimney rose behind the cabin. Its grandest attribute was its four-ribbed wheel.

As Joe handed their packs to the cabin boys, Rose's breath caught in her throat. Her feet padded toward the wheel. She had the strangest urge to climb its structure and see the world from its top.

"A beauty, isn't it?"

"Oh…" She twirled around to find…him again. "You have a terrible habit of sneaking around."

"I know." His caramel eyes twinkled. "I would really like to know your name. Maybe that way I can call out to you instead of startling you every time."

"I suppose since we're traveling on the same boat…. My name is Rose Wood. And yours?"

"Such a suitable name for you."

Rose sneered. "You think you're so charming!"

"I do." He replied smugly.

"And arrogant."

"Well, I think that's a matter of opinion."

"You still haven't answered my question!"

"Dave Clayton, at your service." He gave a mock bow.

"Last but not least, infuriating."

"Ooo, I've never heard that one. One of your thorns is growing too long."

They each stood their ground, eyes trained on the other unwilling to be the first to look away.

"Mr. Clayton! You're needed," a voice from the dock called.

Dave's eyes relaxed from their intense slant, and his lips curved upward. "I need to go." He turned away, then hesitated. "Before I go, what were you thinking about before I interrupted you?"

"I was thinking how I would like to know how this all works." She swooped her arm in an arc downward.

"If you grant me a few minutes of your time later, I'll explain it to you." He smirked and briskly walked toward the dock.

She watched him arrive at his company of men. Many of them hailed him over. At the front of the group was the leader. She crept closer, curious to see whom Dave was working for. She caught a flash of a burgundy coat and then gaped at the raven locks she fantasized running her fingers through.

"I'm here Mr. Shaw," Dave called out.

Mr. Shaw! What a delightful trip this was going to be!

A low rumble traveled through the floor of Rose's room as she unclasped her suitcase. A grinding and then the sound of steam escaping from its chamber compelled Rose to look outside her small square window. Below on deck, many of the men congregated, talking amongst themselves and waving to some on shore. A couple walking toward the boat's quarters caught her eye, Mr. Shaw and Mr. Clayton.

Planning a winning strategy was one of her many talents. How to catch Mr. Shaw's eye? Of course! By playing Mr. Clayton's admirer, Rose would stir within Mr. Shaw many jealous feelings that would be sure to produce some results.

She resumed her task of finding her pocket mirror within the folds of her few clothing. Once found, the mirror revealed a mortifying flaw. A taunting smudge of dirt rested on her cheek.

How's Dave supposed to take me seriously if I look like this!

She dabbed her washcloth in the basin of water provided and wiped off the dirt. She unpinned her curls letting them fall loose and grabbed a curl or two to rest them upon her collarbone. After several minutes of pinching her cheeks and admiring herself in the mirror, she tucked in her shirt. She opened the door and proceeded to find Joe. She knocked on the door—no answer. "Joe?" She knocked a little louder as she whispered fiercely "JOE! All right, I'll be venturing on my own."

A moment later, the door which she was just passing swung open. A gleaming back boot stepped around the frame. Her eyes immediately settled upon the shirtless Mr. Shaw with half of his face smothered in shaving cream. A deadly shaver he held in one hand and a black towel in the other.

"Mr. Shaw." Rose admired the sight before her for a few seconds before she forced her eyes to look into his.

"Yes, I opened my door upon hearing your call."

"I was seeing whether my guide was in his rooms or not."

"You know my name."

"Yes, well, that's a long story."

28

"We've been crossing paths haven't we? Several times." He stepped closer, and his midnight eyes scanned her from top to bottom. "You look refreshed."

"You..." A blush threatened to surface. "You're observational skills are astounding."

Is that the best you could come up with, idiot Rose?

"Doing what I do, they must be. Perhaps over dinner when I'm properly dressed, I could explain."

"Dinner sounds lovely." A small breath escaped Rose's lips.

"Before you leave me, I have need of your feminine opinion. Which do you prefer? A little stubble or shaved?"

She smiled. "Shaved."

His boot inched closer. She suddenly found the top of her hand being kissed by his smooth lips.

"Until tonight," he purred.

After his door closed, Rose heard a faint click down the hall.

There wasn't much in the way of entertainment on the SS Lillooet. She fated herself to having to be content without the opportunity for shopping or much moving around for that matter for the next leg of the trip, as the boat steamed east into the open ocean and then into open mouth of the Fraser River. Rose stepped out for some air. Soon after, a drizzle commenced, inciting her to return to her rooms and write in her journal. Finally, she had some time. She would have a lot of time these next coming days.

An hour before dinner, she wriggled out of her masculine attire to don her only other decent dress besides the one she wore to town in Victoria. Her shoulders were covered by tight sleeves which went down to her elbows. The midnight blue fabric bunched along the sides of her body until it became a slightly ruffled train. Against her better judgment, she had brought it, thinking she would never use it. It took up precious space in her trunk. She couldn't have been more wrong. She pinned up her hair with a few curls framing the side of her heart-shaped face.

A knock sounded upon her thin door. Her heart raced, eagerness threatening to overtake whichever action she did next.

"Mr. Sh…Joe?! For heaven's sakes, where have you been?"

"Asleep, miss."

"Didn't you hear my knocking several hours before?"

"Miss, I'm a hardened sleeper. Nothing can wake me up. Now I knew you were fine having seen you to your rooms and all."

An audible sigh. "What is it, Joe?"

"Miss, what in tarnation are you wearing?"

"It's called a dress."

"You need a fancy dress?"

"Yes, tonight I've been asked to dinner by a gentleman of good standing."

"Who?"

"Mr. Shaw."

Joe ran his cupped hand over his sagging eyelids. "Miss, I don't like the idea of your…"

"You don't have to like it. I do. You're not my father, Joe."

"Ain't that right."

"You may keep an eye out for me from afar."

"Yes, miss."

Rose stepped out of her room as Mr. Shaw stepped out of his. He swaggered toward her, his black finery rustling, whispering her name.

He bent his lips toward her ear and whispered, "You look stunning. I don't even know your name. We'll have to remedy that."

"Yes." Stars shone in Rose's eyes. She wanted to melt into his realm of night.

"Shall we?" He took her arm and cradled it as he led her, not toward the pathetic dining room, but outside.

"Where are we…? Oh!"

On the largest deck space was a square table with two chairs on opposite sides. A lace cover adorned by a dwarf candle were the sole decorations. He pulled out her chair and she sat.

"Mr. Shaw, I…"

"Please, call me Daniel. 'Mr. Shaw' from your lips is a sin to my ears."

"Daniel, this is all too much. I knew what to expect on a boat like this, but you've…"

"Your name?"

"Rose Wood."

"Are you by any chance related to Harland Wood?"

"How did you know? He's my father."

"Harland Wood is a household name in the mining community. Struck one of the richest veins anyone's heard of a year or two ago. Only thing is, no one knows where it is except him. Or so I've heard."

"Well, that doesn't surprise me. Even if I am his daughter, he would never breathe a word of it to me."

"What a shame your father has distanced himself from you."

"How perceptive you are!"

"Please tell me all about yourself, Rose."

Rose proceeded to tell him of how her father had dumped her at finishing school for years, how notorious she was as a prankster, and how only now did her father beckon her to his side. After she finished, she inquired, "And what do you do, Daniel?"

"Ah," he took a sip of his port wine. "I'm in the business of digging up gold."

"Isn't everyone?" Rose drawled.

"Mmm, yes, but I'm very good at it."

"Prove it," Rose's silky dare matched the twinkle in her eyes.

"I'm looking at gold right now." He took her hand and rubbed his smooth thumb over the top, sending shivers down her spine. "Shall we dance?"

"I would love to."

Daniel took her in his arms, and Rose felt as if she could stay there her entire existence. To be so close, close enough to smell his shaving cream…she stopped breathing for a few moments of perfection.

"Are you tired?" His words of concern tickled her ear.

"No, just overwhelmed."

"Is this too much?" He twirled her once and gazed into her heaven-struck eyes. His thumb curved upward toward her cheekbone and down to her lips. Caressing them lightly, he parted them and moved his lips toward hers.

She waited to be kissed, but only felt a brush of his teasing lips and nothing more. "Not nearly enough."

He chuckled. "I will now bid you goodnight." He took her hand and kissed the top of it. "May I escort you to your room?"

"Yes, you may." Any extra minute she could be with him would immortalize this night.

She sat upon her bed and pressed her lips together. She was certain that she would dream the sweetest of dreams tonight and that a kiss would happen soon enough. She wondered what her father would say.

The next few days were an utter bore. Mr. Shaw was nowhere to be seen. Even Mr. Clayton was unusually elusive. She saw his backside round the corner of the hallway a few times, and at mealtimes he sat with his gang of men not bothering to look her way.

Why would he ask for my name if he was never planning to speak to me? Men.

The only available company was Joe. Unfortunately, he wasn't much of a conversationalist. Several times Rose inquired about his family, education, and origins. Always he answered with the shortest answers imaginable or he didn't answer at all. Although he never gave entertaining answers, he became dearer to her heart.

Finally, she was on the last few days of her water-born journey to Yale, where they were to begin their journey on the Cariboo Trail. She decided to spend most of her time outdoors. She approached the paddle wheel, and a few moments later, footsteps followed.

"Mr. Clayton." Arms crossed, she twisted her torso to find her guess correct. She proceeded to face him.

"Rose." He tipped his cowboy hat.

Her lips puckered. "I don't ever recall giving you permission to use my given name."

"From my understanding, that's what friends do." He smirked.

"Is that what we are?" She really didn't need to play the jealousy card after last night.

"Aren't we?"

"We are." She grinned. "Where have you been this whole time?"

"Around."

"How specific!" She rolled her eyes.

"I've been a part of some secret meetings."

"Now I just don't know what to believe."

"Believe what you want. So, are you going to give me a few minutes of your time?" He pointed to the paddle wheel.

"Yes, I'm desperate to, I mean…"

"How flattering!" He strode to her side.

"Ugh, you are one of the vainest men I know." She responded with a chuckle.

He led her a few steps forward, his hand on her shoulder. "What do you see here?"

"I see a wheel fitted with paddles each a certain distance apart from the other. What drives it must be the steam engine…"

"That's it."

"No, that's not it! What about the steam engine?"

"Ah…well, first the boiler. The boiler is a large water tank with pipes running through it. The pipes have water in them which is heated by a fire source. This heats the whole boiler. The steam from the boiler is let into a cylinder which is the chamber where the output is controlled. A piston pushes the steam out, and it's released into the air."

"Now that's what I wanted to know. Thank you."

Dave's eyes darkened. "Rose, I don't think you should see Mr. Shaw again."

"Oh, so you know of our dinner. Why do you say that?"

"He has a lot of lady friends at his beck and call. I just don't want to see you get hurt."

"I can take care of myself, thank you. Have been doing so these past few years."

"I'm sure you can. Still it wouldn't hurt to have someone watch out for you."

"You think you're the one to be that someone?"

"Maybe, if you'll let me."

"We shall see."

They stood together a couple feet apart, breathing in, breathing out in time with each other. The mellifluous sound of the paddles slapping the water graced the rustic scenery.

"Where to when we get on land?" Dave asked, turning his body at an angle toward her.

"My father's home, wherever that is."

"You don't know?"

Rose shrugged. "I'm used to it."

"It's 108 Mile House."

"You are full of surprises, aren't you? How do you know?"

"Your father is Harland Wood. He's a legend. Everyone knows where he lives. I mean… I'm sorry."

"It's all right. As I said, I'm used to it. What about you? What next adventure calls to you?"

He rubbed his index finger against his thumb. "Gold—Mr. Shaw promises us more than we can imagine."

"I'm sure he will deliver. I read a few articles on him when I lived in Victoria. He's a shrewd businessman and is very successful."

"Good to know."

"Will I ever see you again?"

"Why? Afraid you're going to miss me?"

"NO! I'm asking because I'll need some time to emotionally prepare myself for whatever tomfoolery you'll cook up next."

He took a step forward. "I'll find you."

Dusk was setting as the paddle wheeler docked in Yale. She and Joe readied their trunks and brought them outside. Dave swaggered toward her, thumbs in the pockets of his trousers. He tipped his ever-present cowboy hat in greeting. "Miss Wood."

"I thought we would call each other by our given names." She gave a rueful smile.

"You've never called me by mine."

"You're so childish, Dave."

"Ah, hah, now we're mutual friends." He stepped closer. "Really, I'll come find you."

"Good, I'd like a friendly visit."

"Miss Wood, Rose." Mr. Shaw called out to her from behind. He grabbed her hand and coveted it between his own. "My dear, can you ever forgive me for not having approached you these last few days?"

"What happened? Are you all right? Did I..."

"No, it wasn't you. I've been bedridden this last week."

"Oh, I'm so glad you're all right." At the corner of her eye, she could see Dave shifting from foot to foot. "Thank you again for the lovely evening. It was...magical."

"I would do anything for you. We shall see each other again I hope."

"Ask Mr. Clayton. He knows where to find me."

"Does he?" A suspicious suavity stole over Daniel's features.

"Yes, sir." Dave looked him straight in the eyes.

Tension stung the air. "Good day, gentlemen." She kissed Daniel's cheek. She shivered from his exuding torturous essence.

She and Joe stayed in Yale for two days before they resumed their travels. The last leg of transportation was by stage coach. As it rolled and romped over the Cariboo trail flanked by nothing other than trees and rocks so did her heart thunder to its time, wary of what cursed heartaches might come her way.

They are not long, the weeping and the laughter,
Love and desire and hate:
I think they have no portion in us after
We pass the gate.
They are not long, the days of wine and roses:
Out of a misty dream
Our path emerges for a while, then closes
Within a dream.
Ernest Dowson
Vitae Summa Brevis

Chapter 3

The sun had set. Its rays slowly receded from the web of trees on both sides of the Cariboo trail. The last drop-off of passengers other than Rose and Joe had been hours ago. The cool air had turned crisp, hastening Rose to put on her brown leather overcoat. She took both sides of the coat and tucked them into each other with just her weary face peeping over the top. Joe, as always, was in the same position, arms crossed, feet crossed, with an unimpressed expression ever colouring his face.

"Joe?" she asked tentatively.

He stirred slightly. "Yes, miss."

"Where will you go after your duty has been fulfilled to my father?"

"Don't know, miss. I'll probably head to Barkerville, looking for the next job."

"I've never thanked you for keeping me safe during our travels. So…thank you."

"Your welcome, miss." Never gave much, never took much.

"You know, you're more than welcome to stay for a few days to rest and enjoy some good food before you have to leave."

"Yes, miss."

She nodded and decided to sleep a little more until they would soon arrive at her father's house.

A jolt made her neck snap forward. Instantly, she awoke and rubbed her eyes with the tips of her fingers. She fingered the curtains open to see a waxing moon. Joe opened the door and this time remembered to give her his meaty hand to aid her descent. He then turned his attention toward retrieving their bags. She sighted the two-storey mile house and a log shed north of the road. There was no light burning within either building.

My father has retired for the night. How fitting, I can get some undisrupted sleep before having to face him.

The coachman cracked his reins to get the horses going. Joe lighted their kerosene lamp and handed it to Rose before he grabbed their bags. She proceeded to take very small steps toward the house. She opened the creaking door, wincing for fear her father would wake. She had entered a spacious entrance. Whatever wood flooring she could sight by the light of her lamp was scuffed and had clumps of mud scattered about. It must have come in by the boots of her father's clients, boots which would have been slick with mud from the recent rains in the area.

My father is more clean than that. I must speak with the housekeeper.

Before she could view any more of her surroundings, a repugnant smell slowly enveloped her breathing space. The smell of decaying flesh guided her into the sitting area to the right of the entrance. How could it be that an animal had died in here without her father and his clients noticing? It smelled as if it had been dead for a couple of days at least.

Footsteps creaked behind her.

"Joe?"

Silence.

"Joe?"

"Yes, miss," an ominous tone was threaded into his reply.

"Do you smell that?"

"Miss, wait outside. Let me check…"

She dismissed his idea by continuing to follow the scent, furthering herself from Joe's stance in the entrance. She crossed a threshold and found herself in a small study of sorts. Books lined the shelves of one wall. The stench here was overwhelming causing her to cup her hand over her nose and mouth. She started to gag. She swept the lamp from the left to the right until her light alighted upon her father sitting on a chair in the corner of the room. So frightened was she by the sight of him there that she dropped her lamp, and darkness shrouded the room. The smell of death reeked where her father sat. Her voice to call out to Joe was lost.

What has happened here? It must have been days since…

"Joe!" Her voice cracked under the pressure the smell delivered.

Their secondary lantern's light, held by Joe, cast its glow. Since she had met Joe, his expressions had not changed in the slightest. It was the first time she saw fear in his face. This disturbing fact convinced her this was a nightmare.

"Joe, please pinch me."

"Miss, let's go out…"

"Joe!" Rose shrieked, her grasp on reality slipping away. The need to be pinched was fierce, so much so she would go mad if she did not receive one.

Joe pinched her and not softly at that. He pinched her so hard that a shuddering gasp and a cry of a wounded animal escaped her lips.

"I need…to see, please."

He raised his lantern closer toward her father's dead body.

Rose stepped closer to gaze upon the body. His skin bubbled in a most frightful manner. It seemed as if her father had turned into a dead toad. The colour of his skin was like nightshade. His lips, cracked and stained heavy with crusted blood, were parted. A large gash gaped open where his neck was from ear to ear. His eyes were open.

Her fingers shook as she stretched them to close his yellowy eyes. "Joe, we must bury him tonight."

"Yes, miss. Where would you like me to dig the grave? There's a patch of woods not far from here."

"Yes, I'd like him to be laid to rest in a peaceful corner."

"Miss, I'll go fetch a cart from the stables." He plodded away.

Even though the stench of death permeated the entire room, no, the entire house, she could not leave her father's dead body as he had left her many years ago, healthy and alive. No tears threatened to spill. Rose could not avert her eyes from the macabre scene.

At first, she whispered, "Father, what a cruel joke you've played. How could you leave not once but twice?" Her whispering grew into a moan. "Oh, did you ever care about me? Or was I just some petty child you were left to provide for? Hah, I don't even know what happened to my own mother because you never said a single word about her." Now her hoarse and grating voice roared, "I might as well have been an orphan my whole life! What am I supposed to do now? You've left me nothing except this ramshackle mile house in the middle of nowhere! This was your dream not mine. How dare you go and die on me." A slow chuckle deep from within the pit of her stomach surfaced. "Now, there's an idea. You would never have expected me to keep this place running. Well, I'll make your dream my dream and take away the only thing you've ever cared about."

Not a rustle she heard. The rotting corpse was silent.

Rose moved to the entrance as soon as she heard the cart stop in front of the door. Joe lumbered inside to where

Mr. Wood's body reeked on display. Rose bent to pick up her father's legs as Joe inserted his arms around the body's midsection. Together they hauled him up into the cart. Joe started to wheel the cart, and Rose picked up the shovels that Joe had found in the stables along with the cart.

They reached the edge of the forest. Rose found a spot near a cluster of oak trees. She handed the larger shovel to Joe. For the next three hours, Joe dug a five foot deep grave. In the beginning, Rose had fiercely attacked the ground and added a sizeable amount to the mound of upturned dirt. However, the steam of her anger could only propel her so much. After half an hour, she threw her shovel to the side, dropped to the ground and stared at the hole being dug until it was completed. Although Joe took the occasional break to slug down some water and to roll his shoulders, he dug with the tenacity of a mule.

They dropped her father's body into the hole. They then proceeded to fill up the grave. Rose at times would kick the dirt into the grave instead of shovelling it in.

Once it was completely filled, she sunk to her knees and patted the earth into a perfect mound. She huffed, "I presume we must pay our respects with eulogies or sad words. What if there are no words? Is it a sin when there is no good thing you can say about a loved one?"

"Miss, you needn't say anything. You've been through enough."

"Have I? How can you, a stranger, see that, but my own blood, my father couldn't? Please say something in my stead."

He cleared his throat and brought his chin to his chest. "Well, um, the first time I met him was when I was a passin' by. He was kind enough and thoughtful, wanted to do right by all his customers. He took me aside and asked if I would be able to bring his daughter back in one piece. I guess he heard talk from the other customers that that's what I do. He patted my shoulder and told me I'd do right by him."

Rose continued to stare at the grave.

"I don't know what's gone on between you and yer father. It ain't none of my business. When he told me to bring you back home safe, I saw that he loved you. He didn't seem to be a man who showed much emotion, but there it was, plain as day."

"Thank you, Joe, for sharing some words. Now, please, leave me be." Rose heard his retreating steps.

Her body ached from the frigidness that had managed to seep through her oilskin coat. She knew she would need a handful of baths to wash off the dirt and the stench of rotting flesh. Perhaps a few more were in order to rid her from these horrific memories. "Father," she whispered into the night. "I've said all I needed to say." She turned to leave, sure she would never return. "No, there's more." She resumed her position in front of the grave. Her hands were folded in front of her in a pious fashion. She just had to say something…good about father. "I do remember…" she swallowed a growing heaving of emotion. "I remember when we used to live in England the times you were there for me although they pale in comparison to the times you weren't there for me here in gold country. I just cannot let go of my anger. You were a fool to be taken by gold fever. I say this with pity. Goodbye, father."

"Joe!" She called out into the dark night. A minute or two later, she heard his now comforting steps. "I'm tired. Let us return."

They searched the upstairs for a room tolerably unaffected by the smell. Once she did, she paid no heed to her cleanliness, the condition of her hair, or even the condition the bed would be in once she slept in it. She just collapsed onto it. A squeak from the springs and the feel of cotton against her rough cheek were the last little bits she was conscious of before falling fast asleep.

***

Father…father is dead. What do I do now? Wake up.

She stretched her fingers. The rest of her body followed, slowly, each muscle unravelling from its tightly wound coil. It was sometime early evening, judging by the twilight stain of the sky.

I'm so dirty…I need a bath.

The dirt and grime had hardened. Her body wasn't the only thing stained. Her soul was blackening, drowning. She was scared to reach the bottom of this nightmare's ocean.

She braced her elbows and pushed up. Pressure within her skull resounded like a gong. Shakily, she stood and sniffed the air. Death's essence seemed to be receding from the dwelling. She lumbered downstairs and stopped within the private library. All the windows were wide open, a light breeze sweeping through the home. The chair, on which she found her father's corpse, was nowhere to be seen, the small round table without its compatriot. Footsteps behind… "Joe?"

"Miss, I hope you don't mind. I burned it."

"That's quite all right. Thank you for having taken care of it, and for the airing of the house."

"Miss, I've made some stew. It's a simple thing, but it'll do you some good to eat it."

"And you cook?" She didn't have the energy to be surprised, let alone hear him explain the newfound talent. "Lead the way. You must know the house more intimately than I do now since I've been asleep all day."

On the way out of the library, she espied a black and white picture on the desk. She picked it up and saw that it was she. In those childish eyes was true unaffected vivacity and a contentedness that seemed foreign. Rose believed she was physically beautiful. However, she couldn't shake off the feeling that she had lost an inner beauty which she used to carry a long time ago.

My picture was enough for you. The girl herself was too much for you to bear.

Joe and Rose ate in silence, neither bothered by the lack of conversation. Rose gestured for Joe's bowl and placed hers upon it. She grabbed the small wash basin and asked, "Where do I get some water?"

Followed by Rose, Joe grabbed the basin and tromped outside. He pumped the water into the basin and handed it to her. In the kitchen, she got to work on the dishes while he leaned on the counter with arms crossed, a cloth slung over his shoulder.

She chuckled without mirth. "I stole into the kitchen at Angela's College once and poured salt into the oatmeal. All the girls squealed, salty oatmeal dribbling from their open mouths. Of course, no one could prove I did it." She sighed dramatically. "But the cook knew. See, I was infamous for the pranks I pulled. No one else would have dared. So she made me empty all the oatmeal from the bowls and wash them all by hand. It was the first time I had ever washed dishes. Who knew my punishment would be so valuable for life on the frontier!

"I presume, I shall have to look through my father's papers for any sign of a will or legal jargon. I need you to poke around the property and see what needs mending, what needs to be replenished, and just…what needs to be done."

He cleared his throat. "I…um…I know this ain't probably a good time…"

"What is it?"

He cleared his throat, "Well, you'll pay me, right? This wasn't part of the original deal."

Her eyes grew wide. "Of course, payment! What were the details of your understanding with my father?"

"He paid me enough for food and transportation for the return trip. He was supposed to pay me the rest when we got back."

She looked to the study, brows narrowed, "He must have the remainder somewhere. That is if the murderer didn't steal it. Please do as I asked, and I'll see to it."

"Yes, miss. I'll get right to it. Oh and this…" he held up a string of leather with a single key, "I noticed it around his neck."

"Thank you," she murmured. She recalled the gruesome image of her father's lacerated neck.

Joe left to complete his errand while she skirted around the spot where the now burnt chair had sat and started to open her father's drawers. The bottom drawer arrested her attention since it required a key. Rose fitted the key into the hole and turned it. A *click* resounded. She drew it open. Memorabilia had been stashed inside—her baby booties, a lock of her hair, a locket. She opened the locket expecting to find her own picture within but instead found the picture of another woman. Sad doe eyes set within a round face looked back at her. Rose focused on the woman's full bottom lip and raven black hair. Was this her mother?

She had never seen a picture of her mother. Her father had done very well in hiding her past. The woman before her had a touch of Spanish. Could it be that her heritage was founded not only in Britain but Spain as well? Rose closed the locket and clasped it around her neck. The other mementoes she placed upon the top of the desk.

She found a thick envelope with Joe's name. She fingered it open to find large wads of bills.

Looking in the drawer once more, she saw *The Last Will and Testament of Harland Wood.* She sat in the chair closest to the desk and read over the will thrice. The first time, she skimmed it over. Once she read that she was to inherit the land, the business, everything, she read it again. Hardly believing her father's wishes, she read it one last time to be completely sure of his intentions. During the final reading, she saw that the executor of the will was the Hudson Bay Company office in Barkerville, with Judge Begbie (the Hanging Judge) as witness.

My father had many illustrious connections, I see.

She laid the papers on her lap and rested her aching head upon her right hand. A minute later she drifted off into slumber.

She opened her eyes to find the room steeped in darkness save the lantern Joe had burning on the small table beside the sofa. She had to blink a few times, for she thought she saw Joe reading. He was reading! As soon as he realized she was awake, he shut the book with nary a sound and hid it behind his back.

"Joe, I saw the book. Is that Browning? What were you reading?"

"It's not important, miss."

"You know I won't let this go until I know."

"Yes, miss," he said, his face resolutely facing the wall.

She huffed, "Well, your report."

44

"Miss, it seems there were animals on the property. My guess is whoever was here before us purposely opened the latches so they would wander, or they stole them. Other than that, everything is in order. It seems no mule trains or horse drawn-buggies have been here for the last week."

"Joe, I know your only obligation was to bring me back here, but I have need of your services once more. I need an escort into Barkerville. Here…" She handed the envelope to Joe. "I believe this is enough to cover your profit and much more."

He thumbed through the bills. "Miss! This is a year's wages!"

"Will you work for me over the next year? I could use expert hands like yours to continue the running of this mile house. Bed and food will be free of charge."

He nodded, "You need to get to Barkerville? The will?"

"Yes, the matter must be dealt with. However, we have no transportation. Isn't it odd that no one has come for lodging?"

"I'll walk over to 100 Mile House in the morning, miss."

She patted Joe's shoulder and made her way to her room. Even after having napped for the better part of the afternoon and evening, her head ached and her shoulders slumped. As she slipped into bed, she realized the grimy sheets had been exchanged for two woollen blankets.

Joe, how good of you.

He went like one that hath been stunned,
And is of sense forlorn:
A sadder and a wiser man,
He rose the morrow morn.
Samuel Taylor Coleridge

Chapter 4

Rose awakened to the grating noise of rolling wheels, which drifted in through her open window. A groan erupted from the cart. The jostling of harnesses goaded her into spying outside to see what the commotion was all about. The sun had reached its zenith. Once again she'd slept in more than she should have.

Joe threw the driving reins onto the bench and jumped out. The horses stomped their hooves. He drew near them and handed them each a carrot.

Rose turned to dress. She opened her trunk and looked at the clothing within. Usually, she would have guffawed her lack of flamboyant dresses. She was going to Barkerville, one of the most exciting towns along the Cariboo trail. She should dress to impress!

Seeing Death's hand up close and personal had dimmed her need for all extravagance. A dull ache had spread within. The food she ate had little, to no taste. A cloud of stupor hung around her.

She picked the plainest of her dresses and packed them. She donned her masculine outfit which Joe had washed and laid over the small wicker chair in the corner. She also packed her basic necessities and walked out without caring to make the bed or right the pile of outcast dresses on the floor.

As she walked out of the mile house, Joe finished giving water to the horses.

She slid her hand down the back of one of the horses. "Where did you get these fine beasts?"

"Well, miss, I'll tell you what I did. I, also, found out why nobody ain't comin' this way either. I left early in the mornin' to walk to 100 Mile House to rent this buggy. They asked me who I was. Once they knew I knew Harland Wood, they asked me if he be openin' up business once again. I asked who told them it wasn't open for business. He said some man came over several days ago and said that Mr. Wood had sent him to report that 108 Mile House wasn't open for business until further notice. The owner of 100 Mile House said it was slow season anyway and that no one's been up the Cariboo trail for the last few days."

"Did he say what the man looked like?"

"I asked, miss. They said he was plain as can be. Brown hair, brown eyes, about five and a half feet."

"Very clever—that describes a good many men in the Cariboo territory." Rose hoisted her traveling case into the back of the buggy. She looked Joe squarely in the eye with her hands on her hips. "Did you tell them that…" her mouth opened and closed as her eyes struggled to fixate on any point, "that 108 Mile House would continue to be closed for business for the next week and a half?"

"I said a week. We best get on going, keeping north."

It was evening when they reached 150 Mile House.

"Here, miss." Joe set down her trunk. "It'd be best if you didn't wander. I'll bring your meal to you."

Rose slumped upon the bed and stared at the wallpaper, a sickly wheat coloured thing. "You'll get no fight from me, Joe."

She didn't bother to lock the door as soon as it closed.

I know I said I would run the mile house but…what if I fail? I'm so far from home. I guess Joe could teach me what he knows. He knows everything about frontier life. This is a business I wasn't bred for. He, too, isn't a business owner. He's just a guide. How are we going to make this work? My father should have just left me in England with some rich distant relation. I would have had my debutante ball already and probably a line of suitors. I would have been much happier.

Later, when he returned with her supper, he found her in the exact same position. "Miss, are you all right?"

She drawled, "I think that entirely depends. What do you think?" Her eyes never strayed from their point.

"You need to eat. I'll be downstairs."

She replied loud enough, "I don't need to know your whereabouts like some petulant child. Leave me be."

Hours passed before Rose finally arose from the bed, food untouched, and slipped into her nightclothes. The past, the future, the present—none of them mattered since she had laid eyes on her dead father. She could barely remember what she had done, said, or thought. Or was this all some terrible nightmare?

The next three days' travel was a blur. Rose went through the motions of hopping off the buggy, checking into her room, and sitting on the bed both nights they stopped. Joe brought her food which she pushed around until she eventually ate several bites and no more. Her thoughts, like quicksand, pulled her down into an oblivion she could only be aroused from when it was time to resume the journey.

They arrived in Barkerville late in the evening. Their buggy rolled along the street in front of a well-sized boarding house. Joe grabbed her trunk, and she followed him inside.

Time to put aside my moping. I've reached the end of the road. Life must go on.

As she rifled through the little clothing in her trunk, her fingers brushed against a piece of paper. It was Priscilla's goodbye letter. What had happened? She hadn't received word from her. Yet she herself had not settled fully into any one place.

I must go on an adventure so I can tell Priscilla when I see her again.

She brushed her hair and put it up, tucked in her shirt, doffed a hat, and sneaked away into the dead of night. She placed her hands into her pants' pockets, strode down main street while peering at the stores, saloons, and offices, and stopped at a hotel. Merry laughter floated outside from within. As Rose gazed at the scene, fierce whisperings coming from the hotel's adjoining alley caught her attention.

"That ole' hanging judge!" A man spit a wad of tobacco out of his mouth. "He should pay. I say we kill 'im!"

A whimpering voice peeped, "We can't! The Law will find us, that's fo' sure, if we rid it of its master."

The first man slapped the back of his companion. "Stop your slobberin' about. Tonight in the wee hours of the morning, we'll…"

On the balcony above the conspirators' heads, stood an older gentleman. Rose could see, by the light of the moon, his silver hairs swept over the top of his ears and the trimmed beard he sported on his long face. His face looked familiar. She had seen it in numerous papers. The hanging judge…why of course, it was Judge Begbie, the witness to her father's will.

The conspirators continued to prattle on. Her focus shifted to what seemed to be a chamber pot the judge now held in his hands. He proceeded to turn it upside down, its watery contents…

"Ah, Percy, what in God's green earth…" the whimpering man started to cry.

Percy! Not only is he in the business of dishonouring young ladies but also killing lawmen. What a despicable low life!

Percy shouted in rage. "Damn you, Judge Begbie!"

The judge's idea of retaliation was so brilliant that Rose could feel a bubbly laughter set on. She suppressed the urge to squeak a sound. Instead, she crouched down, her back against the adjacent building's wall and stared at the boards beneath her feet as Percy and his henchman retreated out of the alley. The nape of her neck began to sweat as Percy stood next to her. He stood there for a minute, spitting wads of tobacco and wiping his stubble with the back of his hand.

Percy kicked the heel of his companion's boot. "Come on, the boss will want to know what we've been up to." They walked off. Rose felt as if she could breathe once more.

A few moments later, a pair of cowboy boots appeared in the bottom left-hand corner of her view. Her biceps tensed, and she held her breath.

"Hey, there! Are you all right?"

Dave?

He crouched to her level and put a hand upon her shoulder. "You don't look all right. Do you need…? "

She grabbed the hand upon her shoulder and muttered, "Come." She dragged him far into the alley, a few steps away from the puddle of chamber pot contents.

He followed, his steps hesitant and his body slightly resisting her pull. "Now I don't mean any trouble. I just thought…"

Rose brought her face into the moonlight and pulled off her cowboy hat.

His hand tightened over hers and he laughed. "Rose! What are…?"

"Sh," she frantically whispered.

He looked up and down her disguise. "I don't even know how I thought you were a boy! Taking a second look, it's obvious…you're not."

"That's because I know how to blend in, unlike you. Laughing at me in the middle of an alleyway—what are you thinking? Someone will notice."

Still chuckling, he endeavoured to whisper. "Rose, what are you doing in Barkerville?"

"I'm here on business."

He swaggered a step closer. "What kind of business would encourage you to walk around like a boy?"

"It has nothing to do with my business. I put on this disguise because I had to get out of the boarding house. Joe thinks I'm…well…" she shrugged.

50

"Mild, subdued, and silent? Joe…he was your guide, right? I'm surprised he doesn't know you better by now." He smirked.

"He thinks I'm grieving." The words rolled off her lips like thunder.

His eyes prodded hers, seeking the answer to an unasked question. She stared straight through him as if he were no more than a ghost.

"What's wrong?" He clasped her arm.

"I don't care to talk of it." She finally reverted to looking at him and not through him.

"You should talk about it."

"With whom? With Joe who never utters an unnecessary word? With you, whom sarcasm clings to like a lost puppy?"

His resident smirk faded. "Rose, I can listen without talking. Give me a chance."

"Not here, what if someone comes down the alley?"

He nodded. "Follow me."

They walked a few paces apart down the main street, then turned east past the town of echoing dreams. He led her to a peninsula-shaped clearing on the edge of a forest. He sat upon the ground, facing the lighted town, and patted the patch of grass beside him.

She sat down and crossed her legs. Oh, the glorious freedom to do so when one wasn't wearing skirts! "This is hardly proper," she deigned to smile.

A long moment passed before Dave murmured, "I have the utmost respect for you."

"I know."

"You do? How?"

She put a finger to her lips in thought. "Would you have the same playful banter with me if you did not consider me your equal?"

Dave quickly replied, "No."

They both sat in silence. Dave, unwilling to press Rose for the sake of his curiosity, waited until she was ready to speak.

Rose grabbed handfuls of grass. "My father is dead." She looked sideways at Dave, seeing him swallow hard. "I don't know what else to say…which is very strange since I always have something to say."

"You don't need to say anything."

They gazed at one another, saying nothing at all.

Inside those depths, she saw a man who wasn't afraid of her emptiness, who didn't turn away from the corroded parts of her heart. "Thank you, for a listening ear."

He smiled wide. "Not a drip of sarcasm, astounding!"

She elbowed him, "Perhaps there is hope we could speak to each other more often without excessive teasing, hope that our friendship will stand the test of time, no matter how unconventional it is."

"Yes, unconventional seeing how we usually meet in alleyways. People might talk."

"I always relish a good scandal. Don't you?"

Dave turned serious, "How long will you be in Barkerville?"

"A couple days…" All the grass Rose had gathered in her fists, she threw into the air. "I should return to the boarding house." She pushed herself off the ground and roughly ran her hands down her pants, shaking the grass from her clothing.

"Rose," Dave grasped her wrist. "I'd like to see you one more time before you return to the mile house."

Her shoulders slumped, and she turned her head away. "I'm not sure if I will have the courage to slip out again. Things are different for me now. I…I don't know."

"Yeah, I didn't think…you're grieving. Sorry for asking." He smoothed his hat over his hair. "Can I walk you back?"

"If we do, I can't talk. Perhaps you could walk a few steps behind me as we did coming here? You can see to it I arrive safely." A tentative smile peeped from her lips before she turned on her heel and walked away.

His lingering presence, a few steps behind—she could feel the chord strung between them undulate in a rhythmic feel. In whatever direction she stepped, he was sure to follow as if she were the true north to his compass. The bodies lingering in the street became insignificant until they faded completely from her sight. She was only aware of the tug of the chord between her and Dave. Once she arrived at the door to the boarding house, she watched him move down the street. She opened the door to her room, shed the male garb she wore, and lay down to sleep.

***

A knocking, her name being called—she stretched, groaning that her rest had been cut short. She drew the door open a sliver to see Joe's surprised eyes. "Joe, what can I do for you?"

"Miss, you're here!"

"Why, of course, I'm here. Where else would I be?"

"Miss, I looked in on you before I went to sleep. On the journey, you've been..."

Rose opened the door wide, not caring whether her feet were bare or that she only wore her nightgown. She pulled Joe in and shut the door with a bang. "Been what, Joe? Finally I've been a good little girl? Now that my father's dead, I will smarten into a dying breed of polite traditionalism? I will not change for him, never, not even in death!" she whispered furiously. Her hands shook as she ran them down the crumpled nightgown. Her breathing was laborious. " I am not an idiot, Joe. I know the dangers."

"Do you?" he huffed.

Her hand rose to slap the scruff on his cheek, but his defensive reflex was too quick. He looked back into her eyes and saw the fear of what she had almost committed. "Miss, you go too far. Your father would have been proud of your strength and..."

"Do not say that!" Her face seemed to be crumpling in under itself.

"He would have loved your fearsome spirit."

"I don't care!"

"Miss, don't you see? All your efforts to displease your father are because that's what you've wanted the most, to please him. You need to let go."

She shook her hand free. "I let go a long time ago."

"That's a lie."

How can that be? I've been free, taking pleasure in the mischief I've created, free from Father's grasp. What other freedom could I possibly need?

"Perhaps, you're right, Joe. It makes perfectly good sense to lie to oneself." She faced him, a steely gaze protecting another clumsily erected wall.

"Miss, I care about…"

"Joe, you mind your own business, and I'll mind mine. Now, please, get out and let me have some needed sleep. I'll wake when I wake."

Without a word or a glance of anger, Joe left the room.

A dredge came over Rose's soul. Angry at Joe, angry at herself, angry with the world, she lay down and couldn't sleep. What if Joe was right? What if she had lost sight of what was truly pure freedom in this world?

An hour later, she dressed in a plain white dress with light blue stripes and placed her hair in a half up do. She decided to skip breakfast. As she crossed the boarding house's threshold to walk to the Hudson Bay Company's office, Joe caught her arm.

"Miss, where are you going?" he gently asked.

She ripped her arm from his touch. "It's none of your concern. These are private family matters."

He let go. Seeing she was determined to not heed any of his words, he jammed on his hat and kept a distance behind her.

Rose's heart beat fast knowing her venom-laced words directed toward Joe were uncalled for and undeserved. Oh, she just wished she could yell at the people in the street. She felt as if she were drowning in the undertow and gasping for air. Instead, her lungs were filling with death.

She eventually realized she had passed the whole length of town without stepping foot into the Hudson Bay Company's office.

The branches grazed her cheeks as she strode into some nearby woods. She could no longer patch up the dam which held her emotions in check . She covered her mouth with her palms and screamed as loud as she could, as strong as she could muster.

The tremors coursing down her arms and fingertips slowed to occasional twitches. She clenched then unclenched her hands. She touched her cheeks, her fingertips wet from the tears. All thought had been swept away by the violence of her outburst. Her body was a shell, so fragile that one swift blow would crack it wide open revealing the wisp of a ghost inside.

Slowly, she walked amongst the trees, shuffling her feet. She accidentally kicked out a rusted folding blade several feet away. As she picked it up and opened it, she wondered what it would feel like to bleed as her father bled. Would life's cruel enticements fade as her life source exited her body? If so, would eternal life still be hers if she dared take her own? The knife's tip just about to draw blood—the jarring caw of a raven as it flapped away—she gasped and dropped the knife. Her cloud of disillusionment dissipated.

The will.

She gulped and looked toward Barkerville—the unknown, only one step at a time without being able to see where it would all lead. She looked back at the knife she dropped. She was certain, secure in knowing where that action would lead. But had she accomplished everything she was meant for? She kicked it and turned toward town.

The second time Rose tramped down the whole main street of Barkerville, she could see no sign of the Hudson Bay Company office. She opened the door to the general store and ground to a halt at the counter.

A ruddy, round-faced, middle-aged man stood behind the counter with his hands folded upon it. "Now what can I do for a pretty young lady like you today?"

"For heaven's sake, where is the office of the Hudson Bay Company in this town?" The last phrase she uttered was as the sound of the high-pitched whine of a ready teapot.

The perturbed man showed her his palms in a placating manner. "Miss, there's not one in this town."

"How can that be?" She huffed, placing her hands upon her hips.

"The whole town burned down a few years ago. They never rebuilt their post here. Everything was moved to Quesnel."

Her lips moved in a silent *O*. "I see. Yes, now that you mention it, I believe I read about that fire in a paper in Victoria some years ago."

He smiled. "Really? Well, I must say that's swell. To think that we're in their fancy newspapers all the way down there, why…"

His jabbering faded away as she moved to push the door open. She found Joe with his hat in his hands looking into her face with concern. A weak smile barely graced her lips as she followed him back to the boarding house.

Once she returned to her room, she pulled Joe aside. "Joe, I…" Her eyes rested on him then averted once more. "I cannot to begin to express—I mean…Joe." She breathed out his name as if it were her last tether to solid ground.

"There's no need to speak now, miss. When you're ready, you will. I get your meanin'. We'll leave at first light." With a twinkle in his eyes, he turned the knob and walked away, softly shutting the door behind him.

The moon's light was dim, and the street was mottled in shadows. Rose, keeping her head down and her steps close to the boardwalk, shuffled along until she came to the clearing Dave had shown her a night ago. She sat in the same spot and waited, waited to see whether a friend would seek her out. A good two hours passed. Dave had not come. She gathered her hair beneath her hat once more and set off toward town.

She reached the town and was about to pass the alleyway where she had heard the murderous low lives' plot to kill and thought perhaps…Dave would be waiting there for her. She stole within the alley a few steps and saw no one. She advanced further. Suddenly she tripped upon a boot and fell upon her elbows and hands, skinning them. The burn started to fizzle, and she hissed in frustration. "What on earth?"

The boot moved and retracted into a dark alcove beside the building. A man's grunt reverberated within the small space.

Rose froze, not sure if she should just run (look what happened to her in the alleyway the first time), or if she should stand her ground and continue in her disguise.

The man reeked of whiskey. He fumbled around, his arms and legs flailing about in such a silly fashion.

Rose cleared her throat and attempted to speak in the lowest tone she could muster. "Sir, can I help you? Where are you staying?"

"Staying? That's a good question. I…I don't know. Oh, my head hurts."

Rose's blood boiled. Dave?! "You pig! You're just like all the other men."

"Rose? Is that you?"

"Of course, it's me. You're so drunk! I cannot believe it. I was beginning to think you were one of the decent gentlemen in this world. I guess I was wrong." She was about to stomp off when he lunged out to grab her hand and pulled her down so that she landed in his lap. His hands were around her arms pulling her close to himself.

Rose squirmed, attempting to free herself from one of his arms. "Let me go. I'm warning you."

"Rose, please…" He touched her forehead with his own. "I don't know what happened to me."

"Hah, and you expect me to believe you?! Dave, I waited two hours for you at the meadow!"

"You did?" She could hear the relieved smile in his voice. "I meant to go…" He placed a fist to his forehead. Even though she could have shoved herself off and ran, she didn't. "I can't remember what happened."

Dave held onto her as if she were his lifeline. Their noses touched and their breaths mingled. Being in such proximity, she realized he hadn't been drinking. If he had, it was hours ago. The reek of his clothing…it was seeping into her own.

"Dave?"

"Please don't go, not yet." He still clung to her arms.

"I'll wait until your mind clears." Rose couldn't remember when her eyes fluttered and sleep demanded its recompense. She was held by Dave's iron embrace, and she moulded into his form.

The stench of whiskey attacked her nostrils hours later, and her lids shot open. Dave's stubble along his jaw line met her gaze. Her head was inclined upon the muscle of his shoulder. She placed her hand upon his heart and heard its steady rhythm beneath.

Thank goodness he's all right. I hope whatever foolishness present last night has passed.

Dave began to stir beneath her. He turned his head, and his lips grazed her forehead.

The sun had a half hour yet to rise. Rose was thankful that no one had found her in such a compromising position.

She leaned away from his waking form. "Dave, such intimacy…"

He gently placed her legs off his and onto the ground beside him and slowly stretched his way up to a standing point. Then he helped pull her up. "Gosh, I'm sorry, Rose, for everything." He blinked furiously. "Uh, thanks for staying."

Rose shook her head and said more to herself, "I shouldn't have."

He rubbed his eyes. "You're right. I…I should never have asked. I know you might be wondering what happened last night. Honestly, I can't…"

"You don't have to explain." She replied in a dismissive tone. "I'm glad nothing worse happened to you. You look like a miserable vagrant." She softened the sharpness in her voice. "It seems like foul play was at hand."

"What?" He squinted his eyes, his fist pressing against his temple.

"You don't remember anything, and there was no hint of alcohol on your breath. Only your clothes stink. Could one of your men have drugged you and dumped a jug of whiskey all over you?"

He snickered, barely managing to open his eyes. "Why would they do that? How did you come up with such a…ridiculous scenario?"

She gathered up her hair beneath her hat. "I'm not a naive little schoolgirl who doesn't know anything about the world. I've illicitly pocketed my share of gothic mysteries. Maybe I'm overreacting, but I've also seen…things." She looked over her shoulder, disappointed he had mocked her idea. "Just be careful, Dave."

Once she had taken off the whiskey-rotten clothing, she and Joe left Barkerville with nary a word floating on the wind.

Can a man take a fire in his bosom,
and his clothes not be burned?
Proverbs 6:27

Chapter 5

What did it all mean? Rose, the entire trip to Quesnel, was any of the three: empty, full of anger, or pulled along by twisting thoughts. Now, it was the latter which plagued her sensibilities to the highest degree. Priscilla's uncharacteristic and sudden disappearance from school, her father's murder, and Dave's loss of memory—surely all these mysteries had nothing to do with each other. Yet why did she find herself the witnessing party to each one? Suspense abounded in this wild country unlike the tranquil dullness she remembered of overpopulated England. Or perhaps it was part of growing up, the small and necessary mysteries of understanding oneself.

In the midst of her chaotic thoughts, the guilt of having mistreated Joe resurfaced and berated her until it drowned out all her wonderings. The silence between Joe and she (usually not in the least awkward) was close to incapacitating. Joe hadn't brought up her trying to slap him in the face. How cruel and selfish she had been to lay a hand on her faithful worker!

"I'm sorry," she croaked, daring a peek at his face.

Joe kept his eyes on the road and acted as if he hadn't heard her.

"I said…"

His patting her hand with his own silenced her. He gave it a little squeeze, and she smiled.

As soon as they reached Quesnel, Rose jumped off the buggy and marched off with the will in hand.

Joe dropped the reins on the seat and shouted after her, "Miss, where are you going?"

Rose stopped in her tracks and lifted her shoulders as she exhaled a large sigh. She trudged back not caring that the hem of her dress dragged in the dirt. "I'm tired of gallivanting off here, there, and everywhere. I want this crooked business to be done with. When I come back, I want a hot bath ready for my use."

Joe drawled, "Miss, how am I supposed to know when that is?"

"I'll be back in an hour." She walked into the general store and inquired to the location of the desired office. She then left as she was directed and found it. "Pardon me," she said to the clerk, "may I please speak with the lawyer connected to this establishment?"

"What does this concern?"

"It concerns the will of Harland Wood."

Now the clerk was quite aghast. "Harland Wood? You don't mean to say he's dead."

"Quite dead," Rose said with an indignant air.

"That's news all right. Wait a moment please." He scuttled off and disappeared to the back of the store.

Rose didn't wait long before none other than Daniel Shaw appeared behind the counter. Her cheeks coloured, and she instantly regretted not wearing the prettiest, most daring dress she owned (which she hadn't packed). "Mr. Shaw, how charming to meet you here under such circumstances." She raised her hand to shake his, but he brought her hand to his mouth and kissed it. The clerk's eyes opened wide as if he were embarrassed to witness such a passionate greeting.

Daniel's fathomless black eyes bored into Rose's. "Please follow me."

I'll follow you anywhere.

The old excitable Rose was back. She followed him as he fetched a few notebooks from the back office before exiting the Hudson Bay Company. He held her arm as he led her a few buildings down.

"This is my personal office. What a happy coincidence I was checking the Hudson Bay's ledgers when you stopped by!" As he was putting away the notebooks, she surveyed his office. One wall was lined with bookcases housing books on law, the great Renaissance literature, and all the latest English giants. His desk was ebony, and the curtains were a deep crimson. His clothing matched the sable shades of his office.

She was distracted from continuing to admire the setting when she noticed he locked the door and lowered the blinds. He sat behind his desk and motioned for her to sit down on the chair across from him.

"What fine taste you have!" She gestured to the furnishings.

"Thank you." He folded his hands upon his desk and said, "My dear Rose, I'm so sorry to hear of your loss."

"Not as sorry as I. I found him murdered in his home almost a fortnight ago and found this." She slid the will toward him. "It was in a secret compartment of his desk."

Daniel fingered the papers carefully, thumbing through the document as Rose continued on, "First, I went to Barkerville since he had written up the will and had it signed at that outpost. I found out it had been burned down."

"Yes, an unfortunate matter." He put down the will and cradled her hands in his.

She looked at their entwined hands. "It was pointed out that I was to come here, to Quesnel."

Daniel stood up and came to her side, seating himself upon his desk.

"Daniel, I thought you were in the business of digging up gold."

"I am."

"And yet, you're a lawyer, as well?"

He smiled an excruciatingly wicked grin. "Yes, I am. I have a very profitable stake in one of the largest veins ever to be tapped in this wilderness. My company of men run my share day in and day out, leaving me to invest time in what I do, helping those less fortunate around me."

"Truly you are a guardian angel in such a time. I don't know who to trust. I am on my own. To see your face here…"

Daniel stood before her and held out is hand for her to take. He pulled her close, put his large hands upon her shoulders, and took in a deep shuddering breath. "I dreamed of when I would once again be near you enough to do…this." He began to inhale the smell of her hair. His lips brushed her heated cheek.

A fire began to roar deep inside Rose. Her body was tingling with desire. She felt as if control had been wrenched from her grasp irrevocably. This fire would burn everything in its wake. What would be left behind? Could she ride this course to unknown consequences?

His hand slipped closer to her swelling bosom and trailed down to her hip, which he firmly grasped. When his lips hovered over her own, she wanted nothing else but to feel their smooth caress. The meet was devastatingly slow. A cry of ache managed to escape her busy lips. She was now on the threshold of the point of no return.

Dive into the fire? Feel? Or steer clear of its path?

She tentatively moved her hands up his chest and fingered the top of his vest, feeling the planes of his chest underneath his crisp white shirt. Suddenly, he picked her up and placed her on the desk, his hand leisurely sliding up her leg, tracing swirls with his dancing fingertips. A flashback of Percy's hand hiking up her skirts snapped her out of her euphoria. She attempted to halt Daniel's ascent by pushing his hand down.

In response, he crushed her to his chest, and his lips moved to her collarbone. His whispers of abandonment trailed along. His now impatient hand pinned hers to the desk while his other one continued to inch up her inner thigh.

She frowned, her lips ceased. She managed to free her pinned hand and shove him so that he stumbled backward a few steps.

"What's wrong?" His lips were swollen. His face was that of one who had tasted blood and would not relent until he had drunk his fill.

"This needs to stop now." Her voice intoned no weakness, only anger. How could she have gone so far?

"Does it? Isn't this what you wanted?" He grasped her arms firmly and tasted her neck as she struggled to get free. "I want you. Do you want me?" He nibbled her ear.

Her answer surfaced unbidden. "Yes," she breathed.

His satisfied smile danced upon her skin. "Then...since you so graciously proffered yourself for my pleasure, I'll be sure to have it."

"Not like this, I will not be party to this. *This* will not continue. I came here for you to execute the will, nothing more, nothing less." She turned to grab the will and dangled it in his face.

He snatched it in a viper-like motion. "So you did." He pressed his palm against her cheek and teased her with his lips over hers. He suddenly pulled back. "You know, even though you deny it, your lips—I can feel them—waiting to be touched. They search for mine. I want you, and I'll have you someday. Today, I'll extend your leash. Tomorrow, like a dog, you'll be coming back to her master."

"You may think whatever you like. Shall we move on?" A cool facade sheltered the shock within.

"Yes, one step closer to my goal. Let us take a look. Please sit."

She let down her skirts and slid off his desk. She sat in the chair across his, with her back straight and arms tucked in.

Throughout the rest of the meeting, Rose embraced her ability to focus on a calculated, cold action. Neither one addressed the forward encounter, yet he unveiled his rakish gaze in a gaudy fashion.

Daniel read through the will and explained to her that her father had left her everything: the mile house, the business of running it, and even his infamous secret vein. He didn't leave one written clue on how to find the gold vein. She didn't give the gold a second thought. Once she signed a few papers, he authoritatively said, "Well, Miss Wood, I believe that concludes our...affair."

"I believe you deceive yourself into thinking that wit flatters your countenance."

"Believe what you like. I find it rather useful in this business."

The business of bodies, hearts and souls thrown out of the equation.

Rose got up and walked toward the door. "Good day, Mr. Shaw."

"Rose, wait!" He ran to her with such a look of concern, of desperation. Could it be that his conscience had pricked him, that he now sought forgiveness? He smugly smiled. He placed his hand under her bosom to right her clothing. He then ran his fingers through her hair, fixing it in some places. "There, now you look presentable. Wouldn't want your charming and innocent reputation to be put in trouble now, would we?"

Rose put on a steely smile, "You're quite right. Thank you." She opened the door and walked out, never once turning around to see the demon clothed as an angel of light.

Only as she was walking back to the boarding house, did shaky breaths come out.

If I go to the authorities with this, who will believe my side of the story? He's a very wealthy lawyer and gold digger, and I'm the fresh out of school girl known to look for attention in any way she can. There would be a slew of testimonials from school to confirm that fact. Look what has come from my need to be wanted. Dave...Dave told me. I remember now. I wouldn't listen to him. Oh God, in the deepest parts of my heart, I wanted...this, wanted to know the rush. Yet a better part of me, a part that's not even me, wants to hold out for something beautiful. I'm not sure what beautiful even looks like.

She arrived at the boarding house and knocked on Joe's door. "It's official," she said as a sleepy-eyed gruff face met hers.

"Good," he mumbled.

"Joe...I need you to do something for me."

Joe closed the door in her face.

A gasp escaped Rose's lips, so stunned by his uncharacteristic disrespect.

Joe opened the door once more. His face was wet, and water dripped down the ends of his beard. "I'm ready."

"Perfect." She grinned. "We're going to need another hand on deck at the mile house. I want to find someone who can cook well, who likes to do house chores."

Joe smirked, "Because, of course, miss, you can't do none of these yerself."

"Why, I believe my sarcasm is rubbing off on you. You'll be the better for it."

"I don't need no lecture."

Rose's mouth gaped open in amusement. "My, miracles do exist! Now off with you. We'll meet back in two hours to discuss candidates." Her chuckle floated along the short corridor. Surprised to hear her unfamiliar sound of merriment, she put a hand to her mouth and smiled.

She left the boarding house and walked down the road. On the edge of town, a sizzling sound and the smell of cooking beef enticed her to the left side of the road. There in front of her was a small wooden stall loosely covered by a white cloth, its corners tied to the stall's frame. The edges were yellowed and the back overhang had blackened from the smoke wafting from a grill over fire.

The man manning the stall had his back to her. She had never seen anyone like him. He turned her way and gave her the whitest smile she had ever seen. His skin looked like black leather, a face weathered by hardship. Her father had told her of these people, those who had been wrenched from their homes to be overworked daily and many times beaten by the people from the South. His face effused kindness and sincerity.

He put his hands upon his hips and peered into her eyes. He nodded, as if, to himself.

She realized how wide her eyes had become. She didn't mean for him to feel as though he were a specimen she was inspecting.

He smiled, the crinkles in his face fitting into place so perfectly that it seemed as if smiling was the easiest thing in the world for him. "I take it ya haven't seen many…people like me befo, have ya?" His manner of speech was so inviting. The sound of it was created for hospitality.

She shook her head. "I'm so sorry for staring. My father did not bring me up to…"

"Now, don't ya worry yer pretty little head. Many mo' of us 'ave traveled up this way, but I'm thinkin' dat most of us are in de East, you know, where de farmin' is."

"What are you cooking?"

"Now dis here recipe I learned from my momma. It's chunks of beef mixed with onion and here…." He grabbed one off the grill. "Ya spear dem with a stick and cook it over de fire. Now de spices I put on de beef, well, dose are a secret. Here try one."

"Oh, I don't have any money with me at the moment."

"Forget it! Try one, on de house"

"Thank you." She lightly blew on the first piece of meat. Tendrils of smoke wrapped around the stick of beef. She grabbed the first piece with her front teeth and pushed it back to her molars, expecting it to be the same kind of tough meat she was so used to eating. Her teeth came down on the meat, and the meat shredded into pieces. It melted in her mouth. She savoured it and explored the newfound flavours.

"What is this?" She looked at the meat as if it were the holy grail of food itself.

He laughed deeply. "I told you what it is."

After it had mellowed to an unforgettable aftertaste, she turned to him and asked, "Are you here digging for gold?"

"Ah, I tried my hand at it, but dat's not where my heart lies. Cooking—dis is what I oughta be doin', what I need to be doin'."

"You're perfect!"

"Well, I know I'm a saint, but only de good Lord is perfect."

"No, I mean yes. That's not what I mean. Do you have any family, sir? Because they could come along…"

"Whoa, now slow down. It's just me and my secret recipes. Where might we be goin'?"

"Sir, how would like to come work for me at the 108 Mile House?"

"Sure."

"Just like that?"

"Yup."

"I don't know what I can offer you in payment quite yet. We haven't reopened for business. I promise you'll be given fair wages. This is all very new for me. You'll have more than a decent roof over your head and food."

"Don't git yerrself in a big heap now. How could I say no to a pretty little thing like you who's gone out of her way to feed my pride? Things are gettin' quiet around here with de gold rush calmin' down. I've been havin' trouble payin' my rent. You'd be doin' an old man here a mighty fine favour. Lord's been lookin' down on me and finally provided you."

"He has, and He's provided me with you." She stuck out her hand, "I'm Rose, Rose Wood."

"Jack, Jack Smith."

"Mr. Smith, meet my companion and I at the boarding house down the road bright and early. We'll be leaving then."

"Will do, miss. Lookin' forward."

Before an ounce of sunlight touched the town, Joe quietly rapped at Rose's door and gave her a ten minute warning to leaving. Rose had instructed him to do so. She didn't want the opportunity to see Daniel's lusting gaze lurking around. She wanted to steal away while everyone was barely waking. She wanted to run to the only home she had, which didn't feel like much of a home anyway. She had heard the saying *Home is where the heart is.* Her heart had nothing firm she could grasp onto. It was tossed about as if in a stormy sea with no available anchor. The only solution was to choose a home and make do.

As they were packing up the buggy, Rose heard a whistling in the distance. The tune was not a sombre one but one that conjured up dancing and feasting in her mind. Jack focused into view.

He slapped his hands together. "Well, good mornin'."

Rose answered, "Good morning, Jack, I'm so glad you made it."

"Yup, settled everything with my landlady, packed up all my stuff, and skedaddled out o' there."

Joe huffed as he hauled the last trunk into the back. "Who's this yahoo?"

"Joe, this is Jack Smith, the new addition to 108 Mile House."

"Pleasure to meet you!" Jack jutted his hand out to shake Joe's hand.

Joe shifted his gaze from Rose to Jack with an annoyed expression. "Mornin'." He shuffled off to ensure the driving reins and the harnesses attached to the horses were secure.

"You'll have to forgive Joe. He's…"

"A silent fellow, ain't he?"

Rose smiled, "Yes."

Jack threw his bags into the back of the cart. He dusted off his hands as he said, "He ain't gonna have a problem with me, is he?"

Rose touched his arm and smiled. "We could do with a lot of good cheer."

Joe jumped into the driver's seat and handled the reins.

Rose was about to step up when Jack offered his hand. She turned to Joe, skirts in hand. "Joe, you'll never have to worry about being a gentleman again. Jack here will fit the part well enough."

Joe grunted in response, and she gave him a gentle shove with her arm. Jack ascended next. "It's a beautiful day, isn't it gentlemen?" Rose said, trying to relieve the tension between the two.

Jack replied, "Mighty fine day, it is."

Joe rolled his eyes. A mile or two on the Cariboo trail, Jack launched into singing "Swing Low, Sweet Chariot." He was about to sing another from his sure-to-be large repertoire, but Joe had other ideas.

"Mr. Smith, can't we just enjoy the peace of God's green earth?" Joe's arms were stiff at his side, and he held his breath—looking as if he were a teapot ready to blow.

"Miss Rose, I don't think ya told me of all the unpleasant details pertainin' to de job."

"I heard that," Joe huffed.

"Oh Joe! He's harmless. Tell me where you learned your songs from."

Jack gleefully rubbed his hands. "Happy to know someone appreciates 'em. I met a man named Wallis Willis in de Oklahoma County. He was a freedman like me. We got talkin' and he shared dis song he wrote. It stuck to my soul dis song. Once I heard it, I couldn't forget it. I'm heaven bound and dis song...my momma would've loved it."

Rose exclaimed, "How beautiful!"

Joe cleared his throat a couple of times. "You can, uh, sing it if you want again."

Rose and Jack shared a look of mischief. A twinkle in Jack's eyes grew brighter as he hollered the song.

If this is a little picture of what a home could be like, what would the whole picture look like?

A wise man proportions his belief to the evidence.
David Hume

Chapter 6

They arrived at 108 Mile House two days later. This place, which had seemed so ominous, now looked like a run down bed and breakfast, languishing for some crowded company.

"Jack, welcome to 108 Mile House," Rose announced. "I'll show you to your room." Straightway, Rose led Jack upstairs while Joe followed quietly behind. She turned right on the landing to where two separate bedrooms rested away from the other six at the other end of the house. She opened the door to the room on the left. "Jack, this will be your room."

Jack tentatively walked in, "Miss, dis is mighty fine." He whistled in appreciation.

Rose could feel Joe step away from her toward the room next door. "Joe?" She murmured in a disciplinary tone.

"Miss?"

"This will be your room, as well."

"I'll be more than happy with the other one, here."

"No, you will not. It would be highly inappropriate if you slept in my room."

At this scandalous mention, his cheeks turned red as beets as he replied, "Your room?"

"Why, yes! Do you expect me to sleep out in the barn with the horses?" she said, putting her hands on her hips. Jack's chuckling behind her made it almost impossible to keep a stern look on her face and not laugh.

"Don't we have six other rooms?"

Rose quipped, "Which we'll need for our illustrious guests."

"I'm not too sure what illustrious means, miss, but my guess is your guests will be anything but."

"Gentlemen," Rose said, swivelling her head from side to side, eyeing both men. "Do we have a problem?"

Jack piped, "No! How 'bout you Joe?"

"Huh," Joe huffed. He removed his things from another bedroom he had been using and moved them into the bedroom while Jack commenced his unpacking. As she walked toward her room, she heard Joe threaten in low tones, "So long as you don't sing the whole time, we won't be havin' fights. Deal?" The slap of the men's hands clasping together to shake out their deal brought a spark of tenderness in Rose's bosom. She spread the curtains apart to see the surfaces were in need of dusting. She unpacked her suitcase and fished her heaped dresses out of her previous room.

Once she had finished putting everything away, she decided to scour the house and peruse its contents. She now had a business to run after all, and inventory was to be accounted for. She had no clue as to the state her dead father had left the mile house in. She passed by Jack and Joe's room. They were not in sight. She scanned the other rooms she intended to rent out to the miners who would seek shelter. Each room had a sturdy bed made with clean sheets, a quilt, and a down feather pillow.

Father always insisted on having the best.

Each room was also furnished with a writing desk and chair, an end table holding a basin and water pitcher, and a mirror. She wandered downstairs and searched every cabinet, every closet where she thought there would be preserves, supplies. The cellar was full of salted pork, preserves from the garden, and other supplies from wagon trains.

Around the back of the house she found the garden. It had been planted, but the weeds were overrunning every good sprout. Thankful that this part of the property was now shaded from the hot sun, she started to weed. She had been weeding, enough that about a third of the garden was presentable, when she heard footsteps accompanied by a whistle. She turned to the side to see Jack holding a large basket with what looked like weeds thrown in haphazardly. "Jack, what have you got there? They're not pretty enough to put on the table," she said, smirking.

"Miss, don't you know yer medicinal herbs?" he asked flabbergasted, his eyebrows raised as high as they could.

"Jack, we shall have to get better acquainted, perhaps, in front of the fire this evening after supper. Now, would you like to help me finish this plot in silence? I don't like to chatter while I work except…"

Except with Priscilla.

He nodded, put his basket down on the grass, and helped weed the last section of the garden.

She hoped he hadn't noticed her near spill of vulnerability, but…

"Except what?" His long fingers grabbed the plant's bottom and wrenched it from the ground's clasp.

"As I said, I don't like to chatter."

The rest of the weeding, she spent cradled in the soulful tunes pouring through his pursed lips. The feeling of settling in was becoming a more natural occurrence. She couldn't remember the last time she had felt so safe, especially in unknown surroundings.

It was mid afternoon when Rose left 108 Mile House on her own to speak to the proprietors of 100 Mile House. She tacked up one of the horses and proceeded to mount it. At first, her whole body sat straight up as a pin, the muscles in her back, arms, and legs taut as if to snap. It had been a long while since the last time she had ridden. When they had lived in England, her father had snapped up one of the finest riding instructors in the country. She never had a graceful finesse while riding much to the dismay of her instructor. However, she had a natural instinct in connecting with the horse's movements.

I can do this. I need not be afraid. I'm aptly capable of riding a few miles down the road.

She nudged the horse forward, but it only backed up a few feet. "Work with me, horsey. Ugh, I don't even know your name. That's probably why you're not listening, isn't it?" The horse just stared ahead as if bored with the conversation at hand. "Let's try this again," she said nudging him forward once more, only this time remembering not to pull on the reins. He walked a few paces then switched to a brisk trot away from the barn and onto the open road. "I don't remember it being this bumpy," she spurted as she tried to breathe and regain her balance. She began to post in her saddle, making sure that as the horse's front shoulder moved upward she stood in her stirrups. Once she had mastered the timing, the horse moved into a canter. All jostling now morphed into a gentle rocking, such as the motion from a rocking chair. "Now why couldn't you do this at first? This is much easier than trotting."

A line of five log houses loomed into view almost an hour later as she crested the top of the hill. Nearing the establishment, she could see a general store gracing the acreage as well as several buildings in which to house guests. She slipped off her horse and tied the reins to a post. She entered the main house and immediately noticed its roughness and the coarse dirt lingering within the cracks between the boards and in the corners.

At least my father had the decency to keep his establishment clean and elegant.

A china man rounded the corner.

She asked, "Excuse me, could you point me in the direction of the owner?"

"What for?"

"I'm the new proprietor of the next mile house. I must speak with him."

"Yes, Mr. Nelson, is this way. Please follow." He moved toward the back of the building where a man, cuffs up to his elbows and his hands upon his forehead, sat at a desk. "Mr. Nelson, a young lady to see you."

Mr. Nelson dropped one of his hands to wave Rose over without looking up from his paper. "Come in."

Rose sat in the chair opposite him and waited.

Mr. Nelson didn't move but instead mumbled as he further scrutinized his papers.

Rose cleared her throat. "Mr. Nelson?"

"Yes? What can I do to help you?"

"My name is Rose Wood."

He finally looked up and scrutinized her face. "Wood, you say?"

"Yes."

"Harland's daughter! Is your father open for business yet?"

"He's dead."

"Did I just hear correctly that he's dead?"

She gave a curt nod.

He stroked his beard and furtively looked to her. "Please accept my condolences."

"Accepted. My foreman Joe came here almost two weeks ago to tell you to continue to tell people 108 Mile House was closed. I've come to tell you that it is now open for business."

"Good to know. I'll inform my clientele tonight and from now on."

"There's something else I'd like to discuss with you if you have the time."

"Yes, I have the time." His eyes widened as he put his folded hands under his chin.

"The man who told you Harland had sent him over…"

"Yes, I already spoke to Joe and gave him my description."

"Yes, I know. Is there no other information you could give me? Perhaps a mark, scar, disfigurement…"

"No, just that he was on the heavy side. Now is that the conclusion of our business? I'm sorry I don't mean to be rude, but I'm very busy."

"One more thing, I'd like to continue to rent the buggy and horses until I can buy them from you in, say, two months? Would that be to your liking?"

"Yes, tell the new owner that's all right. I've got enough goods here. Any thing to help the next proprietor of 108 Mile House."

"That would be me."

He sat back in his chair and tented his fingers. "Really? I would never have guessed."

"Why is that? Did he really never talk about his only daughter?" Anger began to simmer in her bowels.

"No, on the contrary," he guffawed. "He talked about you all right. Told me that if he ever did die, which he was wary of because of his age, that he would make other arrangements."

"Surely you must have heard wrong."

"I definitely didn't. I wonder what must have made him change his mind."

"Why didn't he want me to have it?"

"He said something to the effect of you were meant to have more than this. He wanted you to be far away from this place because he knew you hated it." His eyes slowly reverted back to his desk.

She slowly stood up from the seat. "Thank you so much for your time." Her eyes frantically searched the door. Her lips went dry. No hesitation was in her steps this time as she strode toward her ride. She kicked the horse's sides, making him gallop from his initial steps. She trusted the horse to guide the way back home.

This doesn't make sense…. I always thought he would pass it on to me to, I don't know, to keep his legacy alive? But Mr. Nelson was quite emphatic about what he heard. There's no good reason why he should lie.

Crickets chirped as the last light of day streaked down toward the horizon, the stars peeped. Too tired to brush the horse, she hastily put the tack away in a haphazard fashion and trudged toward the house. Rose banged open the door, not caring at the moment of the unladylike commotion she was arousing, and plopped onto the nearest sofa. She nearly fell asleep, but Jack's voice boomed from the kitchen doorway, "Miss Wood! Oh…!" He quickly lowered his voice to shushing sounds. "I'm so sorry. I thought ya'd want some of my chicken pot pie. How 'bout it?"

Joe barged in and shouted, "Where is she?"

Rose threw her hands up. "Hush! Your booming voice is loud enough to split my head open. If you must know, I took my sweet time coming back. I heard some unsettling news."

Jack sat beside Rose with his hands clasped together between his knees. Joe hunkered down on the chair opposite, expelling a large annoyed sigh.

Joe huffed. "Well, do we have the horses and buggy?"

"Yes," Rose said, her chin cradled upon her fist looking at a dark corner.

"What is it?" he said, his eyes haggard looking.

Rose replied, "Mr. Nelson informed me that my father had never intended to leave me this land, property, any of it. It begs the question, what changed his mind?" Lazily, she turned her head to look at Joe, "Do you know why?"

Like on, that on a lonesome road
Doth walk in fear and dread,
And having once turned round walks on,
And turns no more his head;
Because he knows, a frightful fiend
Doth close behind him tread.
Samuel Taylor Coleridge
pt. vi

Chapter 7

Joe had no answer. Jack was as silent as the grave, and that was nigh impossible. The fire occasionally spit out its embers. Rose was the first to drag herself up the stairs to go to bed. Slumping onto her bed, she heard Jack's light footsteps walk into his room. She was asleep by the time Joe's hand touched the knob of his bedroom door.

Rose awoke with the sun. She put on a plain dress and a working apron over it and got to work dusting whatever little dust motes remained after Jack's sweep yesterday. Rinsing her rag, she heard a rumble of wheels. Her first customer was here. She peered out the window trying to make out who it was. As the cart approached, she spotted a fair head of curls.

It can't be.

"Priscilla!" She grabbed two fistfuls of her skirt and ran toward the cart.

Priscilla's smile was a balm to her dull, aching heart. She had longed to see her friend again, especially without having given a proper goodbye at finishing school. Priscilla, ever the lady, waited for her driver to help her out. As soon as her feet touched the ground, both of the girls' arms wrapped around each other so tightly they could barely breathe.

"Rose, how I've missed your antics!"

"I have so many questions. I—not now, let's get you inside. You can meet Joe and Jack."

"Two suitors! My, Rose, you've been busy!"

Waggling her brows, she laid her hand over her heart and countered, "Of course not, you know me better than that! I would have a whole string of suitors. I couldn't settle for two. In all seriousness, let me introduce them." She looped her arm through Priscilla's and led her toward the door.

"Joe, Jack!" she hollered.

"Rose, I don't believe this place does you good. You've become even more savage than before."

"I'm just so excited you're here!"

A towel draped over his shoulder and a bowl of batter cradled in the nook of his arm, Jack came from the kitchen. "Joe's out choppin' firewood in de back. Why, hello, dere! Who might you be? I'm Jack."

"Pleased to meet you! I'm Priscilla, Rose's dear friend." She extended her hand out, palm face down.

Jack took notice and swung it down once to acknowledge her greeting. "I've heard some 'bout you."

"Good things, I hope," Priscilla's cheeks coloured.

Jack hesitantly looked sideways at Rose as he said, "Well, I know for a fact she chatters only with *you* when she works."

"That is true."

"Jack, I hope you don't mind if Priscilla and I steal away for an hour to catch up. Oh, but you're beginning to make breakfast! Priscilla..."

Priscilla gracefully interjected, "I'm not terribly hungry, what with all the bouncing of the buggy along the road. I'm afraid if I eat now, I might become ill."

He waved them off. "Run along now. No needin' t'explain to me. My sister was de same with her friends. So long as you come back in an hour or else Joe will have my hide."

"You have our word, Jack," Priscilla said with such solemnity as one who takes a lifelong oath.

As soon as Jack turned his back to continue with the breakfast, Rose and Priscilla giggled all the way up to Rose's bedroom. Both girls sat on the bed.

"My, your father had good taste."

Rose suddenly turned, wondering how her friend could have known. "How?"

Priscilla ducked her head down. When she looked up, her eyes were shimmering with tears. "I'm so sorry that you never had a proper chance to get to know him. It's awful! I—we live near Barkerville. It's spreading like wildfire. I'm sure the paper will be printing it soon. My heart longed to be with you when I first heard."

"Yes, I presume the news would have gotten out since I had legal obligations in town.

"What happened to you? The day we left finishing school? It was quite unlike you to just up and leave with a letter boasting of very poor penmanship."

"Rose, forgive me for upsetting you. My father came early in the morning, hauled my trunks into the buggy in a matter of minutes before he whisked me back home. I only had a minute to pen the letter, and my nerves were getting the best of me."

"Why so quickly? Was anything the matter?"

Priscilla began smoothing some crinkles in her dress. She did so over and over again. "Yes, my brother was on his death bed—the polio. I was never told of his illness before that day. They had hoped…he would get better. They didn't want me to worry. I just wish they had told me sooner. I would have been able to give him a proper goodbye, I could have read to him more, I could have…." Her voice wavered. "We've both lost, haven't we?"

"Priscilla, I'm sure he knew how much you loved him. Anybody who knows you, knows that."

"The rest of my time has been carried out in grieving and comforting my family." She gave a meek smile. "I cannot speak of this anymore, or I'll cry for hours on end. Tell me, what mischief have you been up to?"

Rose relayed to Priscilla all the happenings of the past month. However, she didn't disclose too many details of the night she had found her father dead. That was a night belonging to her alone and the one who had borne witness to it.

"You did this on purpose, didn't you? You filled your life with mayhem so that I would have endless adventures to dream of. You're too kind." Priscilla dreamily sighed.

"I did not. You could have these same adventures." Rose squeezed Priscilla's hand.

"My sensibilities don't complement your experiences. That's why I have you. You said you saw Daniel Shaw several times. Do, please, tell me more."

"Yes, I did." Rose twiddled with a loose thread on her dress. "However, our last meeting didn't go well."

"Why?"

"He's the lawyer I went to, to have my father's will read and dealt with. As soon as I laid eyes on him, he lit a fire deep within me. I was sure to give him whatever he asked. He kissed me…. Then he started to ask for more than I could give. He's less the gentleman I thought he was."

"I'm sorry. Could you have misread him?"

"I don't know how I could have. I want to be wrong. He's everything I've ever wanted in a man. I desire him more than anything else I ever have. Perhaps you're right…maybe I misread the signs."

"Of course, I'm sure it will turn out all right." She started to fiddle with her fingers as if she were in distress.

"Priscilla, what's wrong? Is there some young man you fancy?" She took her friend's hand in her own, rubbing her thumbs over them.

"No, that's just the thing, no one seems to fancy me, not even the older gentlemen. Believe me, they wouldn't be my first pick. There is someone…"

"Oh, now it's your turn to tell me more!"

"It would never work."

"Why?"

"He only sees me as a confidante, a friend, nothing else."

"Have you told him how you feel?"

"You would think that I never would, but I have. He made it very clear there's someone else."

"That may change in time."

"I don't think so."

Rose wished to cheer her up. "Will you stay for a while? Please, I've missed you."

"I'm at liberty to stay for several days. What fun this will be!"

The two girls skipped down the stairs and sat down at the table. A stack of pancakes peeking from underneath the dishcloth sat on the corner of the dining room table.

Jack hollered from the kitchen, "I thought a herd of elephants came stampedin' down de stairs. Ain't you two supposed to be ladies?" He chuckled.

Rose stepped toward the doorframe and squared him down. "Jack, you must never tell another soul about our behaviour." She winked.

Jack winked back.

The rest of the girls's day was spent in walking around the tree line (Rose made sure to steer clear of her father's hastily made grave), lying in the meadow, and doing what all manner of things girls enjoy doing. Rose's soul was knit with Priscilla's.

Like David and Jonathan. How blessed I am to have found such a thing.

That evening, everyone sat round the fire. Rose murmured, "I don't know what a real family is like. It's always been my father and I. Even then, I've mostly been on my own. I don't know if I'm correct, but this feels like family to me. We get along well enough. We look out for each other."

Priscilla hugged Rose while Jack smiled broadly and Joe gave an almost imperceptible nod.

"Joe, if I may ask, what was your family like? I still don't know much about you." Rose asked.

82

"You don't need to know." Joe scowled as he lumbered upstairs.

Ashamed of her unwanted prying, she grabbed her lamp and went upstairs. Priscilla scurried close behind her. She showed Priscilla her room. Once Priscilla was settled, she moved to her own. She laid her lamp upon her end table and proceeded to let down her hair. Lightly humming to herself, she brushed it, put on her nightgown, and lay down to sleep.

A wave of chills swept over her skin (though the covers were still on) as her ears picked up an eerie cry—Priscilla! She vaulted from her bed and hurried to relight her lamp. While she lit the flame, she realized the noise wasn't a scream as she had first thought. Instead, it was the horses neighing uncontrollably, fear lacing their every cry.

She counted herself fortunate she could wake up in the middle of the night if need be because Joe (it seemed Jack, as well) was a very heavy sleeper. She put on her robe and padded downstairs. She made sure to keep quiet.

As she entered the barn, her lamp illuminated the flaring nostrils of both horses. Their eyes intimated they had seen a fleeting spectre.

She attempted to grab the horses' halters. "Shh, it's all right. I'm here. Calm down."

Their eye movements eventually slowed, their gazes occasionally darting toward a dark corner. Their heads hesitatingly lowered, and they accepted her hand of calm.

"What could have made you act this way?" She sifted around the barn. Nothing seemed to have been disturbed. "Goodnight, rest now."

Full of trepidation, she walked to the opening of the barn and peered down the lane both to the left and to the right. She turned to the left and walked a little ways away from the safety of the house and barn. The air was warm and stagnant. Beads of perspiration traveled down her neck. Her hands shook slightly. There was nothing.

The ghost of father...of course not. What nonsense!

A foreboding feeling overcoming her senses, she tripped over herself and ran back to the house. Before she opened the door, she caught sight of an envelope, with red lettering written across, tucked into the door. She grabbed it and dropped it a moment later. The red lettering was clearly written in blood, her name a shattering crimson. She picked it up and ran inside, shutting the door quickly before any invisible assailant could creep in.

She stood in the entrance not knowing what to do with it. She licked her lips and exhaled deeply. Taking two steps at a time up the stairs, she checked on Priscilla. Her friend was sleeping like a baby.

The harmless little creak of closing Priscilla's door made Rose jump.

She sat down upon her bed and stared at the ghastly sight. She took a sip of water from her glass. Her hand shook violently. She spilled a large amount of water on the envelope, darkening the blood lettered name into a mud brown splotch. She ripped open the envelope to find a single sheet with unfamiliar handwriting.

Your father dead, bones to dust,
Remember all the memories you must.
I am not willing that you forget;
For Harland Wood's treasure you must get.

It is not a rumour, it is truth.
Those whispers are your noose.
The more you hear, the tighter
It will wrap, colder than a fetter.

So hunting you must go for me
There is no way out, you see.
You will do as you are told
Or in death you will lie cold.

A groan outside her room—she hastily blew out the flame, hid the note beneath her pillow, and clutched the covers to her nose. Perhaps it was a trick of the mind, but footsteps echoed down the hall. She shut her eyes tight, murmuring to herself that the nightmare would end. She couldn't remember when she had fallen asleep. For the terror of the moment continued to torment her even in sleep.

A lilting voice brought about a sharp pain to her temple. Rose couldn't quite make out the owner of the voice, her head was spinning. She gasped, "What is it?"

Priscilla's voice cleared, "Rose? Rose? Do you hear me? You're giving us quite the scare."

"Priscilla," Rose moaned.

"Oh, she said my name! That must be good, right, Joe?"

"Yup, Jack, go downstairs, get another glass of water." He grabbed the glass on the table and sniffed it. He dipped his finger and sucked on its tip. Once Jack brought the new water glass, Joe grunted. "Just as I thought."

Priscilla laid her lily white hand on Joe's taught shoulder. "Joe, tell us, please."

"She's been drugged. This water has a slight bitter taste to it. Seen it a lot of times when…ah, never mind. Did anybody see any thing?"

Priscilla shook her head as her tears threatened to spill.

Jack raised his voice, "We were all sleepin' last night. Somethin' must ha' happened!"

Joe's voice rumbled in Rose's head as thunder spilling across the land. "We'll have to wait until she wakes up. Give her a few hours. She can tell us then."

Their blurry swirling figures moved out of the room. She meant to call out for them before her eyes closed shut of their own volition, barricading her from conscious thought to be dragged back to her numb cell.

A lamp burned to her left as her lids fluttered open. The pain that had pressed upon her temple was gone.

Priscilla's head lay upon her crooked arm supported by the corner of the end table. Her fair hair shimmered in the low light as she stirred. Her eyes met Rose's and she let out a small, surprised gasp. "Are you all right?"

"Mm, I suppose…." Rose turned to lean on her arm. "What happened?"

"There's really nothing to worry about."

"Priscilla, you must tell me."

"Joe…he said you were drugged."

"Drugged? I'm not surprised." A loopy smile complemented the dark rings under her eyes.

"What do you mean? You didn't do this to yourself, did you?" Priscilla reprimanded.

"I'm not that desperate to liven my life. I believe I've got myself a mad friend."

"Rose, enough with the jokes. I know you're hiding something."

"How you know me too well…someone was here last night. I didn't see any one. I woke to the sound of the horses neighing in terror. I went outside…"

Priscilla interrupted with fierce whispers, "In the middle of the night? It's dangerous outside. You could have been attacked by a bear…"

"There was no bear. Someone was here. Take a look at the evidence." Rose's left hand curled behind her head and felt the letter underneath her pillow. She passed it to Priscilla who turned white as a sheet.

Priscilla's fingers slipped as she endeavoured to release the note from its envelope. Her right hand went to her lips as she read the cryptic poem. "What does this mean?"

"My father truly did care only for gold. There's a treasure, and I'm to find it."

"Where will you start?" Priscilla looked with concerned eyes.

"I'm not going to."

"What do you mean?"

"I will not let this man corner me as a cat would a mouse. I don't care about the gold."

"He'll kill you!"

"Joe and Jack won't let it happen."

"They were asleep last night, and this man drugged you."

"I will not!" Rose shouted.

Priscilla cowered in her chair, her eyes emanating a wounded heart.

"Please, forgive me. I just…can't. I'll be all right."

"No, you won't. I'm going to tell Joe and Jack right now. Perhaps they'll talk some sense into you."

As soon as Priscilla left the room, Rose rolled up the envelope along with the note and shoved it into the opening of her lamp. She watched the threatening words dissolve into ash.

By the time her three protectors had crossed her room's threshold, the last curling scrap had been devoured. Joe's eyes immediately darted to the flame's highest point before it returned to its weak sputter.

"What's going on?" Joe asked.

"I presume Priscilla gave you the details."

"She did."

Rose shrugged a shoulder. "Well, what's all the fuss?"

"We'll help you find it," Jack offered.

Rose raised her palm to stop any more jabbering. "We will not hunt for the treasure, understood, Joe?"

"Yes, miss."

"Joe?" Priscilla stamped her foot. "She's going to die if she doesn't."

Joe retorted in a placating manner. "We'll keep a close eye on Rose. She's ain't going nowhere by herself for the time being."

"Joe!" Rose sat up in her bed with an indignant air.

"That's the condition. Good enough, Miss Priscilla?"

Priscilla screwed her mouth in agitation and her eyes narrowed on a point of the floor, "It suffices."

"Good, now let's all leave Miss Rose alone so she can have a good night's rest."

Rose huffed. "Wait, Priscilla, please stay a moment."

Priscilla stiffly returned to her seat.

Rose said, "I know you mean well, but I just can't!"

Priscilla melted into a tearing girl. "Oh, Rose, I just couldn't bear the thought that…well…I don't think I could live without you." She wrapped her arms around her recovering friend and said, "Sleep well."

"Goodnight." Rose rolled over onto her side and stretched out her arm to sip her water. Her fingers hesitated to touch the glass. The last time they had executed such an easy action, the rest of her body had succumbed to poison.

I cannot live my life like this, always second guessing every thought.

If you don't, you might not have a life to live.

She didn't drink the water. She hoped her fear would slither out her open window to prey upon another host.

The next day around noon, as two teams of wagons pulled up to the house, Priscilla was packing her bags with Rose's help. Rose looked out the window to see at least ten men sidle off their benches and unload their packs. The sound of the clasps closing Priscilla's luggage brought her attention back to her friend. "Joe will bring those down for you once he's done with our guests."

Priscilla walked around the bed and toward the window joining Rose in viewing the newcomers. "It's a shame there's not as many good looking men here as there are in London, or even Victoria. Oh, look at that one! Not sharp and elegant but he exudes such a rugged handsomeness, don't you think?"

"Where?" Being caught up in such girlish fantasies with her friend once again was so simple and pleasant.

"You just missed him. Well, you'll see him soon enough."

Rose turned toward the door. "Let's tell Joe you're ready. I believe I saw your ride coming down the road."

Priscilla followed Rose down the stairs and out the door. Priscilla's ride rolled toward them and stopped.

Joe led the miners inside after instructing them where they could put their belongings, wagons and horses. Many of the men tipped their hats to the waiting ladies.

Joe informed Rose, "Miss, they're plannin' to stay the night. We don't have enough rooms, but some won't mind sleepin' on the floor."

"Good, would you mind fetching Priscilla's things from her room please?"

Minutes later, Joe returned with Priscilla's baggage and placed it into her buggy.

"When will you visit me again?" Rose cupped Priscilla's hands within her own and squeezed them.

"I'll write, now that I know where you live. Perhaps, in a month's time?"

"I suppose I'll have to settle for that. I know your family needs you right now, more than ever."

She smiled sadly. "They do." She squeezed Rose's hands in return. "Please be careful."

Rose smirked. "I will, and I make no promises of changing my mind about the note."

Priscilla wrapped her arms around Rose and sniffled back a few tears. Her driver stood at the ready and gave her his hand to help her up the wagon. A few moments later, the wagon gave a little jolt backwards as the horses started to walk.

Noises from the barn caught Rose's attention. She squinted to see who was inside when Dave walked out. As soon as he saw her, he stopped and raised his hand in greeting. Rose took a step toward him and stopped as she remembered each intimate moment of their last encounter. A small smile played upon her lips. He had said he would come and he did. The distance between them cried for a bridge to be let down, to be walked upon.

Dave looked down at his boots and fastened his thumbs in his pockets. He took a step and another, slowing his pace the nearer he got to Rose.

She felt the wind tugging the bottom of her skirts toward him. "Just a few steps," it seemed to say. One step was all the satisfaction she would give it.

He opened his dry lips then closed them.

"Would you like some water?" she offered.

He nodded. "I hope you don't mind that I'm here. The men and I, we're passing through and...if you need me to leave..."

"It's all right. One friend has gone and another has come. I'd like you to stay."

"About that night..."

She interrupted, "Did you find the person responsible?"

"No, I can't..."

She grabbed his arm and led him toward the small garden in the back. "Here, go on."

He looked around the perimeter and toward the outlying buildings. He took a small step toward her and said, "The only thing I remember is drinking a glass of water at the saloon while the other men were downing whiskey. Next thing I know, I'm out cold in the alley stinking like whiskey. Then you found me."

Her eyes grew. "You said a glass of water? Did it taste a little bitter?"

"Come to think of it, it was. How'd you know? I thought it tasted a little funny at the time."

She raised her hand to her brow and pushed her hair out of her eyes and took a half step away from him toward the great beyond.

"Rose, what is it?"

"You were drugged just as I was two nights ago."

His eyes bored into hers as he stomped toward her, stopping a foot distance away. Beads of sweat trickled down his stubble as he bit his lip. "Were you hurt?"

"No, of course not. Were you?"

"Quit playing around! Were you?"

"I wasn't hurt. What are you so upset about?" She planted her hands on her hips.

"I'm upset at whoever did this!" He grabbed his hat and swatted the side of his leg with it.

"They must be connected, somehow, the two incidents." She said, certain her assumption was correct.

His steam cooled off. "What do you mean?"

She recounted her entire recollection of the night, the spooked horses, the note, and the drug in the water. "Don't you agree?"

"Can I see the note?" He tapped his foot.

"I burned it. I have no wish to go treasure hunting. I will not give in to his demands." She threw her hands into the air. "I just...want to live one moment to the next. I didn't want this place, but I have it now. I see that the shadow of my father doesn't have to cling to this place. I can make it my own. I finally feel like I have a home."

Dave's fingers reached toward hers yet stopped before they touched hers. "It's not safe. You need to leave."

She saw the closeness of their fingers and remembered the graze of his stubble on her cheek. "I can't keep running. I've been doing that my entire life. Running from my studies, my homeland, my father—I need to build my life here."

'Tis all a Chequer-board of Nights and Days
Where Destiny with Men for Pieces plays:
Hither and thither moves, and mates, and slays,
And one by one back in the Closet lays.
Edward Fitzgerald

Chapter 8

That evening, Rose helped Jack make supper for all their guests. They served baked beans, shepherd's pie, and fresh greens which had decided to sprout abundantly the night before. Jack scooped the portions onto the plates, and Rose brought them to the dining room where the men were seated. Raucous laughter engulfed the room.

As Rose went to set the simple china plate upon the rounded corner of the table where Dave sat, he caught her eye. Her throat became constricted. She was unable to breathe a full breath as he watched her every movement.

She had experienced the same immobility earlier that afternoon when she had watched him lunge his horse. His command of the horse was breathtaking, unlike anything she had ever seen. He hadn't been too harsh or gentle, applying the certain pressures and queues when necessary and praising the horse when the job had been done well. She hadn't meant to watch him the entire time he had been in the field. She hadn't meant to watch at all. She had just wanted to take advantage of the shaded garden to weed.

The second before she turned aside, he said, "Thank you."

She smiled. It wasn't a smile coated with sarcasm or a smile she had to put on for the sake of being polite. It was a smile which sprang from the pockets of her heart where remnants of happiness still rang when touched the right way. Those had been few and far between.

A couple men retired to their rooms after supper. The rest, including Dave, decided to pair up and engage in arm-wrestling matches. Joe made it very clear to not upset any of the furniture per Rose's orders.

Believing this was as good a time as any, she played some ludicrously happy tune on the piano. This was the one ladylike gift she had excelled at whilst she was at finishing school. After two songs, she realized Dave had left the room.

Strange, he didn't even say goodnight. Friends, indeed!

Rose's tunes became more morose with each subsequent one. As her finger pressed the last key, a warm hand rested upon her shoulder. She turned to face Dave who now looked very different. He had cast off his sweat-laden chequered shirt for a crisp white one. His brow, hands, and stubble had been washed clean. He smiled expectantly. "Would you like to play a round of chess with me? I see you have a set."

She raised her eyebrows in surprise and admiration. "You play chess?"

"Why would I offer if I didn't?"

"You might have lied to impress me."

"That's one thing you can always count on. I won't lie to you, ever."

Far away laughs and talking floated through the open window from outside. She realized all the men had drifted to the campfire Joe had built for them. "One less liar in the world to be concerned with. How thoughtful of you!" She followed Dave to the chess table. Looking at the chess board, she remembered the last time she had played—with her father seven years ago. She must have been staring at the table for a long time because Dave's hand reached for her fingertips.

"What's wrong?" he asked.

She looked at their fingertips. "Nothing's wrong. The last time I played chess was at this table with my father, and I won."

"Of course, you did."

"No, I only won because he let me. I was very good at the time. My father, on the other hand, understood every glide it took to conquer, every possible way his queen could be taken. He was unbeatable."

Dave let go and crossed his arms. "Sounds like a lot to live up to."

She folded her hands and rested her chin upon them. "I've only just realized that, that's the only way I wish to be like him, unbeatable, invincible. I need to be even better."

Dave moved his first pawn. "You're not just talking about chess are you?"

Rose moved one of hers. "These threats—whoever is orchestrating all this, it feels like a game."

Dave moved another of his pawns. "How do you know?"

Rose replied, "You really should pay more attention." With her pawn out of the way, she slid her queen into position to take over his king, checkmate. She flipped his king off the board with a flick of the wrist. "Just as I see all the possibilities on this board and maneuver it to my will, so is the mastermind who seems to see all the possibilities of my life. I am just a pawn, and I must bend."

Dave whistled. "You really are as good as you say." His face suddenly became very grave. "But, Rose, this isn't a game. If you get hurt, the game is over."

"I can take some losses."

"I can't." His amber coloured eyes burned.

She lifted her shoulders in exasperation not wanting to draw near another potential argument. "I need some rest. I'll see you in the morning?"

He nodded. "May I escort you?"

"Dave…"

A large grunt came from behind them. "Miss, everything okay?" Joe bored his gaze into Dave, as a father would the first time a young man came calling on his daughter.

"Joe, Dave is a perfect gentleman." She turned to Dave. "Yes, you may."

Dave followed Rose up the stairs making sure there was always a foot distance between them. As they rounded the corner at the top of the stairs, Dave looked down and saw that Joe, eyes alert as a hawk's, stood at the foot of the stairs. Dave nodded to him in understanding.

Rose's hand was upon the doorknob as she turned towards him. "Thank you for listening, goodnight."

His hands twitched at his sides. "Goodnight."

Somewhat relieved that his face was the last one she would see that night, she closed the door. She looked around her room to make sure all was in order. She even sniffed at the glass of water on her end table. The crickets sang a continual melody which rocked her to sleep and onward to the land of sweet dreams.

The crickets had stopped. She unclenched the covers around her and left her bed to gaze outside her window. The horses were quiet. All seemed at peace on this side of the house. She exited her room, immediately veering to the right toward the window on the back end of the house. As she looked out, little goose bumps began to appear underneath her sheer sleeves. She rubbed her hands up and down her arms until she assured herself that all was well and that she was all right. The threats she had received were petty at best.

Not having any proper light to guide her back to her chamber, she stretched out her arms, in search of her door. What she didn't count on was tripping on a pair of feet wrapped in a blanket. She crumpled to the floor when suddenly she was being flipped over and pinned to the ground by a man. A yelp escaped her lips. Before she could utter another cry, she heard…

"Rose?" Although his hands initially pinned down her wrists, one traveled the side of her face touching her lips and the other fingered her hair. "I'm sorry." He eased his weight off of her and panted. He lifted himself off the ground. "You scared the living daylights out of me."

Rose, still remembering the weight of his body upon hers as she sat up, whispered, "You're one to talk. You almost cracked my head open." She gently rubbed the back of her head. "What are you doing out here?"

He lay back down and rested his head in one of his hands, his upper body supported by his elbow. "There's not enough beds as you know."

Rose mimicked his position and pouted, "Are you blaming this on me?"

"No," he smirked as he lifted a strand of hair away from her face. "I decided to sleep out here to keep watch."

Rose rolled her eyes. "I came out here and almost slipped back into my room without you noticing. You're going to have improve your guarding abilities. Besides, there's nothing to watch for."

"I disagree…about how there's nothing to watch for, I mean."

Suddenly conscious she was only clad in a flimsy nightgown, she sat up, hugged her knees to her chin and wrapped her arms around her legs. "How did you learn to do that?"

"What?" He smoothed his hair back with a hand.

"Accosting a young lady like an insane person?"

He flashed his teeth. "Oh, that! I fought in the Civil War back home, and it's just…well instinct. I learned to be on my toes all the time."

She started counting in her head. "Wait, that means…you must have been fifteen by the end! How could they make you fight at such a young age?"

Dave lifted his eyebrows in amusement. "They didn't. I lied about my age. At thirteen, I was tall, and I put on a lot of muscle working on farms. I grew a beard so I could pass for eighteen. I ran away from home and joined the North."

"What about your mother? How could you do such a thing to her?"

He exhaled a long sigh. "My ma died when she gave birth to me. My pa—well, he wouldn't care a twit if I had been home or gone. He's a drunk. I did leave him a note. When the war was over, I returned home to find my dad sitting in the same chair with the same brand of whiskey in his hand, his face beet red, hands swollen. It wasn't a pretty sight. I walked through the door. When I did, he took a last swig of his bottle, threw it on the ground, and straight laughed at my face.

"'Another, son, get me another.' His words were slurred. I realized that those broken shards—that's what it had become, broken pieces that could never be whole again. I walked into my room, packed the last few things I had left behind, and walked out. I've haven't been back since, don't ever plan to."

Rose stretched her fingers toward his.

Dave clutched them and looked down at their entwined unity. "When you found me that night in the alley, smelling like I'd been drinking all night long, I can't tell you how…scared I was that you might think those same thoughts I had always thought about my dad. That's why I was desperate for you to stay with me. I thought if you walked away you would never come back just like I never went back."

Rose could never have thought that underneath all of Dave's sarcasm and oozing confidence there would be a tragic breaking and remoulding of a man. The plant of hate which had grown to full length in her heart towards her own father now planted a seed of hate towards Dave's father. "Are you not angry with him?" She pinched the hem of her gown until it seemed as if she could grind it to dust with her bare fingertips.

Dave shrugged his shoulders. "I think I was at first. Now it's just what it is."

Rose huffed, "I don't understand."

"I'm content, aren't you?"

Contentment—am I? No, nothing is ever enough for me.

"That's none of your business," she muttered.

His eyes twinkled as he stood up.

"What?" she snapped.

"You're the most infuriating girl I've ever met." He opened her door and made a mock bow.

She bent down and grabbed his hat. She slapped it on his head before entering her room. Her huffs turned to quiet chuckles, knowing full well that, probably, most people thought the same thing—she was infuriating. Most couldn't stand her like he could. With one of those rare smiles on her face, she fell asleep.

Her sleep had been the best she had in days, even weeks. The weak sun tried with all its might to pry her eyes open. Her vision was blurry at first. Her eyelids fluttered a few times to fully realize what was resting so close to her eyelashes, what was barely slicing them off. She could see her bug eyes in the reflection of the wide blade. It seemed as if an icy hand was grabbing her heart and squeezing it. The need to scream for minutes on end was overwhelming. Paralyzed by the knowledge that she was wrong, she tried to picture what had happened while she had slept in perfect peace. She whimpered slightly to release some tension. Careful to not let the blade touch any part of her, she backed up and almost fell off her bed. The tip of the knife was covered in blood. Quickly, she glanced all over her body and ran to her full-length mirror, twirling in every direction, even lifting her nightgown to scour the planes of her body.

Dave! Please be outside my door.

Her hand shook as she opened the knob. She peered out of her room to find Dave's head buried in the crook of his arm, sleeping soundly. She padded toward his face and felt the soft stubble, a soothing effect on her fingertips. She pressed her fingers upon the jugular artery.

Dave's eyes flashed open, worry etched in the swirling amber lines emanating from his pupils. Dave took her wrist in his hand. "Rose, you look like you've seen a ghost."

"I think I have," she said in a shaky breath. She looked around to make sure no one would see. "Come with me."

He followed her inside her room. His eyes immediately rested upon the knife stamped into her pillow. He guided her behind him, drawing nearer to the weapon as if it would spring to life and harm its intended victim. He didn't touch it but looked at it for a very long time. "Do you know what this is?"

"Dave, I'm not blind, it's a knife."

"It's a hunting knife, with the blood of a deer." Squaring his shoulders, his jaw set, he turned to look at her.

"You are the hunted. Call it a chase, call it a game, you're not safe, Rose."

Why do I feel so safe with you?

"I know that now."

Dave crossed the gap between them and wrapped his arms around her, one arm cradling her back, the other hand buried deep within her hair. "Do you?" he fiercely whispered.

Before she could hold the tears back, they had soaked the top of his night shirt. She couldn't remember how long they stood there, only that it seemed to go on for eternity. If that was to be the end of her life, she could be content.

Not only had she been shaking with the outpouring of her tears, but also Dave was shuddering in anger. "God help me if I ever see his face."

Rose murmured against his chest. "Don't tell Joe or Jack."

Dave put some distance as he looked at her.

Rose looked into his eyes. "I don't want them to worry. I promise, I'll do something."

Dave sat on the edge of her bed, his hands resting on his thighs. "You need to…"

"Do what the note says," Rose finished. "I understand that now. If he can sneak into my bedroom and place a knife hardly an inch from my face, then he can surely kill me. This is his warning."

He took her hands and drew her closer. "I need to leave today. My employer is expecting us soon. I don't know how I can…"

She cradled the side of his jaw with her hand and tilted his face toward hers. "It's all right. I'll inform Joe and Jack of my decision and ask them to be ever more vigilant. They won't deny me, and they'll do their job well." She turned and looked outside her window. "I'll see you at breakfast."

He grabbed the knife and yanked it out of her pillow. "Do you mind if I keep this? Maybe I can track something down."

She nodded her assent with a grim smile. Any help she could get, she dared not spurn. The fact he was so willing…he was her guardian angel. She knew she deserved no such thing.

As she maddeningly continued to stare at a fixed point out the window, she could feel the intensity of his gaze upon her. There was no way he could help soothe any more without being on a much more intimate footing. Could she push this sacred ground of understanding a little further back without complicating whatever *they* were? A moment later, she heard his footsteps retreat. Too much, too soon.

Once Dave had left, Rose stripped the sheets off her bed to burn when no eyes looked her way. She would save the deed for tonight. Washing the sheets—no use when the blood of that innocent game would haunt her the rest of her days if she didn't get rid of it for good.

She moved downstairs to the kitchen where Jack was already up and whistling one of his soul tunes. "Good morning, Jack, how did you sleep?"

He replied emphatically, "Good! How 'bout you? None of dose men touched, ya, did dey?"

Dave rolling on top of her the night before popped into her mind. "No, of course not, if that were the case, you'd have to ship me off to England where the men are all genteel and would never think to put a lady in such a position."

"Some of us are real gentlemen. Would ya like to help me bake some muffins for de breakfast?"

Rose pinched Jack's cheeks affectionately and said, "You are a true gem, Jack. I would love to help you."

Engrossed with the mixing and spooning of the batter, she proclaimed, "Jack, I'm going to do it."

"Do what?"

"You know what." She swatted him with the kitchen towel. "I'm going to find the treasure."

"What made ya come to yar senses?" He wiped his forehead.

She was more convinced than ever not to breathe a word of the knife to Joe and Jack. "That's just it, I think my common sense decided to pay me a visit last night and stay till the end of it."

He picked up a spoon with a spot of batter and licked it, "Mm, if you say so!"

As the men packed up to leave, Dave went outside to tack up the horses and hitch the wagons. When all was ready and the men swung into their saddles, Dave trotted over to Rose. They didn't utter any words of farewell. Everything had already been said earlier. He nodded a promise that he would do everything possible to seek out the predator.

Once all the guests had gone, Joe and Jack went around the property making sure everything was in tip top shape for the next company of men which were not very far off. She could already hear the pounding of hooves on the dust-ridden lines of the earth. She hurried to change the dirty sheets and pillowcases to fresh-smelling ones. The rest of the day was spent doing mundane tasks and some accounting.

Rose settled at her desk and relished the thought of finishing the tasks at hand. Her days of frivolous play and useless tasks were over. She was now the master of her own destiny. Her father had left her a hefty sum, more than enough to continue the business and build upon what was left. She tapped her pencil upon the paper in front of her and thought of the switch in Dave's temperament toward her. His snarky attitude had softened to a fervent sweetness that had taken her by surprise. The way he had pulled her toward himself…an ache formed deep within.

Sleep that night was sweet, unadulterated by phantom predators or strange noises that shook her core. She woke with the dawning of a new promise when a natural perfume tickled her nose. She rose upon her elbows and saw a large bouquet of roses at the foot of her bed.

Did Dave send these for me? Of course not, he's so far way. Why would I ever think he would be the sender?

There was a note folded in half. The overwhelming scent of the roses and the rose-scented letter made Rose open the window. She unfolded the note to read:

My sweet,

Now that you've decided to play along, I'll give you your first clue. It was found in your father's coat, the one he wore when he died. Stray from the path determined, and you'll

find your body in the same unholy grave you dug for your
father with your bare hands.
    Please don't bring this relationship to ruin. I would
hate to mourn your passing.

Your passionate admirer,
X

    The "X" had been crafted with the most beautiful penmanship. Although this note was the most frightening touch of the predator to date, she cradled it and studied its contents and hoped to find some clue as to the identity of this madman. She placed it in a secret compartment of her valise.

    She turned to the given clue. It was a piece of paper, quite worn from, she was sure, the thumb strokes her father must have bestowed upon it. All that was written upon it was *Nevermore.*

    She didn't know the terrain of this wild country. Yet she did know her father, no matter how much she had tried to shut him out. It was a reference to Edgar Allan Poe's *The Raven.* It wasn't much to go on, yet it must have been extremely important if it had been found in his pocket, not the one on the outside of his coat but the secret inner pocket which she had noticed had been ripped open and rid of its contents.

    The next few hours she lay on her bed and pondered upon *nevermore.*

Even such is Time, this takes in trust
Our youth, our joys, and all we have,
And pays us but with age and dust;
Who in the dark and silent grave,
When we have wandered all our ways,
Shuts up the story of our days:
And from which earth, and grave, and dust
The Lord shall raise me up, I trust.
Sir Walter Raleigh

Chapter 9

The sting from a rose thorn snaked its way beneath Rose's skin—a pin-sized drop of blood. She brought her bouquet downstairs and hung them upside down to dry. She cared not to have them sitting in a vase. No, she would make them a relic, by which to remember the reason why she had changed her mind. When this was all over, she would crush the brittle petals under her boot.

Joe rounded the corner. "Miss, where'd those come from?"

She pasted on a bemused smile. "I found them in a rose garden."

Brows furrowed, he folded his arms, " I ain't seen no rose garden."

She threw her hands into the air. "Why, Joe, I've been taking many walks. All right, I'm exaggerating on the garden part, but there is a rose bush in a quaint little nook, where the fireflies skitter and dance all night and…"

"Don't you want to enjoy them then?"

"I will when they've dried."

He slapped the air in front of him while turning around, "Women."

The whir and *ticking* of the telegraph machine drew her attention away from the hanging bouquet to the message at hand.

Mark dead accident. Funeral at Barkerville two days - Frank

She peered at the message. "Joe!"

A moment later, he reappeared and said, "Yes, miss."

She bit her lip. "Do you know a Mark and Frank?"

It was the first time she had ever seen his eyes light up. "Telegram?" he stretched out his hand and stepped forward expectantly.

Once he read the contents, the light instantly died in his eyes.

"When do you wish to depart?"

He looked away as he replied, "I'll finish up what needs to be done here and leave bright and early in the morning."

Before he could leave the room, she stated, "I'm going with you, Joe."

"No offence, but I'll head out on my own."

"Joe, I'm not asking."

He looked at the floor and nodded, "All right, as soon as it's dawn, we leave."

"Understood." As soon as Joe left the room, she strolled out to the garden where Jack was weeding. "Jack?"

He was wearing a wide-brim straw hat and gardening gloves. "Fine morning, ain't it? Here, why don't ya join me?"

She smiled. "I'd love to."

They worked in silence for a few minutes. "Jack?"

"Yes, Miss?"

"Don't tell Joe I told you this or that you even know about this…"

"Miss?"

"Mm?"

"I thought ya don't like conversatin' while ya work."

"I don't. Teasing aside, this is important. Joe's friend, I believe a very good friend, just died. His funeral is in Barkerville in two days. Joe is heading out at first light tomorrow, but I believe he'll leave tonight."

Jack shrugged his shoulders. "What's de problem?"

Rose wiped her forehead with the back of her hand. "I told him I was going with him tomorrow morning. He begrudgingly let me, but I think he's going to give me the slip by leaving tonight instead of tomorrow. If I'm wrong, the horses and I will have gotten to know each other a little better. If I'm right, well then that's that. I just don't want you to be alarmed when you don't find us tomorrow."

Jack placed his hands on his knees. "And who's gonna be lookin' after dis place for ya?"

Rose kissed his cheek. "Why you, of course! I couldn't ask for anyone better."

"Well, now, I guess I can accept de post on condition ya give dis ole man another one a dose when ya get back."

"I wouldn't expect you to demand any less!" A deep laugh resonated from within her body. The sound easily flowed from her lips. Was this contentment?

Before she went to bed, she packed a small valise with two changes of clothing and hid it under a pile of hay in the barn once Joe had finished with the barn chores. She had directed Jack to firmly place the tall wooden ladder they stored on the side of the barn under her bedroom window. After everyone retired for the night, she quietly slid her window open and climbed down the ladder. She hit the ground and strolled toward the haystack corner and lay down, waiting until the moment Joe would arrive to steal away into the night.

Hours later, Rose heard the heavy footfalls of Joe's hardy boots upon the gravel. He carried a lantern. Ten steps into the barn, its light fell upon Rose's erect posture.

Joe showed no surprise. Instead, annoyance coloured his face. "I should have known," he muttered.

Rose stood up. "I knew you would try to give me the slip. So I made my own plans."

He tacked up his horse. "Ya know, you remind me of a dog who won't let got of the bone in its mouth."

Rose followed suit and tacked up the other horse. "Although I didn't know you very well, I'm glad you were there when I found my father the way I did. It seems you already have a friend to grieve with in Barkerville, yet I must repay the favour you paid me. I promise I'll be as a shadow, there and gone the next moment. Besides, I have another reason for going."

He huffed, "It's the treasure."

She cinched the girth. "Yes, I don't know what exactly I'm looking for, but my father did spend a lot of time in Barkerville."

"Where you going to start?" He moved the bridle onto his horse's head.

"I'd rather not say. If this goes sideways, they have no reason to go after you or Jack."

They both finished saddling the horses and walked out of the barn with the face of the moon to guide them.

Joe mounted. "It's going to be a long ride."

"Obviously!" She rolled her eyes. "I expect to set up in a nice hotel so I can soak my sores in a hot bath."

They galloped a good ways before slowing down to a trot and then to a walk. All night they rode and onward to the morning. They reached Quesnel a little after noon. Rose didn't feel an itch dismounting her horse. Her legs didn't shake as she enjoyed a delicious meal of chicken pot pie and bacon. They each paid for a room just so they could sleep for a few hours before hitting the road again.

When Rose awoke from her nap, her screaming leg muscles forbade her from rising.

An insistent knock came at her door. "Miss?" Joe's muffled inquiry reached her ears.

"Joe, I knew it was going to hurt, but not like this!"

Suddenly, his hand slapped her door twice as he chortled. Rose's mouth dropped open at his surprising response to her complaint.

"Joe!" Her body now ached from the ripples of laughter emanating from the pit of her stomach. "Give me a few minutes!" She managed to sit up and rub her legs until it was barely bearable to get up from the bed. After several failed attempts to mount her horse, they were back in their saddles and riding onward to Barkerville.

Once they arrived, Joe held his end of the bargain by booking Rose into a fine room with its own bath. He left to find his friend and to inquire as to the time of service.

Rose settled into the hot bath, embellished with salts. She rested there for an hour before she heard Joe's familiar knock. "Yes?"

"I'll be leavin' within the hour for the service."

"Understood. I'll be ready."

"You don't have to come."

"I want to go. I have some scouting to do anyway."

As soon as his steps faded down the hallway, she slowly rose from the water's depths and cried a little as she bent to exit the tub. It took her a good fifteen minutes to dress and just about as much time to do her hair. Once she was finished, she slowly walked to the front entrance where Joe had just arrived.

He walked down the main street in front of her, and she followed, allowing ten paces between them. She didn't want him to be mindful of her. He needed to grieve without worrying about her.

They headed past the town's borders down a little lane. Minutes later, they arrived at the entrance of the cemetery. Beyond the little white gate attached to the picket white fence surrounding the headstone-filled plot, there was a ring of men on one side of the grave. The widow and her companions were on the other. Joe moved between the men, many looking up at him and putting a hand upon his back. Joe sidled beside (whom she presumed to be) Frank.

Frank stood below an oak tree and had a face which seemed to have a permanent bewildered expression. His shoulder touched Joe's, and he smiled. There were no tears in his eyes. He and Joe seemed like brothers.

When the preacher stopped speaking, there was an interlude of silence. The cawing of the ravens, death's serenade to the mourning party, intensified as they all alighted upon the tree's branches. The cawing became incessant. Somehow, she believed that, perhaps, it was a message for her to leave, not the cemetery, but Joe's friend's grave.

Nevermore...the ravens...there must be some connection.

She slipped away from the funeral party undetected. Even Joe, who always seemed to have an eye on her even when he wasn't directly looking at her, was wrapped up in the emotions of grief as he shovelled some dirt into the grave.

She tread amongst the rows of graves, careful not to disgrace any markers by walking on top of the graves themselves. She came upon one which said: "Sacred to the memory of Peter GIBSON, of Vankleekhill, County of Prescott, Canada West, who died July 24, 1863. Aged 31."

The poor man...so young—what of his family?

The cawing of the ravens bade her move further along the trail. So many names, ages…the untold promises of gold…every earthly object and body disintegrated to dust never to return again.

Where does my treasure reside?

Once she reached the end of the line, she would have given up if it had not been for the single raven cawing at her, not from a tall branch but from the ground. Its beady black eyes never strayed from her face. It cocked its head to the side as if to question her sanity. She could have sworn it was trying to speak to her. Its harsh *caw* made her jump. Her hand flew to her heart. As it cawed, it swivelled its beak behind itself. She followed its line of sight to a small tombstone, nothing surrounding it. Curious why the bird would bid her go, off she went. The closer she came to it, the more it seemed to have been made for a baby. She stepped round to see it…and on the tombstone's surface was *Nevermore.*

And my soul from out that shadow that lies floating on the floor shall be lifted—nevermore!

Rose looked back at the raven who had followed her to this cursed ground. It hopped backward, head down as if in obeisance unlike the raven from Poe's work. Rose nodded and off it flew. She stayed a minute longer and determined to return to this place at night to uncover what other secrets her father kept.

She returned to the funeral gathering and found the men talking quietly amongst themselves. Joe and Frank were in deep conversation. Rose caught Joe's eye and rolled her eyes in the direction of St. Saviour's Anglican Church. He dipped his chin.

She strode toward the retreating figure of the preacher as he wove through the crowd and entered the church. Reverend? May I ask you a question?"

He turned and smiled, "Of course, what do you wish to know?"

She asked, "Who paid for the headstone with the words *Nevermore?*"

He paled immediately. "Oh, miss, I…I" He couldn't find his words. "I can…can…cannot. You see, I was told…there was a…large settlement…gi…given to the church for my silence."

Her face was stone cold. "Do you know who I am?"

The reverend lifted his hands and shoulders.

"I am Rose Wood, Harland Wood's daughter. It was he who paid for it, wasn't it?" She stepped toward him.

In fear, he stepped back. "I…I…please understand."

She continued to step toward him until she had him cornered. "No, you understand. You know there's someone after it, don't you? My father trusted you, but I won't. Tell me at once because my life depends upon it."

Sweat beaded upon his forehead although the temperature was on the cool side. He gave a curt nod.

"Good, now, understand this. I'll be back within the week. I don't want any interference." Disgusted by his weakness, she turned away. "Has anybody else come asking about the grave?"

He squeaked, "No."

She shrugged her shoulders back. "Next time someone else comes asking about it, do me a favour and don't be the shivering mouse you are now. Get some backbone, good day."

The heels of her boots clacked against the scuffed wood flooring. As she exited, Joe and Frank walked toward her. She waited for Joe to make the introductions.

Joe started, "Miss, this is my good friend Frank. Frank, this is Miss Rose."

Frank stuck out his hand. "Hiya!"

"Good day, you're not from around here, are you?"

He chuckled, "You could say that."

Her gaze slid sideward to Joe, "You have very interesting friends."

Before Joe could say anything in response, Frank blurted, "He says the same thing about you."

Joe nicked him in the side. Frank's face had the air of not knowing what he had done wrong.

She smiled mischievously, "I like you very much, Frank! You've earned my respect in the space of two minutes which is more than I can say of other people."

He returned his hat to his head, "I'll take that as a compliment."

Joe interrupted, "Miss, we're off to chat at the saloon. See you this evening."

Frank chirped, "Want to join us?"

Bemusement now coloured her face. It was far from custom for a man to ask a woman to accompany him to a saloon unless he were interested in courting her. Although she would do so any other time just to make tongues tattle, she needed to plan what was next in the hunt.

"Thank you, but no. You're too kind. However, I would suggest you don't go asking other young women to join you. You might have to catch them mid faint."

Rose moved to her room where she sat upon her bed, the poem of the raven repeating in her mind. It was her father's favourite. What would she find underneath the dirt? She looked upward. Would she find help?

I know you're there. I'm just not ready yet. It's been too long.

She swung her face into her pillow and fell asleep after wrestling with her thoughts.

The next morning she went to the front desk of the boarding house. "Excuse me, can you tell me if Dave Clayton is in town?"

The old woman squinted. "No, miss, you just missed him. He was rounding up the last of Mr. Shaw's men in these parts before he moved out to Quesnel. Why are you asking?"

Rose offered the woman the sweetest smile she could muster. "A matter of boring business, I'm afraid. I must have been mistaken about our meeting place. Thank you." As Rose walked away, she could hear the old woman mutter, "What would a girl like that need to do any thing with business? She's a pretty little thing, needs to get married!"

Ah, marriage— the state of living which all women were pressured to pursue, the one thought waking or sleeping which must forever be in the centre of a young lady's mind. Once it had seemed more work than it was worth, but then she had thought, that perhaps with Mr. Shaw...she shook her head. Maybe Priscilla was right. Perhaps there was still a chance.

After noon, Joe and Rose packed up and rode off toward Quesnel. Once they slowed to a walk after having galloped a good distance, Rose huffed, "When we get to Quesnel, you'll be going on without me."

"Your daft if you think I'm leavin' you behind." He pulled to a stop.

She did the same. "Joe, I'll be taken care of."

"Who's going to take care of you, miss?"

"Dave. What we must do next, you cannot know."

"Miss, I don't think it's a good idea."

"Why? You must admit he's a gentleman, and he's treated me with the utmost respect."

"You're right," he begrudgingly admitted.

"Why, Joe? I believe I didn't hear that quite right. Could you say it again, please?"

"You're right, but..."

"Yes, what will people say? We'll travel as cousins, my reputation untarnished. Please, this is important. I wouldn't do this if it weren't."

Joe looked at the ground for a long while. "You need to be back at the mile house in a week. If you're not, I'm going to hunt him down and kick him right…"

"Joe, spare me the gory details. We'll be back within the week."

Welcome, thou kind deceiver!
Thou best of thieves; who with an easy key,
Dost open life, and unperceived by us,
Even steal us from ourselves.
John Dryden
V.i

Chapter 10

Joe (with Rose's money) paid for two rooms at the inn and grabbed a whiskey at the bar while Rose asked the clerk where she could find Dave Clayton.

"He's at the Hudson Bay Company, been shadowing Mr. Shaw all day on business."

She was about to open the Hudson Bay's door, but retracted her hand and sat upon a nearby bench to wait for Dave to come out. She wasn't ready to face Daniel Shaw and all the flustering feelings he alighted within her. She wore a wide-brimmed hat to shield herself from the fierce sun. Her hands were quiet, still in her lap.

Some time later, the door swung open. Instead of Dave Clayton, Daniel Shaw swooped out, devilishly handsome as ever. He sprung down the steps and drew to full height at the sight of Rose.

"My dear Rose, how are you?" He took her hands in his. A spark of lust stoked the coals of the growing fire within her body.

She looked into his ebony depths, and they expertly lured her in. She was lost and didn't want to be found. She tried to grasp what he had just said, but it eluded her as if his words were water running through the cracks of her cupped fingers. She swallowed hard and answered with a safe bet. "I'm well, and you?"

"Come inside, let me get you something to drink."

She followed him like a loyal dog.

...like a dog you'll be coming back to your master.

The words he had spoken at their last meeting resurfaced and made her shudder.

"Please fetch a glass of water for Rose," Daniel asked the clerk.

He smiled thinly at Rose before doing as he had been asked. Just as he disappeared to the back, Dave appeared from upstairs.

Shaw rubbed his hands. "Ah, Mr. Clayton, finished the work?"

Dave's eyes alighted upon her then darkened when he saw how closely Daniel stood next to her. "Yes, sir."

The three looked at each other. An awkward silence settled.

"Well, Mr. Shaw, Mr. Clayton and I must discuss some business matters, if you would excuse us."

Daniel looked perturbed. "Of course! May I be so bold as to ask to see you this evening to discuss some more…personal matters?"

Flustered, she quickly looked to Dave before making a decision. "Yes, I believe I can spare an evening."

Daniel flashed his brightest smile. "Perfect! Where are you staying?"

"At the boarding house just down the street that way."

He took her hand and kissed it. "I shall see you at seven." He handed her the water and departed.

Rose turned her attention to Dave. "Shall we?"

Dave replied, "After you." He held the door open for her as she stepped out. After a few steps, he offered her his arm. "Everything all right?"

Rose made sure to moderate her pitch so that only he could hear. "There's been a development. We leave tonight. We'll travel as cousins. Does that suit?"

He snorted, "We don't look anything like each other!"

"All right, then we're distant cousins, second cousins."

"What does Joe think of all this? You must have come with Joe."

"Yes, I did. He'll relay to you the terms when you meet me at the boarding house tonight."

His voice shaded, "After your dinner." His arm stiffened.

She tried to keep a neutral face. "Why so suddenly angry?"

"I have some news on the hunting knife. I'll tell you about it tonight."

They came to the boarding house. Rose let go of his arm. "Dave, what's wrong?"

He avoided her gaze, eyes clouded. "Hope you have a nice time." He tipped his hat and left her staring after him, no words chasing him down.

Punctual, Daniel arrived and escorted her to the best restaurant in town. She hadn't brought anything especially worthy of a fine dinner. She donned what she thought was best, a simple white and blue striped dress. As soon as they were seated, she felt underdressed to say the least. She fiddled with a front button. "Forgive me for not having worn something more appropriate. I wasn't prepared."

He clasped her hand in his own. "Don't be. You're the most beautiful creature here."

His disarming smile and stirring compliment made any self-conscious thoughts fly away. Throughout dinner, she asked him about his gold-digging business which he avidly discussed.

The evening is going quite nicely. He hasn't touched me in ways that I'm uncomfortable with though we are in public...ugh...I'm over thinking this. Priscilla was right. Last time was an unfortunate mistake.

By the time dessert came, he shut down completely. "Daniel?"

He turned his eyes back to hers after having looked at the wall behind her for a few moments. "Forgive me!" His smile made her stomach flip. "I wanted to ask you to forgive me for the way I acted before, at our last meeting. I wanted you so much in that moment that when you weren't ready, I lashed out."

This confirms it.

Rose began to be dizzy. Could a man want her this much, this dangerously? "Truly?" He formulated the perfect words. However, his intonation—was that a cold methodical rhythm?

He nodded.

"All is forgiven."

"I beg you to consider attending the ball we'll be having in Barkerville in two months time. I'll probably not see you until then, but will you do me the honour?"

Her first grand invitation, how could she say no?

"Could I consider it over the course of this week and then send you a telegram with a response when I return home?"

His jaw clenched as he narrowly looked at her. The thin line of his lips was quickly replaced with a suave smile. "Of course, take all the time you need."

"Thank you." She swiped a look at the time and saw that she was to meet Dave in half an hour. "I think it's getting a bit late now, don't you?"

"The night is young. Shall we go for a stroll?"

"Yes, you may escort me back to the hotel."

"Would you not rather I showcase some of the sights?"

"Oh, Daniel, I really would love to, but I must get some rest. I leave as soon as it's dawn tomorrow."

"How thoughtless of me to not be informed of your plans. Shall we?" He took her arm, drawing her so close that the curves of her dress pressed against his suit.

The stroll was short. As Rose turned to say goodnight, Daniel's lips met hers perfectly, hard and insistent. She couldn't deny the attraction, the inability to resist what she responded to so instinctually. There was the factor that it was done so publicly. This, she wasn't comfortable with. As their lips, quivering with thirst, parted, she saw a drawn curtain flutter in place.

As if the kiss he had planted on her lips wasn't enough, he now took her hand and did the same there. "I look forward to your answer in a week."

Rose chuckled, "And what if I say no?"

He wrapped his arm around her torso and pulled her close so that their lips were but an inch apart. "Something tells me that won't be the case." He lessened his grip slightly.

She couldn't help but bridge the gap between their lips once again. The taste of him had a great power in sending her into a frenzy of needing his lips and tongue to be entwined with hers.

Hesitantly, Rose tore herself away and traipsed to the door in a heady dream state. She hurriedly dressed into more comfortable riding clothing. She walked back to the lobby where she found Dave slumped in a single chair. His hands were clasped in front of his face, and his eyes were downcast and brooding.

"Cousin?"

His slit eyes looked her way above his stone cold posture.

"Joe would like to see you now."

Without a word, he launched into a standing position and followed her to Joe's room. As they walked down the hall, she felt a cold front drift from Dave's rigid walk. She opened Joe's door to see Joe pacing like a hungry mountain lion.

He paced a few more steps, stopped, and pointed his index finger straight at Dave. "You make sure she's safe. She says you're a gentleman. I expect nothing less."

Dave froze.

Joe continued, "You better be back in a week's time. If you're not, I'll come after you with the Mountie."

Rose covered her forehead with her hand, all the while shaking her head. "Really, Joe? Are you done?"

"Yes."

"Good, let's get on with it."

Joe grabbed the cowboy hat sitting on the dresser. He stood in front of Rose and placed it on her head. "It'll be a boon. Take care of yerrself."

Rose threw her arms around Joe's neck. "Don't fight with Jack, and I expect the mile house to be in tip top shape when I return. I'm going to miss you, old bear." She put her hand upon Dave's arm, eyed the hall to make sure no one was around, and guided him to her room a few doors down.

"Aren't we cousins?" he whispered as soon as she locked the door.

"Yes, we are now!"

"Then why are you sneaking around like that?" He stuffed his hands into his pockets.

"Because even cousins can become…more than cousins," Rose said, as she finished throwing the remainder of her things into her satchel. "You're unusually quiet this evening."

He opened the door and peeked out.

She then slung her satchel over her shoulder and joined him.

He looked down at her and said, "I've got nothing to say."

Was he the one at the window? How come he hasn't said anything about it?

He opened the door wide, and she stepped out. Just as they swung onto their saddles to ride to Barkerville, a low voice boomed behind them, "Are you Miss Rose Wood?"

Rose turned to Dave. Then she glanced back to see the town Mountie, his hands on hips. "Yes."

"I'm sorry, miss, you won't be ridin' out this evening." His bulldog expression was firm.

"May I ask why?" The sweat on her palms increased to the point that the right rein slipped from her hand.

"There's some questions I need to be askin' ya…alone." His eyes shifted to Dave.

"Sir, this is my cousin Mr. Clayton." Rose gestured.

The Mountie's gaze intensified. "Mm, mm! Come follow me, miss."

"Yes, of course." She whispered to Dave. "Take the two horses and wait for me on the edge of town. I'll meet you there in an hour."

A hard flint settled in Dave's eyes. He took the reins of her horse and trotted off with both of them.

The Mountie led her to his office. It was large enough for a desk and two holding cells. He gestured to the chair across from him, and she sat down.

He leaned back in his chair and put his folded hands across his torso. "You're a hard one to find, Miss Wood. I've been lookin' for ya ever since news of yer father's death."

Rose didn't blink. "I've had to attend to business."

He shook his head. "Oh, I know. So have I. I've been busy goin' after a gang for a long time. Finally caught up with 'em last week and delivered 'em some justice." Seeing this had no effect on her, he brought up his original intent. "As I said, I've been needin' to ask you some questions 'bout your father's death."

Rose folded her hands in her lap. "Go on."

He raised his folded hands to the top of the desk and leaned forward. "Where were you when yer father died?"

"I was on my way home with the man my father had entrusted with my safekeeping."

"When did you arrive home?"

Rose tried to remember the approximate date. "I believe it was Thursday eight weeks ago."

"Why wasn't any lawman told when you found the body? Why wasn't there a proper funeral?"

"I didn't call for anyone because when I found him, he was bulging, blue, and utterly dead. He must have been dead for three, four days! The stench was unbearable. Joe and I, we dug a hole and put his body in it. His body was so decayed that it was the perfect festering ground for maggots."

He tapped his finger upon the table. "And what about after?"

"I found his last will and testament. Once I disposed of his body, business was at hand. It couldn't wait."

"It's a shame ya didn't wait. Was it foul play?"

The slit in his throat re-emerged in her mind. "Yes, it was."

"D'y know why and who could have done it?"

"Sir, I haven't been to the mile house since my father took possession of it. I know nothing of what his life was like out here. He could have had many enemies for all I know."

The Mountie shook his head confidently. "Not a chance, everyone loved Harland Wood. He was everyone's help. But…there's a rumour floatin' around he had buried treasure, a huge vein of gold."

Rose smiled bitterly. "I assure you there's no such thing. Stop the rumours. People will be better off without them."

He leaned back once again and looked long and hard at Rose. "All right, is there anything else you can think of?"

"I didn't know my father so I don't see how I can be of any help. Are we done?"

He slowly nodded.

She rose from her seat and walked out. Once she was a good distance away from his office, she ran to the edge of town, a phantom gliding in the shadows. As soon as she neared Dave and the horses, she slowed down and breathed deeply.

Dave, already off his horse, walked over and let the reins of the horses fall to the ground. "Is everything okay?"

Rose threw her hands into the air and plastered a smile. "Oh, so now you want to talk?" Hands trembling, she stooped to the ground. Meanwhile, the horses nibbled on the grass ignoring her. She felt Dave's hand grip her shoulder. A fury took hold of her and she flung his arm away and faced him. He held both her arms captive. Struggling to go free, she beat his chest with her fists. Instead of bending to her wish, he held her to himself. Immediately, tears she hadn't let fall free in a long while, fell of their own volition, breaking the stronghold of control she had built. Dave's stubble, a stroke of comfort, bristled past her cheek.

Dave loosened his grip over her once she yielded to his touch. He stroked her hair over and over, smelling her scent, rosewater mixed with a touch of lavender. He murmured, "I'm sorry."

She chuckled against his coat then lifted her face to see his. "For what? For holding me bound when all I wanted to do was run?"

He lifted his thumb and stroked her cheekbone, "For caring too much."

She folded her arms over her chest. "If that's all you're guilty of, you're a saint, and I worse than a sinner."

He walked to the horses and picked up the reins. "We're all sinners, some of us saints."

She took her horse's reins and vaulted onto her saddle. "Aren't we fine company, cousin?"

He did the same. "Yup, we are. The company of a sinner and saint are all I need."

"Ha!" She flicked his hat, making it topple off his head.

He jumped off to retrieve his hat, swung back on, and encouraged his horse to gallop. He hollered, "Last one to that bend in the road is a thorn in the side."

For the first time since riding a horse, Rose gave her horse free rein to race to answers, to run because of freedom, and to rally for the task ahead.

Ill fortune seldom comes alone.
John Dryden
1.392

Chapter 11

An hour's distance from Barkerville, Rose's eyes drooped and threatened to close if she didn't lie down in some fresh grass and sleep. She could feel her body lean to the right. Before she could jolt awake, a large hand grabbed her cloak. Her sluggish response effected a huff from her companion. His hand was quickly replaced by his arm encircling her shoulders.

"Rose." He shook her gently. The rocking motion induced her to nestle her head in the crook of his shoulder. "Rose, we're almost there. Do you think you can travel another hour? Without falling off the horse?"

She chuckled as if she had drunk a good pint of whiskey. "Of course, I can." She shook her head and willed her eyes to open. "See."

Dave tried to hold in his laughter. "Your eyes are bloodshot. They're as big as an owl's."

She frowned and kicked her horse forward in a clumsy manner. "You'll see."

As soon as they reached town, Dave aided a very haphazard Rose into her room. He helped her to the bed and sat her up as he took off her coat. After gently laying her down, he placed the coat on top of her. He got up and found, to his surprise, that his hand had been claimed. Her fingertips had closed around his before she had fallen into a deep slumber.

His thumb stroking the top of her hand, he leaned forward and memorized the look of pure peace on her face as she slept. He allowed his lips to touch her brow for a second before withdrawing to his own room.

Rose and Dave slept until the evening. They had dinner together in the main salon. A quiet stillness had settled between them despite the merriment of the other diners. Once they had eaten the main course, Rose remembered that Dave had news of the knife.

"Dave, before we left Quesnel, you said you had some news of the knife."

He leaned forward his eyes trying to maintain stillness. "I took the knife because I thought I had seen it before at the Hudson Bay Company. Sure enough it was right there in the display case." He wiped his mouth with his napkin, "I asked the store owner if he had sold any in the past month. He did to a few people. One of them was a young girl. I asked him to describe her. He couldn't, couldn't remember the colour of her hair, height, anything. Just as I was about to leave the store, a runner boy told me he, at least, remembered that she was buying it as a gift for her father, a Mr. Brown.

"Funny thing is, Mr. Brown doesn't exist. I mean I talked to all the Mr. Browns in the area and surrounding homesteads. None of them had a daughter that had bought a knife for them."

Rose finished the last bite of her chocolate cake. "She could have been a drifter, maybe the family moved on. She could have made up the whole story. Maybe it doesn't even tie in after all. It could have been any of the other customers."

He murmured, "You're right. Just, it's strange. The whole thing feels off."

"The master tempts us with a clue that leads to more questions, or to keep us busy in the wrong spot. We have to let it go." She cleared her throat. "Thank you for looking into it.

To tell you the truth, I don't know how I could do this without you, especially tonight."

"I could get used to the sound of that."

She smiled tiredly. "Don't. I won't be feeding your pride any longer."

He shook his head, his eyes twinkled. "You don't understand."

"I don't? Then tell me, what is it?"

"It's not about my pride. It's about the privilege."

"The privilege? To be a pain?" She waggled her eyebrows.

He stroked his hair back and smiled, "The privilege to serve you, to show you I…."

"To show me what?"

He gave her a pointed look. "We should get some rest before tonight. Whaddy a say?"

"All right," she said, her eyes contesting his. His bulldog expression was relentless.

At one in the morning, when the whole town had quieted, they slipped from their rooms. Looking like large ravens in their black pants and midnight billowing cloaks, they sprinted from building to building. They swiped some shovels from a barn and stole away to the cemetery.

They dared not light any lanterns lest they be caught in the middle of their search. The moon had disappeared behind a dense movement of clouds. They strode side by side only to be separated by the maze of tombstones.

Dave huffed, "Rose, give me your hand."

She reached toward his voice and felt his fingers close around hers. He took the lead and she followed. He gave her directions of where to step and what not to bump into. Just as he was giving another direction, he hissed and bent to rub his shin.

"What happened? Are you all right?"

"Ugh, don't go there…NO…here." His abrupt pull made them both land upon the ground.

"Dave, you're hurt. Let me take a look."

He chuckled, "How are you going to do that? We can't see anything! Let's do the job, and I'll deal with it later."

Miraculously, they reached the stone of *Nevermore* without another incident. Rose could only go by memory of the general direction of the singular tombstone. Dave lit a match near the headstone emblazoning the words in a chilling glow. Without a word, they began to dig, the sound of metal cutting the earth. Their heavy breaths—they heaved the dirt to the side. The further they went, the faster Rose's heart beat, afraid to find anything tangible. Anybody could have written the word. It could be termed a coincidence. This was the point of no return, where she couldn't deny the treasure's authenticity any longer.

Her hands shook more perceptibly the more they dug into the earth. They shook to the point that the dirt in her shovel spilled to the sides. Dave led her to the side. He continued to dig. He threw off his coat five minutes into digging. Another thrust, then…the clang ringing through the air. He jumped down, pawed through the ground, and released its hold upon the mystery contents. He threw it out of the hole. It landed a foot away from Rose's feet, making her jump a step back.

He hoarsely whispered, "Are you going to open it?"

Shaky breaths escaped her lips, "Yes." She kneeled upon the ground and inched closer to her Pandora's Box. The tip of her middle finger felt the ridges of dirt on the exterior of the metal. Her fingers trailed along the sharp corner of the box to the middle of the other side when she felt a hindrance. "I can't open it. Padlock."

The swipe of a shovel—"Rose, stand back."

She put a hand to his arm. "Light a match."

The small sputter of flame revealed the padlock to be in good condition and free of rust.   She slapped her thigh. "We need to find the key."

He huffed as he slammed the tip of the shovel into the ground. "And where are we going to find it?"

The shrivelling reverend—he had the key, she was sure of it. "I know where it is. First, we need to take care of this mess."

"Agreed." She could barely see the planes of his back turn toward her as he began to cover the hole.

She grabbed her shovel, and helped him return the dirt to its resting place. The light of the moon began to seep through the cracks of the clouds. They patted the ground with their hands and turned to leave. Suddenly, a whizzing sound grazed their ears. They looked around the gravesite to see an arrow embedded in the freshly overturned ground.

Though the darkness reigned, it couldn't hide the fear shining in their pupils. Dave grabbed Rose's hand and ran. Their breaths heaved as they wove left and right to steer free of the headstones. He swept her into a copse of trees and used his body to guard hers from imminent danger.

Dave's hand gripped the bark of the tree next to him. His heavy breathing resounded in her ears.

A rustle of leaves and twigs far into the woods startled them. He placed his arms around her, pinning her to the tree.

Rose whispered, "It's probably just a rabbit."

Dave brought his finger to his lips and shushed her. He grabbed her hand, and they sprinted back to the edge of town. They stole into Rose's room. Arms crossed, his eyes deep in thought, Dave leaned against the door.

Rose paced the length of the room.

Dave walked over and grabbed her shoulders. "Where's the key?"

Rose shook off his grip. "And the hurry is?"

"Someone's trying to kill you."

"No, they're trying to scare me off. Remember, I'm doing exactly what I've been tasked to do. This fiend will only kill me when he has no use for me. I have to figure out how to turn the tables before then." She sighed. "I strongly believe the key is with the reverend for safe keeping. We'll walk over tomorrow. Wait…no. I'll walk over tomorrow. You'll stay here until I return. I don't want to implicate you in this mess furthermore than necessary."

He turned on his heel and opened the door to the hallway. Without looking back, he murmured, "Lock your door, Rose."

Rose didn't see Dave in the dining room for breakfast the next morning. Every time she would see an entrant at the corner of her eye, she would completely rest her attention on

126

that spot. Every time, she was disappointed she didn't see Dave's sarcastic grin. She picked at her food for an hour before determining to break the reverend's resolve even further.

The sun shone brightly, not a trace of a cloud in the sky.

Why couldn't you have made the clouds stay away last night? Please move some things that I can't in my favour.

She grasped the handle of the church door and shoved it with the force of her entire body. The ominous creaking was one you'd expect to hear from a mausoleum door, not a door pertaining to a symbol of faith and salvation.

Someone should really fix this.

The emptiness of the church mirrored the emptiness in her heart she had known of for some time. Her steps clacked against the wood flooring. "Reverend?" Not a sound answered. One of the doors to the back rooms was slightly ajar. "Reverend?" she called out again as she opened the door. "Oh, dear Lord, what happened?"

Littering the floor, pages of books had been torn out. A knife had been embedded in the wall behind the gasping reverend. He tried to massage his red imprinted throat. She scurried to his side and tenderly moved his neck about, checking for grave cuts or bruising. It looked worse than it was. "Who did this to you?"

He couldn't speak. Instead, he pointed to the open window, its cream-laced curtains blowing in the wind.

"Wait here." She ran without hesitation (her dislike for the reverend pushed back) to the inn and banged her fist against Dave's door.

He opened the door looking down while he buttoned his shirt. A triangle of tan skin peeked through until his fingers buttoned the last button. "Rose, I'm sorry, I…"

"Dave, get the doctor and bring him to the church. Now!"

Seconds later, he was behind her putting on his coat. They parted ways at the entrance, and she ran back to the reverend. She found him passed out. "Reverend!" She shook him. "Reverend!" Aghast he was still not awake, she whispered, "Lord, please forgive me." She slapped him hard, and his moist eyes fluttered open. "I've fetched the doctor, he'll be here soon. Who did this to you?"

He shook his head lightly and raised one shoulder to feign ignorance.

She heard two sets of steps pounding against the entrance floor. "The key, reverend, where is it?"

His eyes darted back and forth, trying to find their bearings before they rested upon the flooring situated in the corner of the room.

She put to memory the spot he had fixed his eyes upon just as the doctor and Dave entered the room.

The doctor flew down beside her and checked the reverend's vital signs. "What happened?" His white moustache wiggled as his mouth moved.

"I entered the church to speak with the reverend. I found him like this. It seems the perpetrator exited through the window." As the doctor opened his bag to pull out his stethoscope, she asked, "Who would do this?"

He shrugged his shoulders and listened to the heartbeat for a minute. As he was putting away his instrument, he replied, "This is quite a peaceful town. It's frightening to know someone would want to harm the reverend. This hasn't happened before."

Arms crossed, Dave looked down upon the scene. "Is he all right?"

The doctor replied, "Yes. Knowing his medical history, his heart is my first priority. Other than that, he seems to be fine. The bruising and redness will go down eventually. Thank you for promptly calling me to the scene. Would you, sir, help me carry him to my clinic just down the street?"

"Of course." Dave placed himself on the other side of the reverend and wrapped the reverend's arm around his shoulders. Together, the doctor and Dave lifted him up onto his feet and dragged him out of the church.

Rose watched them leave. She was about to take a step when the fluttering of the curtains snapped her attention back to the open window. The spot the reverend looked at was right beneath the window. She and Dave would return at night.

Two hours later, Rose picked up the sound of a tentative knock on her door. She lay on her back on her bed reimagining what it must have been like to have beefy hands closing upon her airways, to have each remaining breath strain to see the light of day. Would she find it easy to succumb? "Come in."

Dave walked in glaring, "I thought I told you to lock your door."

She lifted her hand to protest, but it slumped back to the covers. "I forgot. I'm sorry. How's the reverend?"

Dave sat at the end of her bed. "He'll live, really, by a miracle the doctor said." He glanced at her limp form and smiled. "I've never seen you this quiet."

Those ghost fingers pressing upon her artery vanished. "I haven't lost my fight, not yet."

"I don't think you ever could. I'd bet my life on it."

She sat up, not able to fathom the depth of his words. "You believe in me that much."

He turned his body toward her. "I do and the One who works in you however much you believe you're a lost cause." He unclenched his fist and gave her his hand. After she took it, he helped her rise to her feet. "So, where is this mystery key?" Dave met her questioning gaze. "Did you have a chance to ask him?"

She nodded.

They strode toward the back of the church once dark had fallen. They were relieved to see the window still open. Dave got down on one knee and placed his palms over each other.

Rose chuckled. "Surely you're not proposing, are you?"

Dave smirked. "What if I did? I don't think you could refuse my irresistible charms."

"Hah!" She placed her boot into his foothold. "You have much too high an opinion of yourself." She grabbed the bottom ledge and heaved herself over into the room.

A moment later, Dave landed beside her. "So do you. It's nice to have the old Rose back."

She looked around to see the litter of papers hadn't yet been tidied. "Yes, I gather I am although I don't know how long it's going to last. It must be the mischief of this whole affair that's awoken the beast inside me. Who's footprints are these?"

Dave squatted to inspect. "Must be the Mountie's. Heard he came by an hour after the attack. Looks like he stepped in fresh horse dung. So, where do you think it is?"

"Right underneath me." She held up a crowbar. "That's why I brought this."

"Good, you're prepared. My lady?" His open hand gestured to the tool.

Rose gave it to him and began to lightly stomp upon the floor. A hollow echo resounded, and she knew she had found the place of interest. She bent to her knees and knocked upon the same spot. "It's here. Try not to damage the wood."

Dave managed to wedge the end of the crowbar in between the wood slats. With a grunt, he heaved backward. A crack sliced the air. Dave tossed the crowbar to the side while Rose proceeded to completely free the wooden board. The light flooding through the window spotlighted a single object, the key. She picked it up. Dave returned the wooden board to its place without it seeming to have been opened. Both, not saying a word, slipped out the same way they had entered.

The box on the bed, the key in her hand, the man beside the woman—Rose took a step forward and took a deep breath. "My father planned this all these years, he must have known…must have suspected…"

Dave put a hand on her shoulder. "Would you like me to do it?"

"It's all right." She kneeled before the bed and placed the key into the padlock. She turned it to the left and heard a small click. The padlock removed, she opened the lid to see another box within, a music box. She held her breath as she opened it and was afraid she would see some token, memento from the past. Instead, the sombre foundational notes of *Moonlight Sonata* rang through the air. The treble notes undulated in a pattern of despair warring against hope—a minute in which only the music filled every crevice of the room. Once done, Rose opened a little rolled piece of paper to read…

"The Tell-Tale Heart," she breathed. "I don't know what to make of this."

Dave rose his hands to suggest, "There must be something he said or wrote to you in a letter?"

"Maybe…it's the only thing I can think of that might…"

Dave jammed his hands into his pockets. "What is it?"

"There's a locket I have (not her late mother's) back home in the shape of a heart. But is *Moonlight Sonata* a clue, as well? If it is, I don't know how they would go together." She sat upon the bed, scrunching her forehead.

Dave sat beside her and put his arm around her drooping shoulders.

Her head gently fell upon his shoulder. He turned his nose to smell her hair and kissed her crown. Rose couldn't understand why she nestled her face right against his chest, why when her senses were filled with his earthy musk tones, her hands felt the need to touch, to ascend. Her fingers rustled his stubble and rested on his jaw line. "You should leave."

He breathed into her hair. "I can't."

"Leave, please."

"I don't think you mean it."

I do and I don't. I'm not the same girl anymore no matter how hard I try to be. The queen has been ousted by a foe greater than she could have anticipated. My girlish wants matter not when lives are at stake.

She lifted her head, her face not an inch apart from his. She placed her hand upon his beating heart and felt its power flowing into her own. She fixed her eyes on his. "Dave, how you make me wish…that things were different…that I could be different."

"They don't have to be." His hand moved to cup her cheek. "You certainly don't have to change."

"Yes, they do. I do. Please go before I don't have the strength to ask any more."

Dave tilted his head to brush his lips across her forehead. "I'll go only if you have a witty remark to send me on my way."

She looked down and smiled. "I don't know if I have any of those at the moment, but oh, how Joe would whip you if he were here."

"Good thing he's not."

As soon as Dave exited the room, Rose exhaled a large breath she hadn't known she was holding in. She stayed where she was, trying to recollect the exact position his body had been to hers, remembering the touch of his lips, the curvature of his body, his smell. She allowed herself five minutes to dream before she wrapped it up, shoved it into a musty room in her mind, and built the wall with brick and tar so it wouldn't spill out without permission.

An hour before dawn Rose sneaked out of Barkerville and rode back to 108 Mile House on her own. The closeness she and Dave had shared—it should not, would not happen again. She hadn't even known she wanted him to be hers, to be more than a friend. Only until recently had she felt a deep-seated connection, one which spanned from the excitement of her fingertips to the warm comforting thoughts of his presence, to the erratic beatings of her heart. Or perhaps it had been there from the start, from the moment his hesitating touch was in earnest to protect her dignity. Perhaps it had been masked by her selfish need to indulge in Daniel Shaw's overt romantic displays. She had put more effort into the shell of who she was than what she knew was good for her soul. Now she knew better. And now she couldn't have it.

Look for me by moonlight;
Watch for me by moonlight;
I'll come to thee by moonlight, though hell should bar the
way!
Alfred Noyes
The Highwayman

Chapter 12

Dave rubbed his hand over his drooping eyes. He would pay for lack of sleep.

He couldn't stay away. If there was some opportunity to put aside work and help her find release from the demons that seemed to constantly be poised for attack, he would act. He would persevere to the end, even die for her, if it ever came to it. She had suffered so much. The suffering—to be held in a madman's grip—he would prevent.

The curve of her exposed neck down to her collar—the memory of this image crept into his mind as he dressed. He fought hard to contain the strong physical repercussions he felt when she was near. To draw her form close and mould it to his, to run his fingers down the sides of her dress, to always have the smell of her hair wafting to his nose—he blew through his nostrils hard. He pressed his hand to his forehead and closed his eyes shut.

God, I need your strength.

The night before, he thought that perhaps they could move past the indelible friendship they had, that he could show her how much he loved her.

He tiptoed to her room and gave a knock. No answer. He tried the door, and it opened. The bed had been made, her suitcase was gone. A single sheet of folded paper taunted him to open it and read its contents.

Dave,

 Thank you for taking the time to aid me in my mission to recovering my father's gold. Your help has been indispensable. I couldn't have been as brave without you.
 Before I left, I visited the reverend to see how he fared. I noticed how the door to the church had been fixed. The reverend said (in such a hoarse voice) that you were the one who had taken the time to do such a kindly act. I'm so blessed to have a friend such as you, who cares not only for himself but for those in need around him.
 Please forgive me for having left on my own. I promise I won't do anything rash.
 I believe we are on the brink of falling deeper than what I'm ready for. I didn't realize how quickly it came upon me. I would not ask you to wait. There must be a line of girls aching for you to look their way, as I feel this moment. I wish...I look forward to seeing you again soon, alone or accompanied.

Yours truly,

Rose

***

Once Rose reached Quesnel, she rested at a saloon where fashionable young ladies could eat a good meal, where rioting and heavy drinking were not to be found. After, she asked the driver of the stage coach if she could ride alongside him and his passengers for her safety's sake. He, a good-natured man, gladly bobbed his head and signalled she could ride on whatever side she liked.

Her equestrian skills were now at a level she was comfortably and confidently capable of matching whatever stride or gait the hitched horses took on.

Eager to keep her promise to Dave, she travelled the whole way to 108 Mile House with the stage coach. That was the one promise she could give to him and keep. As soon as she arrived home, she handed the reins to Joe and swayed upstairs to her room to get a few hours of sleep before evening fully set in.

Incessant shaking bade her eyes open to see Jack's broad smile.

"Howdy, I thought I'd wake ya up for some nice chilli stew. I know yer tired, but ya can git some proper sleep in a couple o' hours."

His sweet, simple gesture brought a smile to her lips. She propped herself up with her elbow. "Did it ever occur to you that I was getting some proper sleep?"

He slapped his knee. "Now, now, ya need rest and good food. I'm not sure how much food ya've been feedin' yerself."

"That's true, you coot. Thank you. I'll be down in a minute."

She slapped her face with cold water from her basin and sat at the table. Jack blessed the food, and they silently dug in.

Joe was the first to speak. "Where's Dave?"

Rose took a bite of her chilli before answering. "He couldn't accompany me on my return."

Frowning, Joe asked, "What happened?"

"Nothing."

"That boy would do anything for you, even get his hide whipped." He pointed his finger at her.

She rolled her eyes to mask the turmoil she felt inside at the reasons why she had left on her own. "Really, Joe, I..." His glare stopped her in her tracks. "I left without him knowing."

The men exchanged glances. Jack nodded his chin in Joe's direction, encouraging him to pursue the matter.

Joe continued, "Was he...did he do anything to you?"

Flabbergasted, Rose hollered, "NO! Of all things! I left because...because,"

Joe and Jack's expectant faces waited upon her answer.

She looked back at her chilli. "I left because he is too good for me."

The rest of the meal Rose was content to hear Jack prattle on about the different recipes he created over the past week. He excited Joe into a quiet desperate fuming.

The rest of the week was characterized by the hardy tasks of running a mile house in the wilds of British Columbia. Day in and day out, Rose would welcome new miners. Her duties of running the house were to change the sheets daily and wash them in the large wooden basin kept outside behind the house. She would separate the sheets and whites from the darker clothing of Jack's and Joe's (whenever their laundry needed washing) and put them in the basin of hot water,(after having boiled the water on the stove top). She would grab the handle of her dolly stick and swish the clothing around. Then she would grab the washboard and scrub until her arms ached. After having rinsed the laundry in another tub of water, she would hang it out to dry.

Another job of hers was to weed the back gardens. Jack usually accompanied her. She, in turn, would help him pickle eggs, beets, and can whatever other necessities he deemed important. Jack was in charge of all things to do with the kitchen and cooking. Joe was given charge of the horses, chickens, and mending of anything broken.

Rose would hum whilst she swept and dusted. The first time she hummed astounded her; for she had never been so happy or carefree that she had let her voice find a tune on its own. Even though the cares of the previous week threatened to burden, being home and following a routine had a calming effect on her soul.

Joe, Jack, and she dined on their own, apart from their guests at breakfast and lunch. Once the day's tasks were mostly at an end, the three of them would mingle with their guests. Rose would put away her working apron and change into an evening dress. Every time she made her way to the table, she looked for Dave's face, wondering if he had, perhaps, taken no heed to her letter and paid her a visit. Every disappointing time solidified her respect for his character because he respected her wishes. Every time her heart hurt with a pang.

Once the supper dishes had been cleared and she finished her rounds of mingling, she would retire to her study (it had been her father's study) and keep the books. She had always excelled at mathematics at finishing school, with what little they taught. She had always wanted to know more. Some of what she was doing, she taught herself with her father's books.

Her daily chores were what she had wanted to be useful in, not to sit, look pretty, and embroider. She then realized she didn't need a man to make something of herself. She was now the proud owner of a thriving business. Perhaps she could have learned more under her father's tutelage.

He's gone, and I'm happy. I wonder if I would have been happier had he been alive. Unlikely.

Once her bookkeeping was done, she would pull out the music box and listen to the haunting melody tinkle over every surface of the study. She'd close her eyes and imagine she were on the banks of a lake at midnight, watching the light of the moon on the water's surface. When the music's spell ended, she squinted her eyes while studying the piece of paper. She tried to conjure what her father could have meant by it or by both the music and the phrase.

Rose was surprised that her silent assailant, her invisible force of brutal encouragement, had played the passive card the past week. Had she shaken them off on her unexpected ride alone back home? Rose feared it was another game, a change of the rules to keep her on her toes so that she would not get comfortable with whatever was the next play.

Two weeks passed by. The first week, she enjoyed the time she had to just live, to experience what a simple life could offer. By the middle of the following week, she grew uneasy and restless and waited for some sign that she had been inadequate in her job of figuring out the puzzle. It now became a twisted dependence upon danger. Also, no word or telegram from Dave…she, once again, began, in earnest, to seek an escape from her life.

Her nervousness now was to the point that she could not sleep in the middle of the night. Her eyes, try as hard as she might to close them, were wide open. She wrapped her large shawl over her nightgown and walked over to the back window. All the men were in bed. Some of the miners snored so loudly she could hear them through the walls. She leaned against the window frame and stared out toward the moon. Its dark pockets in contrast with the light plains made her wonder if ever man could see such wonders in person. Her eyes stayed upon its surface for a long time.

As she turned to go to bed, she gasped. She had never noticed the proximity of the two trees right below the window nor how their branches positioned so perfectly under the light of the moon created a shadow, the shape of a heart (as perfect as it could be). She chuckled under her breath and couldn't believe she had stumbled upon the answer without ever having tried to search for it. Yes—*Moonlight Sonata* was the clue for the moon's light; the *Tell Tale Heart* for the design she now saw rendered before her.

She was overcome with excitement and turned in anticipation to see the look on Dave's face. The emptiness around the room brutally reminded her that she had put herself in this position. She had let go of her partner in crime. She turned back to look at the shadow dancing upon the grass. Biting her lip, she weighed the options before her. She could always uncover the next play another night when the moon made its same appearance with Joe beside her so that if her assailant should choose to prey upon her, they would think twice. Yet the unknown buried beneath the heart's centre

called to her basic instincts of needing to know, needing to hunt. Once these instincts had been called, all good sense was thrown out with the dish water.

She trotted to her room and shoved on some woollen socks and the plainest, stain-tattered dress she could find. Tiptoeing down the stairs, she dared not breathe. She tried to hear the subtlest of sounds which would warn her if another watched her every movement. She made her way to the barn and grabbed a shovel.

After the earth gave way to twelve of her thrusts, the clang of metal met her ears. A chirp of laughter, frantic hands removing clumps of sod—her prize at last. When she brought it into the light to take a look at it, her brows furrowed as she crossed her arms. There was no keyhole. How on earth was she to open the box? She inspected it. Engraved on the side was a chessboard and its pieces in their proper starting order. To play the game, she would have to press the buttons within the grid to execute any chess moves.

If Father didn't want me to inherit this place, to find his gold (if there is any), why would he tailor these clues to me? No one else would understand him the way I do, would they?

She pressed one of the buttons. Small grinding noises emanated from the box. The button remained down while the noises continued. Once they stopped, the button moved back into place, and the box remained closed, unwilling to be another Pandora's Box.

She looked toward the woods and thought she saw the glow of a lamplight being extinguished. Quickly she picked up the box and ran back into the house. She didn't care if she had left the hole unattended. She would explain in the morning.

Although her fingers ached to rifle through her father's books to see if she could find a guide to opening the mystery box, she knew the minute she would sit down her mind would fog. She was sure she would fall asleep at the desk. She cradled the box and pushed it beneath her bed. This conundrum might take some time. It seemed, with her assailant at ease, she had some time to spare, time to beat her father at his own game in which he was king and now she would become queen. Queen of her own destiny, queen over her enemies—a queen who sought the heart of her King.

Our deeds determine us,
as much as we determine our deeds.
George Eliot

Chapter 13

"Looks like a large dog dug a 'ole in our yard!" Jack hollered from the kitchen at seven in the morning.

Rose had risen early and gone to her study to finish the task she had wanted to begin after her midnight dig. She jammed the palm of her hand into her bleary eyes and groaned.

Having just come in from checking in on the horses, Joe whispered hoarsely, "Shut yer barkin'. Some of the men are still sleepin'! Besides, there are no dogs here!"

"Well, then, what is it?"

The men continued to argue back and forth. Rose wearily pushed herself up from the chair and leaned on the doorframe as she said, "It was me."

Both men immediately stopped quarrelling and turned to stare at her.

Jack asked, "What for, child?"

Rose replied, "That's where the clue led me."

Joe asked, "What clue?"

Rose sighed, "It's high time I tell you what happened in Barkerville. Jack, would you make us a pot of tea, please?"

Jack nodded and did as asked.

Holding their teacups and saucers, they all sat down. Joe looked ridiculous sipping from such a tiny cup. He tried to place his fingers in a comfortable manner.

All before sipping a drop of tea, Rose relayed to them the dig at the graveyard, the reverend's attack, and the discovery of the key as a result of the reverend's indication. She made sure to leave out the part about the arrow being shot into the ground by a skilful archer.

"It's been a couple of weeks since then. I only understood the meaning of the last clue last night. I took it upon myself to find it."

She left out the part of, maybe, having seen a lamplight being extinguished within the embrace of the forest. That fact she could not trust, would not. It could have been a trick of the eyes.

"I'll cover up the hole right away." As she rose, a hand stayed her.

Jack gave her a squeeze. "I'll do it. Go to bed. You look like you haven't slept a wink."

Joe was eerily silent.

"All right, gentlemen, I'll sleep a little while longer. I trust you can see some of the men out if they plan to leave before I wake."

Joe replied, "Yes, miss."

When she awoke several hours later, half the company of men had already left. The last few stragglers were packing up while another company of miners checked in. Rose's job was to be at the front desk (so to speak) and collect all the necessary information and payments from the men wishing to stay at the mile house. Every time she did this, she searched for Dave. Every time she didn't see him, she wondered if she had made the right decision, turning him away.

The last man she ever wished to see in her life, the man who had almost stolen her honour now stood before her. This time he was sound and sober. Their eyes met, and she immediately looked down. He walked toward her and asked for meals and a room for the night. Rose endeavoured to not let it show on her face the disgust which boiled within the pit of her stomach. He didn't seem to recognize her.

"Eh, haven' I seen you before?"

She gritted her teeth as she smiled. "No, sir, I believe you haven't."

As he fished out his payment, he boasted, "Well, I've seen a lot of pretty girls like you. They give a good show in every town I've been in." His grimy, stubby index finger touched hers. "I just thought you might have been one of 'em. Maybe you could give me a tour of this fine 'stablishment."

She jerked her hand away. "Joe can give you the tour. I have business to attend to. Good day."

Even the leer on Percy's sober face made Rose's insides ripple in revulsion at the sight of him. She'd have to be careful while he remained in her home.

Thank you, Lord, he's only here for a night.

Joe rounded the corner and brought Percy upstairs to show him to his room. Rose waited for Joe to come down again. When he did, she said, "While that man is in this house, I'd ask you to keep a close eye on me, please."

Joe's bushy eyebrows drew together in concern. "Miss?"

With her head held high, she said, "He sprang upon a good friend of mine while I was in Victoria and almost ripped away her honour before some men found them. She was devastated from the attack. I don't want the same happening to me."

"How do you know he's the one?"

"Trust me, I know."

"All right, miss."

"Thank you, I know I can always count on you."

She walked back to her study while images of her first encounter with Dave replayed in her mind—the way he had gently let down the hem of her dress, their sarcastic banter after such a brutal attack. She realized she couldn't have recovered any better if any other hero had saved her that day.

As Rose reached the stairs that night to go to bed, a firm knock sounded upon the door. She rolled her shoulders back, a crick escaped. Walking to the door, she called out, "Jack, we have company. Could you get the…" Her hand turned the knob and opened the door as a gasp escaped her lips. "Miss Craig?"

"Miss Wood, good evening." Rose had never seen her teacher outside school property. Miss Craig had switched her usual austere bun to a looser bun at the nape of her neck with a lovely sweep of hair on the side. Her golden tresses shimmered in the candlelight. Her horrid principal's clothing had been exchanged for a decent dress with a beautiful crocheted shawl flowing over her shoulders. "Well, will you invite me in? I hope you don't act like this with all your guests. I would be surprised if you received any business at all."

Rose resumed her composure. "Pardon me, of course, come in. I just never imagined to see you standing at my door."

Jack rounded the corner. Dutifully, he picked up her bags and heaved them upstairs. Joe, who usually attended to this chore, was fast asleep. He had come down with a cold, and Rose had insisted upon him going to bed an hour earlier. He was to drive into town early in the morning to pick up some supplies.

"Here, let me take your shawl." As soon as Miss Craig had entered her abode, Rose was at attention to her manners and civility, excepting her blunder in the beginning. Although she had always scorned Miss Craig's corrections during her stay at finishing school, she now understood, being an owner of a business and now having seen more of the world, that what she had been taught was for her betterment. She was the chunk of glass, shards poking out every which way. Miss Crease and the circumstances she had gone through, her glassblowers, had refined her edges into a smooth sculpture. Life wasn't a game anymore. In all seriousness, it was a matter of life and death, the growth or destruction of love and friendship.

"Would you like some refreshment before I show you to your room?" Rose asked as she put Miss Craig's belongings to the side.

Miss Craig answered as she looked around. "Yes, please." As Rose led her to the dining room, she remarked, "Your father had excellent taste."

Rose turned to look at her.

Miss Craig explained, "I read about it in the papers."

Rose, satisfied with the explanation, went about filling the kettle with water to boil. She gestured to a chair and said, "Please sit." Rose returned to the kitchen to grab the saucer, milk, and sugar. "Here you are," she said as she handed the items to Miss Craig.

Miss Craig quietly prepared her tea and sipped. "You've made a good life for yourself."

Rose checked her posture. "Yes, I have. I enjoy it here very much. I didn't think I would, but then again one can surprise oneself."

"Yes, I understand that sentiment clearly. I didn't think I would travel here to see you until the last possible moment."

"Pardon me for asking, Miss Craig, but why did you come? We were never on the best terms. Truthfully, it was I who never gave you due respect as my instructress."

Miss Craig sighed and drew from her breast pocket an envelope. "I was instructed to give you this, by your father, if ever something should…happen."

Rose looked at it, yet didn't reach out to accept it.

Miss Craig laid it in front of Rose and said, "I'm sorry I didn't deliver it sooner. I've been preoccupied with institutional matters, and I heard from different sources that you were running around the Cariboo doing God knows what. I'll not ask, it's not…"

"Any of your business? That's right." Rose glared at the envelope. Would her father never let her rest in peace? Still in death, he had a knack of hounding her spirit. She suddenly stood up and said, "Shall I show you to your room? I'm quite tired. Breakfast is served at seven."

Miss Craig drank the rest of her tea and followed Rose to a ready room upstairs.

"Goodnight, Miss Craig," Rose clutched the letter all the way to her room.

How could he? If he knew she were in so much danger, why didn't he just whisk her away back to Britain? Why keep on playing the game of coveting gold?

She drew out her letter opener. A single sheet of paper slipped out with nary an entire page to its contents.

Dearest daughter, (bile started to rise in her throat)

I hope this goodbye isn't too frivolous for your taste. Your directness will be your strength in the days ahead.

As you may imagine, having obtained the gold I have, I have made many friends and, unfortunately, many enemies. Many of these enemies have been disguised as friends.

You're reading this because I have met my demise. Perhaps, you believe I stayed in the Cariboo for selfish reasons. You believe I wished to increase my already plentiful bounty. That's not true. I've stayed because I love this land, the wild heartbeat of its geography. The wind's moan, the rivers' songs, and the way I see your mother in every moment of beauty.

A hint of danger should never drive you from the things you love most, home, family, love. This is my home. If you desire to see the world, to find your home elsewhere, that would bring me great pleasure, even in death.

Your loving father,

Harland Wood

A ripping cry sounded from her throat. Her hand clutched the pillow, and she buried her face in it. Her shuddering body did not still until an hour before the sun came up. Even then, her sleep was wracked with painful dreams of what could have been.

When sunbeams skirted playfully upon her lids, she awoke instantly with not a single shred of clinging fatigue. She hid her father's message where she hid the music box and ached to start some menial task of keeping house. Joe thumped downstairs a few minutes after she did and went straight outside to tend to his tasks.

Miss Craig followed several minutes later. Concern spread like a taught map on her face. "Rose, are you all right?"

Rose didn't have time to answer, for the opening of the front door disturbed whatever fake answer could protrude from her lips.

Joe entered, muttering, "More of the lead ropes are missing."

"Again?" Rose's palm cradled her forehead. "Why would any of the miners steal them?"

Joe turned around to answer after having closed the door. Instead, he stood stock still as he swept in the view of the back of Miss Craig's chignon and slender frame.

Rose saw another moment to implement one of Miss Craig's introductory statutes. "Miss Craig, meet Joe. He's been my key protector and helper on these grounds. Joe, this is…"

"I know who she is."

Drat! He ruined the moment.

"You do? How?"

Joe took off his hat and bowed his head. "Emily, I…I"

Miss Craig extended her arm to Joe, "Shall we take a walk?"

Joe gulped and took her arm in.

Miss Craig said to Rose, "Please excuse us. We have much to discuss."

They were out the door in a second, leaving Rose to trap the nearest fly buzzing round her mouth.

***

Emily gently tugged his arm to the right. She could see, at the corner of her eye, Joe's lips slightly puckering even though his deadpan expression didn't match. Within a minute of their walk, she saw his hand move up to grab hers but then stiffly return to its safe place. She knew he needed time. So she would not speak until he was ready.

Five minutes into their walk, Joe asked, "How have you been?"

She smirked at the most obvious question he could choose to ask. "Well, thank you. I now teach and am headmistress at Angela College in Victoria."

He took off his hat to smooth back onto his head. "I didn't see you there when…"

"No, you wouldn't have. I was having a meeting with a certain girl's parents. And you?" She chuckled. "How did we meet here? Cross paths when I thought I'd never see you again?"

He stopped slowly and faced her. "I've wondered what I would say to you if I'd ever see you again. Simple truth is I'm sorry, sorry for what I asked you to do, sorry for the mistakes I made. Bein' here at the mile house with Miss Wood, it's been my way of makin' up."

Emily turned her face to the wind and nodded. "I see that. You've done right by her. She's changed, and I think some of it has to do with you."

Joe's eyes didn't rest on her for long before he looked at his boots.

She touched his arm. "I've forgiven you a long time ago. Let's just walk in silence."

***

Rose moved the curtain to the side and observed the couple slowly growing the distance between themselves and the house. They didn't look like lovers. Rose could tell that much from the comfortable divide spanning between their bodies. There was a much stronger bond she couldn't quite put her finger on, a bond forged by circumstances so much greater than themselves.

She turned away from the window when she smacked into Percy's round belly. "Oh, goodness, you scared me." The tension slowly oozed from her arms as she put them down. "What can I do for you, sir?"

He jacked his thumbs into his pants. "Well, now I was hopin' for that tour."

"Ah—uh—we don't exactly do that here. See, we're very busy."

"I knew you looked familiar. Yer that gal in the alley." He backed her against the wall. "We never finished our business." He curled a strand of her hair in his pudgy finger.

"I don't know what you're talking about."

"I think ya do, pretty darlin'. Now gimme that tour." The muzzle of a gun rested against the bodice of her dress. Then he cocked it and stuck it back in its holster. "Don't try to do nothin'. I'm one of the fastest gunslingers in the West."

Oh, please.

Determined not to be the victim again, she rammed the heel of her palm into his nose. Percy doubled over as blood pooled onto the floor. Then she kicked him toe first in between his legs. He howled. The men in his company came rushing in from everywhere, including Jack from the garden. She seethed, "This isn't the Wild West. This is British Columbia. Know the difference." She looked around at all the faces of the still silent men. "Would anybody else like a tour?"

A few of the men looked at each other and shuffled off. Some continued to stare at Percy as he whimpered like a child. Percy screamed, "Do somethin'! Get the sheriff!"

"You mean the Mountie? You got what was a comin' to ya," one said before the rest returned to what they had been doing.

Jack was grinning from ear to ear and clapped his hands. "How'd you do that? Yer full o' surprises."

Rose led Jack away, back into the garden where she joined him in the weeding. "Before I came here with my father, we lived in England. My father always believed that life was to be experienced and was for the taking. He provided me with riding lessons, which ended within the year's end. He also made sure I studied under a fencing master. Not only did my fencing master teach me techniques of the sword but also those of self defence. I never thought I'd have to use them until last...I mean today."

"It wasna yer friend who he took that day, was it? It was you."

"Joe told you. You're right. I was ashamed. See, the first time I was in shock. I didn't…this time was different. Also, he was sloppy in his hold."

"I'm mighty glad your father gave you them learnin'."

"Jack…please tell Mr. Percy he is to leave the premises at first morning light. He's already paid for the extra night. And I would very much appreciate it if you slept out in the upstairs hallway."

"It'll be my pleasure, miss! What a fine idea, sleepin' in the hallway! Who woulda thought o' that?"

I wish you were here, Dave.

A few minutes later, after having basked in memories of her and Dave, she asked, "Jack, has Joe ever talked to you about his past, mentioned any particular names?"

Jack chuckled and whistled, "No matter how many a time I knock on that head o' his, he's as dead as a doornail. He definitely won't tell me anythin' bout himself."

At mealtime, all the miners ate a hearty meal. However, Percy sat brooding and cast feverishly hateful eyes whenever Rose walked into the room with a platter of food.

When all the men had retired to bed, Jack and Rose got out the extra cot they had stored in the cellar. Rose made the bed while Jack changed into his night clothing. As soon as Rose got to her bed, she knew she could sleep peacefully with a guard at her door.

The next morning, Jack ousted Percy, looking like a drunk pig, from his bed. He threw his bag out the door and bid him a good morning saying he could wait down the road for his company of men.

Let other pens dwell on guilt and misery.
Jane Austen
Mansfield Park
ch.48

Chapter 14

Ever since Emily Craig walked into the mile house,
Joe had become unusually withdrawn. He had never been a
very talkative man in the first place. However, he usually
conversed well enough most evenings with Rose. He would sit
in the living room across from her and tell her of what
improvements he had made to the property that day. Or
whenever he had been sent to fetch emergency supplies from
the 100 mile house, he would reveal all details.

Every evening since her arrival, he was in the barn
working harder than the day before. The evening of the day
Percy left, he stomped in at quite a late hour and said, "Good
night, miss, Jack, Emily."

Rose smoothed out the pages of her book before she
asked Emily, "What is the connection between you and Joe?"

Emily looked up from her book with an air of scrutiny
and replied, "Pardon me, it's none of your business."

Rose put her book down and braced herself with both
arms upon the sofa. "I believe it is. He's not himself. Ever
since you've arrived, he has a strange air about him as if a
witch has cast a spell upon him. You're not lovers, I can tell

that much. He does walk around as if a cloud of constant guilt hangs over him. You're good at that, aren't you? Making others feel guilty."

With a steely gaze, Emily replied, "You don't know what you're talking about."

"Then enlighten me." Rose threw her hands into the air. She noticed that Jack was no longer in the room.

Emily remained silent.

"All right then," Rose continued, "tell me this. Why did you come in the first place? Other than my father's letter? You've stayed past the necessary amount of time. You've always made it rather clear you never liked me."

Emily stepped away from her seat and paced in a clear, determined manner. "When I see you, I see a mirror of myself when I was a young woman. That young woman dealt with more than she bargained for."

Rose stood, as well. "I see, this has something to do with your past with Joe. Absolve him of any guilt you may hold against him, for your sake." Rose grabbed the tea set and marched into the kitchen.

Emily followed behind and stood at the frame of the door. "I never intentionally hurt him. I am not the monster here. What binds the two of us was a sad throw of Fate, circumstances which were beyond our control except one. Now that I know he's here, I hope you'll be open to my staying a few days to bridge, with kindness, the great divide."

Rose wiped her hands on the cloth in frustration. "I've begun to feel protective over him though I know he can take care of himself. I've not replaced my father with him in any way, but…he's treated me well.

"I know you're not a monster. Recently, I feel as if, at every turn, there is one lurking in the shadows."

Emily's eyes narrowed in an enquiring fashion.

"That talk is for another night, goodnight, Miss Craig."

Emily followed Rose upstairs and glided into her room while Rose went to hers.

The next day, Joe stomped over to Rose's desk as she checked the books. He held out a telegram. "What's this?"

Rose gingerly took the telegram and read its contents.

I've completely forgotten.

"Thank you, Joe. You may leave."

"I was very tempted to burn it."

"I'm sure you were. I'm so very proud of you for not having done so. Is that all?"

He grunted, "Mm, mm."

Before he crossed the threshold, she blurted, "Are you all right?"

He turned slightly.

"I mean I've seen a change in you since Miss Craig arrived and...I don't mean to pry. I just wanted to say please bring the old Joe back. I miss him."

"Duly noted, miss."

Once she was alone, she perused the contents of the telegram.

Rose, I want your company at dance. Say yes. Waited too long.

Her first instinct was to say yes. She could do with a fine escape of a man wanting all of her. She even thought it was a fine way to make Dave jealous, for him to see Daniel fawning all over her. She could have him on a tightly wound string.

God, how could I be so base?

She searched for an answer not to the immediate question on a corruptible piece of paper but to the one that had been troubling her heart for the last couple of months. Her eyes seemed to bounce to and fro until they landed upon the family Bible. Slowly, her fingers reached toward its cracked leather, and she slid it closer to her chest. She couldn't remember the last time she had read it. It was long before she was left at boarding school. She exhaled deeply.

I will not go back to the way I was. I've been without life for too long. Restore unto me the joy of your salvation.

Before she sent her answer to Daniel, she closed the door to her study and read until her already brittle heart shattered into a thousand little pieces by the sword of correction only to be forged together again by the gentle hand of grace.

Wisps of Gold

***

Emily did up her hair in a simple bun. The day was incredibly hot enough for her to push up the sleeves of her dress. She did not. She could vividly remember the stains of time when she did up her hair and hoped to appear elegant as a full grown woman—the way her flustering hands pressed a hair against here and undid a strand there. Another memory— the way another pair of hands moved with hers to undo the buttons of her dress and how much later they were done up again—her face hot with guilt.

She found Joe chopping at logs. Most of the logs were felled in one swoop. Only a few were stubborn enough to warrant a second chop. His jacket had been flung to the side. Sweat coated most of his chequered shirt. A few buttons were undone.

She called out, "I thought I'd find you out here."

Joe didn't answer immediately. Instead, he chopped one extra block with such a force, she surely believed it would fly into the already chopped pile by itself. He wedged his axe into the stump. "You found me."

"I've come to tell the truth about what happened those many years ago. I know you didn't want to hear it then. I believe you do now."

Joe looked up at the darkening sky. "Just in time. I know a place."

Past the empty stalls and a mound of hay, Joe motioned for her to climb a small wooden ladder leading to a small room in the rafters. She settled herself onto a small stool while Joe sat on a bale of straw. She folded her hands together and stared at the wooden floorboards, seeing the cracks were inhabited by a few scuttling spiders. The pit-pattering of the rain helped soothe her racing heart.

She said, "After you left, I went to my parents to explain the situation. I told them I wanted to keep the baby even though you—but they didn't see it the way I saw it. They told me I'd have to give up the baby. So I went through the pregnancy locked up in my room. They would only let me out in the evenings when the curtains were drawn, and the visitors were sent away. They told everyone I was very ill, contracted some rare disease. The story was that I survived and was cured.

"After he was born, I felt as I had never felt before. A bond so instant, deeper than the deepest chasm, it filled me in every way. No part of me was left untouched.

"My mother told me I could have a few days with him before he was to leave. Those few days were the most precious of my entire life. I spent my time wholly devoting myself to the life who would never know me.

"One night I woke up to find the dresser I had emptied for him and stuffed with blankets empty. My door was locked from the outside. The next morning, my mother told me she had given him away to a good family in Summerstown, a week's travel from my home back east. They were aristocrats of sorts she said, people who could give him all he needed. I knew they could never give him the love I could.

"I tried to find out about the couple after my 'recovery,' but they had moved far away and hadn't told anybody where they had gone. They were a very private couple. I tried, I really did."

Joe nodded, "I'm sure you did. You've got the tenacity of a bull."

She smiled a weak smile, "You were never really one for compliments."

They continued to sit for a few minutes in silence. She could see Joe needed to know, truly know. "I forgive you, Joe, for wanting me to murder the child inside my womb. I forgive you for leaving me cold in the dust, forsaking me, placing me in a position to have no one on my side. Be in peace." She rose and placed her hand gently upon his shoulder. She climbed down the ladder, walked to the front door of the barn, and stopped to touch the heavy rainfall. Just as her foot crossed its threshold, a groan sounded from the upper room. It was a sound which would forever play in her reel of painful memories.

The wheels of the coach sloshed through mud and slithered to a stop. Rose stood by the window and watched Emily carry her valise and wait for Joe's hand to help her up. Joe grabbed her hand and mouthed a few words. Then he hung his head as if in shame. Rose had never before seen Joe so affected in such a tender manner as Emily could possess him to. Emily lifted his chin with the tip of her finger and moved her head so that their eyes met. Then, she was gone with a step and a half and a slam of the coach door. Joe just stood in the rain. Even when the rain became an onslaught, he just stood there.

Rose opened the door and shouted, "Joe! Joe!"

He still stood there as if he hadn't heard her shouting.

"Joe!" She stomped her foot and looked up into the sky before grabbing her heavy coat and fetching Joe herself. She grabbed his hand. "Come inside, Joe. I'll make you a nice hot cup of tea." She dragged him in like a stubborn mule. Once they entered, Rose hung up her outerwear and shrugged Joe out of his. "She's quite the woman isn't she? I was wrong about her. I thought she was the devil, but now I realized there's quite a bit more to her story, isn't there?"

"She's a woman, been cheated out of life."

O, my Luve's like a red red rose
That's newly sprung in June:
O my Luve's like the melodie
That's sweetly play'd in tune.
Robert Burns
My Love is like a Red Red Rose

Chapter 15

"Jack, do we have everything? Oh, I think you've missed…"

"Now, young lady," Jack swaggered in with that wholesome smile he always wore. "Didn't anyone ever tell you hollerin' is unladylike?"

"Didn't you realize I don't care?" Rose smirked. "Or at least not at home when there are no guests around. Which reminds me…" She whipped her head around to find Joe. "Where's Joe?"

"He's out with de buggy, miss."

"Do you know if he spoke with Mr. Nelson of 100 Mile House?"

"Dat he did. Mr. Nelson's more than a happy to keep any potential guests we might get for de next week or so. Business is slow now so we be doin' him a favour."

Rose put her hands on her hips. "Good, I'm happy to oblige him." She looked around the house, content with its cleanliness. "All right, Jack, off we go."

"Tell me why I'm goin' too."

Rose placed an arm around his back to guide him outside. "Everyone needs a good time out, including you."

Jack knew better than to spout off in song on a long ride such as the one to Barkerville. Ever since Emily left, Joe had been particularly easily set off.

The road to Barkerville always left Rose awestruck with its beauty and wildness. Carrying the same sentiments as her father did for this land—she was reluctantly brought closer to him.

Ever fibre of her being stirred with a buzzing. She was eager to partake in some good tidings, one of the grandest affairs of the year in this part of the world. Yet, nothing excited her more than the possibility of seeing Dave again. Too long had she gone without his sarcastic wit and his presence. The longer she thought over all their past encounters the more she became confused.

Is this infatuation or the beginnings of love? Did he wait for me even though I told him not to? How long can a man wait if he isn't in love? How long can he wait if he is?

Jack interrupted her from her musings. "Miss Rose, ya must be thinkin' of somethin' vary serious. Yer face is screwed up tight."

"I'm, perhaps, thinking too much. Would you sing one of your songs for me please? Joe, you'll have to endure."

Joe hadn't even caught a word she said. Even when Jack raised his voice so that the whole surrounding countryside could hear, he didn't seem to notice. His face seemed devoid of any annoyance or anger.

The excitement rustling throughout the streets of Barkerville infected Rose so that she lightly bounced her feet. Jack continued his singing and whistling down the main road until they pulled up at the hotel where they would be staying for the week. As Joe helped her down, Rose eyed her surroundings.

Ladders were placed throughout the sides of the street. They bore men hanging up banners. There was an odd woman here or there watching with glee as the town was transformed into the most decadent setting it could be. Most of the women (whatever women there were) were trapped within their homes. The occasion's need for a feast was their enslavers.

A rabble of miners emerged from the direction of the mines. Dirt covered faces, tattered clothes, and belaboured postures—in the crowd, she could spot *his* face even though it was just as dirty as any man's. The way he held himself and the kindness of his eyes were some of her dearest memories.

Dave wove through the crowd and headed into the only quiet spot in town, the church. Her gaze didn't stray from his form until he stepped inside. She took a step forward acting upon instinct, to see him right away and dazzle him with her sarcastic wit. But she withheld herself and bit her lip. When did this all seem so complicated? She didn't know whether she should act or not, whether her actions would encourage his affections or aggravate him.

Jack's hand upon her shoulder. "Ain't ya gonna see 'im?"

"Later, Jack. Right now I need a long hot bath."

"One comin' right up, miss."

"Thank you."

When it was time to go to dinner, Rose was suddenly nervous. What if she saw him at the restaurant? What should she do? What should she say? What should she wear?

A knock sounded on her door. "Jack!"

"Miss, yer ready?"

"Maybe we shouldn't eat out? Let's have dinner in our rooms."

"Now, now, ya said ya wanted to eat out."

"Fine, give me five minutes." She unpacked her suitcase and pulled out the same dress she had worn on her escapade throughout Victoria, the first dress he saw her in. She let out a deep breath.

There's no need to be nervous. We'll muddle through this together whatever this is, if there is even anything.

The restaurant was packed full. Rose, Joe, and Jack meandered through until they were presented a table far in the corner. As menus were passed out, Rose found Daniel Shaw's company of men seated together. Dave was amongst them. Her heart skipped a beat as she looked him over. He was clean shaven and put together tidily with clean pants, a cream shirt, and a plain brown vest over top.

From afar, she saw him laugh and crack a wide smile at a joke one of the men made. He took a quick look at the menu and looked up. He saw her in the corner of his view. He opened the angle of his body toward her and stared at her. It seemed as if time had frozen still and they were the only two who moved in the same wavelength. He granted her his most charming smile then—

"Miss, what would you like?"

"Oh, whatever he's having," she said, pointing in Jack's direction.

As soon as the waiter left, Jack sent Rose a questioning look.

"What? You have excellent taste."

Throughout dinner, Rose became less self-conscious and more Dave-conscious. At one point she couldn't keep him in the corner of her view because Jack was sharing the most ridiculous story she had ever heard of his travels in the Midwest. When her laughing had calmed down, she looked over to Dave's table. He wasn't there. Suddenly drops of water splattered her dress and she heard Dave saying, "Oh, I'm so sorry, sir. I wasn't looking where I was going. Here let me…" Dave took the towel hanging from the man's belt and started to mop up the floor. As he stood up to return the towel, he slipped a note into Rose's hand. Once he patted himself down, he said, "Joe, Jack, Rose, fancy seeing you here. Here in town for the annual festival?"

Joe acknowledged him. "Dave."

"Well, I'll be seeing you around. Have yourself a good evening." He winked at Rose.

Throughout the rest of dinner, the note burned as a constant reminder to check it contents later that evening.

As soon as Rose had a minute to herself in her room, she opened the note and read, *Meet me at our spot.*

Half an hour later, she alighted upon him on the edge of the forest. She stopped a few feet away from him.

He turned to face her and said nothing. The way the shadows of the neighbouring trees hung over him, his features were unreadable.

She couldn't bear to say anything in her defence to having left him without a word. She would only verify the fact that he had successfully wheedled his way past her defences. "I saw you enter the church earlier on. Have you been visiting with the Reverend?"

Dave took a step closer, his face was still in the shadows. "Mm, hm."

"How is he after his attack?" Rose looked down, ashamed of the reminder.

"He's good. I've been helping him fix some things up around the church." Finally, he stepped out into the moon's glow, a smile of peace transfixed on his face.

Despite being fearful of facing him because there was the chance he wouldn't want to be with her, she couldn't help but smile when she saw him.

He stepped closer every few seconds until he was inches away. As he stood there looking into her face with acceptance, she couldn't turn hers away. She felt the hesitant surface of his fingers stroke her cheek, and she leaned into his touch. His fingers wound their way to her hat that covered her mound of hair underneath it. He took it off, and his other hand plunged into her raven hair. During all his advances, they had come so close that barely a sliver of light could be seen past their bodies.

Dave inhaled deeply and said, "You came back."

She smiled wickedly, "I couldn't miss the social event of the year, could I?"

Dave took a step back, not yet letting go. His face was thoughtful, cautious.

Rose immediately remembered that Dave had known of Daniel Shaw's invitation. "I said no. I'm so sorry to have dabbled with your affections in the beginning. I was so engrossed with pleasing myself I didn't think of how you would feel. I couldn't foresee *this*."

Dave closed the gap once again. "I knew after our first meeting…I couldn't let you go even if you broke my heart into tiny little pieces." He drew her in and laid his head on top of hers. They stayed in that position for several minutes, the both not knowing how to proceed after having revealed already so much of what was in their hearts. He murmured in her ear, "I want you to go to the dance with me."

Rose's head was in perfect placement for being able to hear Dave's heartbeat. Hearing it drum erratically against the wall of his chest, she knew she had the power to shatter or strengthen. She thought of how blessed she was to do the latter. "I'll go with you." She cradled his head nearer hers and brushed her lips upon his cheek near the corner of his lips. His lips...so close...feeling so necessary to seal her affections...so easy to lock with hers. In this grip, she could feel how willing he was to participate, how long he had waited for their touch. The beautiful tug and pull of temptation was so infectious that she knew she would give in if she waited too long. She let go and resumed her head against his chest. The starry host was the only witness to the union of their longing hearts, or so it seemed.

The next day, Rose walked around town to soak in all the sights of the townsfolk readying for the big party the next night. The decorations were all put up, even those that had come from the Orient. Crinkled paper lanterns danced in the wind near some homes and shops. A man walked out of one of the homes carrying such decorations.

"My darling Rose!"

She swirled to the origin of his voice and saw him strut out of an office like a peacock with his brightest feathers on show. The confidence he carried and his breath-defying looks still struck the carnal chord within her soul.

He took her hand and kissed it as always. "It is so good to see you have come despite your refusal to go as my escort. Why?"

Afraid to whisper any note of an emotional attachment to Dave for Dave's sake and hers, she kept her lips sealed.

"No matter, all women have their secrets. If you won't go with me, will you at least save one dance for me?"

She pursed her lips. "All right, one dance. I'm free to dance with others, am I not?"

"Of course, we shall see." He took a step forward.

She took a step back. "It was good to see you again, Daniel." She turned away from him and felt the intensity of his gaze. She wouldn't give him the satisfaction of looking back.

When she returned to her room that evening, a large box lay on her bed. She looked back at the door she had just closed and wondered where it had come from. She opened it and found a dress within. She gently picked it up and surveyed the gift. She had never seen one such as this.

The bodice was crimson red silk, and it swooped to the left diagonally bunched at the corner with red ostrich feather. The bottom swoop of the dress was covered by cream lace. The sleeves rested on the pinnacle of the shoulders, a wine red bunching of material. She turned it over to see a large red bow, the apex of the train. The cost of this dress would be…ridiculous. It must have been imported from England, and it seemed to have been custom made. Truly, it was one of a kind. She laid it on the bed and found a letter at the bottom of the box.

Dearest Rose,

I had this especially made for you. No other is worthy enough to wear it. Wear it to the ball tomorrow night. If you do not or if you alter this dress in any way, your escort will vanish. Do not disappoint me.

Your watchful eye

Her blood chilled. It was back.

Man for the field; woman is his game:
The sleek and shining creatures of the chase,
We hunt them for the beauty of their skins;
They love us for it, and we ride them down.
Alfred, Lord Tennyson
v, 1.147

Chapter 16

"My, Rose, where did you get such a thing?" Priscilla, who had arrived late afternoon the day of the ball, fingered Rose's dress. So awe-struck was she by the sight, she couldn't utter a word for a whole minute while she gawked.

Rose's hands smoothed it down as she took in the sight. It fit her perfectly. Most of her hair was piled in luscious curls. A few locks hung down the nape of her neck, her look the most elegant she had ever contrived.

Rose reached over to the letter, which had accompanied the gift, and gave it to Priscilla.

Priscilla turned white as a lily. "How...how can you wear that? It's been tainted by blood."

Rose faced her resolutely. "I must."

"Who is your escort?"

"That can be a surprise!"

"Surely it's Daniel Shaw! How he's fawned over you since he laid eyes on you!"

"It isn't," Rose said, as she put on the ruby inlaid earrings which had come with the dress.

"Well, what a strange turn of events," Priscilla muttered.

The two girls walked over to the main hall where already a giant buzz could be heard from within. Joe and Jack had arrived early to help set up whatever last minute details needed tending. As the girls neared the door, Rose caught sight of Dave coming from the direction of the miners' squat housing. When they met a few feet away, Rose made introductions. "Dave, this is Priscilla, my friend who is like a sister to me. Priscilla, this is Dave, my escort."

Dave stepped forward. "Very nice to meet you, Priscilla."

Priscilla put out her hand. "Likewise, I'll see you later, Rose?"

Rose nodded absentmindedly as she took another step forward in Dave's direction.

He took in the sight of her. "You…this is the first time you've made me speechless, absolutely speechless. I've never seen anything on God's green earth more beautiful than you."

"Thank you, you are…you have exceeded my expectations in every way. That bowtie…here…" Rose moved closer to him and straightened it. The temptation to fold into him was so great.

Dave offered his arm, "Shall we?"

How different this all looked compared to the balls she had heard many women gloat about back in England when she would sneak into her aunt's sitting room. She had always dreamed of swirling silks and men in stiff suits circling round the ballroom with their dames on their arms.

This was a real party! No stuffy manners, just good old jolly fun. Even though many of the women from the different towns had come, there were still not enough for all the men present. So, as Rose entered the hall, she saw many men dancing together and stomping their feet with linked arms, circling round in place.

To one side of the room were all the refreshments including cakes, pies, and cookies. The tables were covered in chequered cloths. This place, with all its rowdy merriment and rustic charm, felt more like home than England ever did.

She and Dave danced the first two reels together. She was never at rest; for the men were constantly in line to dance with her. She didn't mind being on her feet all night. It was a celebration for her, as well. The life she had made for herself despite the broken pieces her father left behind was something to be treasured.

Just as Priscilla came up to her to speak, Daniel Shaw walked in. With every step he took, all eyes were drawn to his enigmatic presence. As he walked toward Rose, his eyes never left hers. The deep chasms were endless, and she feared plunging to her death. He took her hand and swept her into a sensual dancer's embrace, fierce and unrelenting, and whispered into her ear, "I knew this was the only dress that could do you justice. You glorious creature!" As soon as the last word had fallen from his lips, her palms began to sweat, and the room began to spin although the focal point of his eyes did not. She tried to speak, tried to close her eyes, tried to fall to her knees. His arms, ice-cold prison bars, held her up.

His honey-smooth lips touched her ear sending electric shivers throughout her body, "My darling Rose, don't make a scene here. I knew..." He lowered his hand down her back and drew her closer. "You would figure out sooner or later." He sighed. "I was disappointed when you came with my cousin. I could have accepted the fact that you wanted to come alone but..."

Out of the depths of her muddled mind, the word "cousin" sent a jolt through her heart. "What do you mean 'cousin?' Dave isn't..."

"Shall we take this elsewhere?"

"Do I have a choice?"

"You do although I'm sure you would like to see your dearest friend again...unharmed."

Rose gritted out of her teeth, "You, pig!"

"Ah, what a feisty nature! I knew you and I were the same through and through when I first met you. Come, let us take this to a more private location." He grabbed her wrist and began to weave through the thickening crowd.

A blast of cooling wind whirled Rose's skirts as they walked down the road to Daniel Shaw's Barkerville office. Once arrived, he backed Rose against his desk and drew his curled finger down the side of her face. "I wish you would relent…give me what I want." His hunger was apparent in every feline movement he made.

As his hand reached for the top lace in the back, she said, "Could we sit and have a proper conversation?" His fingers continued their appointed work. She leaned into him more, conjuring whatever sultry feelings she could, and whispered into his ear, "Please?"

He stopped, his fingers sliding down the front of her dress, and said, "Of course, anything for you, my pet. We can continue this after business is taken care of." He walked to his cabinet and pulled out a bottle of port and two glasses.

Rose took a sip and stated, "You will not touch Priscilla."

Daniel put on a mocking smile. "She's of no use to me at the moment."

"There are so many things that must be said."

"Speak, dear Rose, for the sound of your voice… I could listen to it all night."

"That won't happen." She gathered in her hands the folds of her dress and scrunched them. "You said, 'cousin.' What did you mean? Surely there would be some resemblance if that were the case."

"I mean what I say when I say it. Dave is my cousin."

"How?"

"You know the story of his fighting in the Civil War. Well, he forgot to tell you he was a war hero."

"How did you know about that?"

"There are some answers for you to find on your own. His mother was my mother's sister. See, my family disowned his mother when she went off and married someone beneath her. Turned out she had a terrible life. When my parents found out that his mother had died and that he had walked away from home a war hero, why, they reached out right away wanting to make amends. He's been, or I should say was, under their care ever since."

Rose looked at the floor, thoroughly confused, and said, "If what you say is true, why would he not have told me?"

"Why would he? He's intimately connected to your puppet master."

She flounced out of her chair and ran to the door to escape.

He was too fast. "Rose, the evening isn't over. I have more to say if you'll let me."

"I want to see Dave."

"That's not possible at this time. You're part of the game, and you can't walk away until I say you can."

Strangely enough, all the fear she had harboured over the past few months, now washed away as she faced her tormentor in the waning light of the candle. The office was mostly covered in shadows, night's cloak heavy upon them.

Rose picked up her glass. "You've been behind all the threats all this time. Did you murder my father?"

"For that I cannot take the credit."

"Who did it?" she whispered.

"Who do you think? Who's in the best position to receive orders and carry them out?"

Dave…his cousin, a man skilled in the art of modern war, a man part of Daniel's company, a man who drew close only to use my secrets against me.

Her lips went dry. "It cannot be."

Daniel smirked, "It could, couldn't it? Your father was in the way, and I needed him out of the way."

"How could have he been there before I was?"

"Have you seen the man ride? He was born in a horse's field!"

"I can't believe this," she reiterated.

"Well, you'll have plenty of time to process this information later. Right now, on to business."

"I have more questions. My father's will…"

Daniel interrupted, "Those questions can be answered at a later date. We can see each other again. Now for your mandate, you're to find your father's treasure."

"What rubbish! I assure you it's not real."

"Oh, it's very real! Why don't you make your own inquiries into the matter?"

"Why do I have to be the one to find it? Why can't I give you the last clue I found and let me leave this place?"

"There are three very good reasons why I won't do neither. First, I need someone with intimate knowledge of Harland Wood to follow the trail. Second, it brings me great joy to watch you scurry about, playing our little game. Third, I'm not letting you go anywhere. You're mine, and there's no escaping my hand. Don't you see that it must be you?"

"All the clues so far haven't required a special knowledge of my father."

He gritted through his teeth, "Don't test me. Fail to meet the end of the game, and I'll take away everything you love."

There's no way out. I fell into the lap of a madman willingly.

"Thank you for laying out the terms so articulately. I suppose I must be going to start the search for your treasure immediately." She stood up and twisted the doorknob to open the door.

In a flash, Daniel was beside her and shut the door forcefully with his palm. "Why, the night is young…" He fingered the silk of her shoulder sleeve. "I would like to revel in your pleasures." He sank his lips onto her shoulder and began to move them toward her clavicle.

Rose said in a strained voice, "Could I leave you with a token of my passion? One kiss and then you must let me leave."

His face inches from hers, he replied, "I suppose it'll have to do this time."

Her lips quivered, not from the anticipating delight but from the horror she would have to perform to leave this place intact. "It'll have to do," she whispered before joining her lips with his. She forced her hand to caress his face as their kiss grew in intensity. "That's enough, goodnight, Daniel."

"I don't want to let you go," he said, as he grasped her wrist tightly.

"You have to." She put on a fond smile and twirled her finger around one of his locks. "Distance makes the heart grow fonder."

Strumming the melody to the beat of his heart managed to get her out alive and somewhat untouched. She didn't know how long she could keep up playing *this* game. The game of finding her father's treasure, she could play for a long while. She was here in the Cariboo country, and she was here to stay. Somehow she would find a way to turn the tables and take the upper hand so that he couldn't find leverage to grow the influence of his power.

Joe, Jack, Priscilla, she would do anything to protect them. Dave...she would have said the same. Now it was clear where his alliances now stood. But perhaps...Daniel was wrong, he was lying. She would go find Dave right now and demand an explanation. Perhaps this was all part of some horrible nightmare.

Goosebumps formed on her flesh, not because it was a cold night but because even playing the charade of being infatuated with Daniel that last moment brought about even deceit she would rather not dabble in. She had changed so much, and she knew it wasn't of her own doing.

No one was on the streets. All the merriment screamed from within the dance hall. A few men stood at the threshold of the entrance door. She looked into each of their faces. They were well on the verge of tipping into drunkenness. None of them were Dave.

At a quarter to twelve, the party had increased to its loudest tempo. She scoured every corner, every dancing couple for his face. He wasn't there. She spotted Priscilla speaking with a very awkward young gentleman, not more than nineteen years of age. Rose neared her friend and eavesdropped a little on their conversation.

"...the mines everyday. Ya know, it's mighty different from what I thought it was gonna be." The young man's face blushed a deep red. "Maybe I can show ya around, you know?"

Priscilla, the picture of innocence and gracious as ever, replied, "How delightful that all sounds! It would be fascinating to have a tour of the mines. Unfortunately, I'm only in town until tomorrow. You see my father will be needing my help around the farm. Tomorrow is my only day to spend time with my dearest friend. Speaking of which, let me make introductions. John, this is Rose, my friend. Rose, this is John, whom I've just met this evening."

John, flustered, grabbed her outstretched hand and planted a slobbery kiss.

Priscilla smiled in slight embarrassment. "John, could Rose and I have a few moments to speak?"

"Sure," he replied, bobbing his head enthusiastically but not moving an inch.

"Alone?" Priscilla piped.

John zipped out of there as if his coattails (which were incredibly large on his slight body frame) were on fire.

"He's a sweet soul," Priscilla smiled after him. "Where have you been all evening? I've been looking for you everywhere! I didn't see you…it was right after Mr. Shaw entered the hall. I thought I saw you leave with him."

Rose hung her head.

"Rose, you don't mean to tell me that you…well…I can't say it!"

"No, Priscilla, but there is much to tell you, not here, not now. Meet me tomorrow morning in my room. There's much to explain."

Priscilla took her hand, "Of course."

"Before I go, have you seen Dave anywhere? Is he here?"

"I'm sorry, I haven't seen him since you left."

Tears began to spring up. Rose endeavoured to control them lest they fell.

Priscilla said, "You won't be staying any longer? Oh, please say you'll do."

Rose brushed away her imploring hands, "I can't, goodnight."

The mass of frolicking bodies she had to push past to leave became a mass of colours washing over each other in waves. Her vision only cleared when it was just her and the brilliant mosaic of stars in the sky.

As soon as she entered her room, she struggled to remove the dress, heavy with deceit, lust, and blood. It was a shame that such a beautiful piece would have to be so tainted. She was down to her undergarments when she finally realized a note sat upon her bed. Relief flooding her chest, thinking it was an explanation from Dave, she rushed to the bed, jumping upon it and grabbing it. Reading the first line, her balloon of hope deflated.

He means to taunt me, to break me. Whether Dave is the one who...or not, I will win this game.

She threw the note to the floor in disdain and proceeded to take off her undergarments. The curtain suddenly fluttered from a light breeze, catching her attention. Immediately, she drew the window closed and made sure no one could look inside from any angle. Even then, she felt the intense hunger in Daniel's eyes rake over her as she disrobed completely to slip into her nightgown.

Joe's frantic (as close to frantic as Joe could get) rapping at the door awoke Rose from her restless sleep. She slipped on another layer and opened the door with a yawn. "Joe, have you seen Dave?"

"No, miss, haven't seen him since early last evenin'," Joe replied with a grim look. "I wanted to make sure you were all right."

Rose rubbed her eyes in irritation, "I'm...never mind."

"When would you like to leave, miss?"

"After lunch."

Stubborn as a mule, she decided to see whether she could track Dave's movements after the dance. Yet every moment he didn't appear, her firm belief in their intimate connection dwindled to broken pieces.

Deciding to skip breakfast, she walked toward the church. A silence greeted her as the door opened, again reminding her of Dave. As soon as she turned to face the podium, an "ah," made her jump.

The reverend's mousey voice was low. "I'm sorry I'm scared you. I thought I might see you."

Rose asked, "Why is that?"

"After what happened last time you were here..."

"It has nothing to do with that."

He breathed a sigh of relief. "Oh, good, I have such a hard time…"

She interrupted him, "Where is…?" She stopped herself suddenly, realizing what she had just done, shutting him up because deep down she believed that what she had to say was vastly more important, that she was more important. She bit her tongue. "I'm sorry I interrupted. Please continue."

His small eyes screwed up a little in confusion. "I have such a hard time reliving that moment when I truly believed it was my last moment on earth and I was about to meet my Maker."

"Reverend, do you fear death?"

"It's not the idea I fear; but, perhaps, the method of death. Everyone wishes for a peaceful death in their sleep after having lived a full life, no?"

"Yes, I'm sure they do."

Will I have that luxury?

Rose asked softly, "I know you said you don't wish to relive the moment, but you never saw your assailant's face?"

The reverend shook his head, "No, I didn't. I'm sorry."

"Have you seen Dave?"

"He's finally told you, hasn't he?"

"Told me what?"

The reverend sat down and motioned for her to do the same. "Dave and I have become friends ever since he's come in with Daniel Shaw's gold mining company. He even fixed the front door."

Rose smiled to herself, "I thought so."

"Ever since he's met you, he's been in agony over telling you that he's Daniel Shaw's cousin. The thing is, I can't think why it'd be such a problem. I would think being related to him is an advantage in this town. On another count, I don't see how they could be."

"What?"

"Cousins. They don't look anything alike."

Rose couldn't remember if she and her cousins looked anything alike. "Thank you. You've told me a great deal."

She left the church and went to the only other place she could think she might find him. She sat under the shade of the trees bordering their small meadow for what seemed like eternity until she saw the sun reach its apex in the sky.

As Rose opened the saloon's door, Priscilla was reading the menu. Rose hurried to sit. "I'm sorry I'm late."

Priscilla looked to her, a ready, forgiving smile on her face. "It's all right. I've just been seated and given the menu. I was looking forward to this all morning."

Rose grabbed her menu. "How was the rest of the party?"

"My dream came true. Daniel Shaw came up to me..."

"He did?" Rose blurted. "I mean go on."

A slightly injured look on Priscilla's face, "Yes, it's not that incredulous. As I was saying, he asked to dance with me." Stars shone in her eyes. "It was the most magical time of my life."

Knowing what she knew, Rose's insides roiled violently inside. She was determined to shield her friend from the awful truth. "I'm so happy for you. Did he say anything about seeing you again?"

"No, he didn't; but maybe.... Now what did you want to tell me?"

Rose replied, "I received a visit from the man who has been behind all the threats."

"You know who it is?" A look of horror stretched across Priscilla's face.

"I don't." A lie which put a strain on Rose's mind. She needed to protect her friend. "He was wearing a large cape with a hood. His face was covered over by the shadow of his cape."

"Surely his voice?"

"It was muffled. He must have been wearing some sort of cloth over his mouth. From the lower tones of his register, I assume it must be a man."

Doubt of the veracity of Rose's story showed on Priscilla's features. Priscilla said, "What now?"

"I was mandated to find my father's treasure...and taunted to figure out who was my father's killer. Supposedly, they're not the same people, my father's killer and the man behind all this."

"Rose, promise me you'll be careful."

She nodded. "Let's eat."

The rest of their lunch, Rose asked to be updated on Priscilla's family life and how her family was faring after their loved one's death. After Priscilla left town, Rose hastened to do the same. There was no more time to lose, chasing after the sun's rays and frolicking in newfound dreams.

There was a hunt to commence. There was a devil to catch in his own play. There was a treasure to be had. There was a queen to rise.

Experience is the child of Thought,
and Thought is the child of Action.
We cannot learn men from books.
Benjamin Disraeli
bk.v, ch. 1

Chapter 17

As soon as Rose's boots scuffed the fringe of the entrance carpet of her home, of her business, a darkness seemed to crawl up the building's cracks and cloak her paradise, drawing from her a suffocating gasp.

It was evening, the twilight dusting every surface beneath the windows. Joe and Jack were busy unhitching the horses and bringing their goods inside. They had taken the opportunity   to restock on their way back home.

Before Rose could run up the stairs and grab that metal box (her fingers itched to play its game), she checked the telegraph roster for messages that had come in while they were gone. There were a few from their suppliers saying they had just shipped some items. Only one truly caught her interest. One on which was written that the owner of 100 Mile House was coming up to visit the next day on his way to Barkerville.

Curious as to his request but wanting to be helpful to her partner along the Cariboo Road, she replied saying she be would delighted to have him for a short visit.

The steps to her desk were slow and non deliberate. She struggled to conjure a sense of purpose. Reaching her study, she forced her rigid body to sit, to grasp her father's ink pen in her fumbling fingers, to record the list of supplies they had bought. A tear droplet splashed onto the page; her perfect penmanship was now desecrated. She pushed the ledger away and allowed the fountain to flow, tears over Dave's betrayal, tears of being trapped within her own fear, tears of what could have been. Exhausted and limp, she dragged herself up the stairs and fell into bed. Tomorrow she would be strong.

The next day, Rose struggled to balance a few glass jars in her arms in the cellar when she heard her name being called. "Coming," she aggressively hollered as she rolled her eyes. She thumped the jars onto the storage shelf in the cellar and went upstairs to ask, "Jack, what is it?"

"De owna from de 100 Mile House is here to see ya."

Rose wiped her hands on her work apron. She unwrapped it from around her waist and hung it on a peg on the wall. She greeted Mr. Nelson at the front door. "Mr. Nelson, how do you do? What brings you here?" She stuck out her hand for him to shake.

He shook it and crossed his arms. "Well, I was just passin' by on my way to Barkerville on a matter of urgent business."

"Oh, I hope nothing has gone incredibly wrong at your establishment."

"Not in the least, miss. I was here to see how you're getting along since, originally, you weren't…"

"I've been doing very well for myself, sir. I have two men as full-time workers who work alongside me. I found out I have a knack for business and bookkeeping just like my father before me."

"And he really did pass the mile house down to you?" Mr. Nelson inquired with raised eyebrows.

There were still many unanswered questions, the answers to which Daniel still held. She truly believed the matter of the will was one of them. "That matter has been dealt with."

Mr. Nelson threw his hands up in the air. "Well, then, I guess that takes care of that." He turned to exit out the front door.

Rose laid a hand on his retreating shoulder. "Mr. Nelson, do you mean to say you would swipe this establishment right from under my nose?"

He swivelled, a look of horror plastered upon his face. He planted his fists on his hips. "Miss, I would never on my honour—true, I wanted this place and true, your father insisted he would have me first in mind when it came to leaving me this mile house."

Not only did Daniel Shaw rob Rose of a fresh start but he also robbed this man of the business he loved. Yet she knew Mr. Nelson's life would be in danger if she ever disclosed the awful truths she was privy to. She would find a way to make it right.

"Mr. Nelson, I'm so sorry that things didn't turn out the way you had hoped. They certainly haven't turned out the way I had hoped. I give you my word that when I decide to sell, I'll give you a fair price."

"Humph, it's more word than your father ever gave me. See, he never gave his word, but he strongly hinted at the bargain. Shake?"

"Shake." She had come to love this place she had made her own; but change would always come. This change could benefit her and her competitor. "I'm sure we could come to a fair price when the time is right."

He looped his thumbs into his belt. "You've put me in a mighty fine mood, miss. Good day!"

As he walked out, Rose believed it was a proper assessment that this man seemed to have been the closest to her father. If anyone would know about the treasure, it would be him.

Just as he was entering his wagon, she called out, "Mr. Nelson, perhaps, you could answer a question of mine?"

"Anything."

"Did my father ever speak to you of a gold vein he kept hidden? Of a treasure?"

He roared with laughter and slapped his knee. "That treasure's a myth, been circulatin' for a long time. I'm sure there's no such thing."

"Some people seem to think it's as real as that horse right there."

He drew his eyebrows high, "Imagine that, a horse made out of gold. You could live like a king! Nah, don't go wastin' your time on foolishness. Better spend your time making a fortune out of this place. That's where the real money is!"

Rose bid him a good day. She couldn't afford to not chase after the myth; for her life and the lives of those she loved depended upon it.

That evening, Rose, yearning for some company, brought out the metal box, with the chessboard etched on its side, to the living room where Joe, after having brought the horses into the barn, now sipped on a hot cup of coffee. Rose thought coffee was too strong of a taste although she did quite enjoy the smell. Tea was the drink she allowed herself indulgence; her English roots held firm.

Jack was patching up a hole in his pants, a rip that happened two days ago.

"You know I could patch those up for you," Rose said, as she glanced sideways.

"Ha! I've seen yer work. Nona yer fingers gonna come near my pants. Anyway, my momma taught me a long time ago."

"It's true. I never enjoyed sewing, embroidering, or any of the fine female arts they taught us in finishing school."

There were no other persons in the room other than those just described. No miners had come through that day needing food or shelter. Hence the reason Rose felt comfortable and safe bringing downstairs the atrocity in front of her.

"Well, how's ya gonna open dat thing?" Jack asked.

Rose threw an entreating glance his way. "I'm about to find out. I've tried a little before but…I wasn't motivated as I am now. Before I undertake this, I need to fetch some paper and pen." She moved to her study to get the necessary objects when she noticed a folded letter that hadn't been there before.

Ready. Get set. Go.

"Really, that's it?! How original!" She groaned in frustration and stomped her foot. She drew her curtains to the side to peer into the inky blackness which was occasionally alleviated in some spots when the moon decided to break through her prison of clouds. She threw the note in the wastebasket, grabbed her things, and tried to calm her nerves before she sat down in the living room.

She let out a deep breath. "I believe my father set this up so that I would have to figure out the most complicated game he could conjure. Or perhaps the shortest? Let's see." Her first move was to create the shortest game. She made the same moves she had shown Dave that night only a few weeks ago. The memory assaulted her already wounded spirit, rendering her unable to perform what needed to be done. Every detail of that night began running through her mind— his tone of voice, the length of stubble on his face, his charming yet irritating smirk, the way his body had been in proportion to hers, the way their fingers had touched. In the end, this memory produced a single tear running down her cheek.

"Miss Rose?"

"I'm going to need a lot more paper, Jack. Please be a dear and fetch me some."

"Sure thing." He returned with a huge stack.

"Now I'm ready." She proceeded to make the first set of moves ending in a win. Once completed, she could hear the whir of tiny mechanisms and gears moving, grinding, and changing positions until they stopped with the box still closed. It was ready to be tried again.

Rose began to play both white and black and record every single move she made with always the same result, the mocking movements and then silence. By the time Joe and Jack had gone to bed, she had written game plays on fifteen sheets of paper double-sided. She put her pencil down and decided to run her hands over every inch of the box to feel whether there was any kind of protrusion or dent that would hint to a certain button needing to be pushed; but no such thing did she feel. She went to bed exhausted with the promise of tomorrow hanging heavy on her shoulders.

The next night she was at it again. Her hand was severely cramped from all the fiddling and writing. Enraged by the lack of visible results, she threw the metal box against the wall and yelled with a force which grated her throat. "How many plays do I have to make, Father, before this wretched box is opened?" She slid her shaking hands down her cheeks. Suddenly she heard…the taunting sounds of gears. She swiftly stepped toward the box, afraid to touch it, leaning forward with eyes wide open, skin prickling with the possible finality of the moment. It had never rearranged itself for this long. Was this all this old box of junk needed? A good shaking and clunking around to rid the gears of their set goal? At last, the sounds stopped. She leaned down to pick it up, just waiting for it to fall apart and reveal what was inside its precious walls. She turned it over, nothing. She tried to pry it open with her fingernails, ripping one in the process. Nothing, nothing had changed. She dropped it onto her desk, defeated, not caring that her blood was pooling where the fingernail had torn too deeply.

The task of opening the box so consumed her that she racked her brain almost incessantly throughout the next days for plays she had forgotten to try. When she thought of one, she would grab a piece of paper and write it down to try that night. Five days passed, the insanity building day by day. So desperate was she that she could barely think a straight thought during the day and definitely none at night. Her ledgers and bookkeeping were untouched; her food many times the same.

On the sixth night Rose slumped in her chair and stared with eyes full of hatred at the thing that had made her last few days a nightmare.

Jack piped, "Maybe the answer is staring you right in the face."

Rose didn't flick her eyes toward him. "What do you think I'm doing right now?" she retorted. Aware of her unkindness, she closed her eyes. "I'm sorry, Jack. I know you're trying to help. Maybe you're right." She picked up the box and again ran her fingers against all the grooves on the one side of the chessboard. Each square on the board was outlined. Perhaps she didn't need to feel the answer, maybe she needed to see it. She moved the box under the light of the standing lamp beside her chair. The straightforward chessboard on one side, the top and bottom sides were smooth metal, the sides bordering the chessboard showcased various etchings of the different chess pieces, but the opposite side of the board...there was a single etching, still dirty from the soil. She hadn't paid any attention to it before. Rose bolted forward in her chair. "Jack, can you get me a wet cloth, please?"

He jumped right out of his chair to do her bidding.

Joe's eyes wavered from the newspaper in front of him.

As soon as Jack returned with the desired cloth, she rubbed at the etching. After a few strokes, the queen image within a square border stared back at her. She breathed, "Of course, how could I not know this? It's been that simple! All those hours—I could cry!"

Jack asked impatiently, "What? What is it?"

Rose replied, "The queen. She's the most important asset to the army. She was my father's favourite." She sat there in contemplation.

Both Jack and Joe's attention were now fully fixed on her and her cryptic sayings.

Joe asked, "Which one?"

"The white one," she said, as she pushed on the corresponding player. Again a series of whirring and clicking motions sounded from within the box. Suddenly, the single etching of the queen protruded from the box's side.

"Why the white one?" Jack asked.

She replied, "It was always in reference to my mother. That was the only thing he ever said about her. White for purity. Gentle as a dove, wise as a serpent." Her finger hovered over the protruding square etching and pushed. There were no minute noises to greet this action, only a loud click. Then...it opened.

The whole side of the chessboard swung out from the box, creating enough room for her hand to reach in. The sides of her hand brushed against the rough edging of the gears until her fingertips finally touched a piece of paper. "Ah!" she declared as she pulled it out. "Another clue," she smiled grimly. "When will this hunt end?"

Jack slapped his thighs. "Ya want us to git?"

Rose pondered for a moment before she returned the piece of paper to its hiding spot and pushed the side back against the box before she said, "No, tonight I'm going to taste some sweet rest. There's time for intrigue on the morrow." She shut her door and surrendered to an uneventful sleep.

It has long been an axiom of mine that
the little things are infinitely the most important.
Sir Arthur Conan Doyle

Chapter 18

The twittering of the birds accompanied the sun's rise.
Rose could feel the corners of her mouth lift in contentment.
She grabbed her sheets and stretched. Perhaps, today she
would sleep in, read the novel sitting on her bed stand, treat
herself to a normal day in the life of a frontier woman, no,
more like a normal aristocratic woman of England.

She turned toward her window—all her simple
musings dashed by a note, pierced through by an arrow,
tacked to her wall. Again, someone had intruded, someone so
quiet and full of stealth—it was some of the best sleep she had
in a long time. It couldn't be Daniel. He was a businessman,
tied to his professional demands in Quesnel and Barkerville.
He was getting someone to do his dirty work. Could it be…? It
had to be Dave. He knew her, her fears, her strengths, her
weaknesses. He knew her and violated her in the worst way.
She threw off the covers, stomped to her wall, cried out as she
grabbed the arrow, and pulled.

How could she have been so stupid? She thought she
had played them really well in getting the attention she had
wanted. Then she grew, and she thought there was something
real between her and Dave. Reality struck—they played her so

well, fed off of her need for male attention—a man for momentary pleasure, a steady man to hold her heart. The brilliance of it…made her sick to her stomach.

Hesitantly, she turned her eyes to the note.

There's no time to waste. Get to work.

She wished she could burn away the wretched memories of his visage; for it came unbidden too many times, more than she could take. Would they have never met! Her breaths were shallow. Her heart squeezed so tightly by the pain—could she rip her skin to shreds and crawl out of its sorry carcass to be swept up away in one large gust of wind, return to ashes?

If she were to survive, she would have to enact the great divide. No more could she utter his name or even think it. He would become a spectre, the one she must vanquish. She would rebuild her walls one brick at a time until his name held no sway at all.

Now, to work! How did he know she hadn't looked upon the next clue? Did he lie in wait outside, watching her through the windowpanes? If he could come in like ghost and shoot an arrow, he could most definitely know her every move.

Anger propelled her toward the box. She opened it as she had the night before, reached inside, and pulled out the paper. Its edges unfurled, it was a…sketch. The skill her father had to draw this picture—it seemed alive, a perfect rendition of what could be. A range of mountains was featured. A stream flowed along the foot of the mountains and was met by another at the base of a particular mountain of the range. The two streams connected and continued to flow as a bigger stream away from the mountain. All the mountains looked the same except for the significant geographical difference of the one where the two streams met.

She overturned the paper to find a small triangle at the lower right corner.

A triangle…where have I seen that symbol before?

She threw on a simple dress. She took the steps two at a time. She found a few customers being served some breakfast, some miners who must have ridden all night to come so early. She gave them a quick greeting, then shut herself in her father's study. She strode to his bookshelf and scanned the titles. She was sure she had seen it in one of these, the science books. She pulled out the physics and chemistry books. Page after page, she rifled through a physics book. The symbol didn't appear. Finally she found it in the chemistry book.

Change...to change into. Father...of course.

"Jack!" she yelled.

He poked his head through the doorway. "Good mornin', miss, did ya have a gud sleep?"

"Yes, I did, thank you. I need a lemon to.... Do we have any? Oh, and a candle?"

"Lemon we got. A candle? There's daylight, miss."

"Jack, would you like to see a secret code?"

He rubbed his hands in excitement and nodded.

Minutes later, she squeezed the lemon into a bowl and brushed the juice onto the sketch. After the candle was lit, she put the paper close to the flame. Lettering began to appear in various sections of the sketch. At the top, the phrase "Fifty miles northeast of here" appeared. Where the streams converged was the phrase "marker". The last phrase to appear was "gold". The fine calligraphy was positioned about two-third of the way up the specific mountain.

"Finally, no more riddles."

Jack put a hand on her arm.

She inclined her head toward him and saw profound sadness in his eyes, those eyes usually alight with joy. It broke her heart to see him so.

"What is it?" she pleaded.

"Is dair no way out o' dis? I need ta go with ya. Ya can't go alone."

Rose braced her hands on his shoulders and looked him in the eye. "Jack, I need you here, to run the place for me. I couldn't have brought the business to where it is without your help and Joe's. And don't tell Joe."

"He'll help ya."

"You know very well he won't. He'll rope me up here if he has to and check it out for himself. This is very personal.

I need to do this. If I don't, something…horrible could happen to both of you. Because of me—they're not petty threats. They're very real."

"Then let me pray a blessin' on ya."

As he laid his hands upon her shoulders, as those tender words of care rose to heaven, she shuddered at the thought of the journey ahead of her.

Before the hooves of her horse could take their first step, Joe stepped in the way. His arms were crossed over his chest, and his brow was furrowed. It was the first time he had made her feel like a child doing a naughty thing…and she was going to lie. "Where do think you're going, miss?"

"Joe, really, I'm off on an errand. I'm meeting with Mr. Nelson."

His unusually grim face didn't seem convinced. "How come you didn't tell me?"

She offered a carefree smile. "I couldn't find you. I've been looking for you…seems like ages."

I can play this game to keep you safe. No one will rip this family apart.

His eyebrow rose. "One more question. What did the paper say?"

She looked at the road and then straight into his eyes. "Another random clue. It'll probably take me days to figure out. I believe this ride might…help me clear my head."

He took one long hard look at the road, almost as if he were trying to see the true destination of her day. "All right. Be back before sundown."

With a nod of her head, she set off toward the unknown, toward the singing thrum of adventure. She had packed a light lunch and canteen that she hid in her small saddle pack. She couldn't risk tipping off Joe in any way of her true intentions. She had also brought her father's compass. At first, she rode toward the 100 Mile House. Once she was sure Joe could no longer see her in the distance, she cut across the forest at a slower pace to go in the needed direction. Her detour cost her time, but it was necessary to keep the suspicions at bay.

Wisps of Gold

Two hours into her ride, her breathing became ragged as she thought over and over at the closeness of it all, how she could be done with it all from here on out. No more hunting, no more games, freedom. No more Daniel, no more...Dave— no, that ship had sailed a long time ago. It sailed that night he had left her in Daniel's clutches, had disappeared without a word. It had been about three weeks...three weeks she had secretly checked for telegrams every day from him, imagined him stopping by. Those eyes that had looked into hers with longing and told her silently it was going to be all right, those hands which had worked alongside hers to fight the unknown. Oh, they had played their game well; so well that she could say something had broken inside her. Trust for anybody other than Joe, Jack, and Priscilla—even then...could she truly say she trusted any of them wholeheartedly, completely? Dave had been part of their inner circle, and treachery was found. Would she find it again? One day at a time, she would move and endure.

She came to the base of a mountain range. She hopped off her horse and dug into her measly lunch. From here on out, she would walk. She slung the reins around the horn of her saddle and let her horse graze. He wouldn't go far even if she were gone for an hour. The greedy thing would stay and eat the whole field of grass if he could in one day.

The one stream was now before her. Easy, all she would have to do was walk alongside it until she found the other stream it met with. Simple.

As she walked alongside the stream, its bubbling and occasional gurgling quieting her weary soul, she realized how her father had come to love this land, how she was now coming to know the same love. Her fingertips grazed the waist high bushes beside the stream. Now if she were given the choice of leaving, would she? This land untouched, the pureness of its riches, not just the gold but also its simplicities—it was now hers just as it was her father's.

The crack of a twig—her head whipped around, seeking the origin of the sound, almost half expecting Daniel, or even worse Dave. It was only a deer. She dared not breathe for fear of breaking the spell its eyes cast upon hers as it looked upon her intently. This moment of stillness brought back to mind the first time she had set sights on the deer in Victoria. It wasn't that long ago and yet seemed like another lifetime ago. She was a completely different person back then.

As the deer pants for streams of water, so my soul pants for…You. I've finally returned home, back to Your heart. There is where I'll stay.

As if the deer had heard her heart's resolution, it walked toward the stream to drink. Even though she was sure the deer would let her pass, she stayed in her spot and watched. Only when it returned to the forest shadows did she feel she could pass and continue on her way.

A few minutes later she found…not two streams converging into one. Instead, she found the stream emptying into a…lake? Rose didn't remember seeing any kind of lake on the sketch. Did she have the wrong range? Perhaps she hadn't read the compass correctly? Maybe her detour had compromised the true direction. She couldn't very well tell if it was the correct place just by looking at the mountain. All the mountains looked the same to her.

Disappointed that her lying to Joe hadn't brought her one step closer to ending this mess, she sighed as she stared at the lake. How would she find another excuse to get out for another whole day? There were only so many stories she could make up. Then Joe would try to corroborate her story with Mr. Nelson whenever he saw Mr. Nelson next. This was a complete disaster.

She returned to the exact spot where she had left Horse except…he was nowhere to be seen.

Planting her hands on her hips, she spoke to herself. "Where did he go? This is impossible." She looked all around. "This can't be happening. Horse! Horse!" She felt incredibly stupid now not having given Horse a better name than exactly what he was. "I definitely have no sense of imagination. Horse!"

I can't believe this. I'm stranded with no food, no water, and…I left the compass in my saddle pack.

Horse had not gone the way she had come (toward the lake) so she decided to go the opposite way. She hoped that by attuning her ears intently to any familiar equine noises she would find him. After several minutes, she heard no neighing and saw no way of returning home before dark. Well, there was no time to mope. All there was to do was walk in the direction of home, or what she thought was the right direction. Her sense of direction was a little off because of the detour she had initially taken.

She occasionally called out to Horse with no answer in return. Her feet were sore, aching when she heard a feint whinny. She believed her mind to be playing tricks. There it was again with a more satisfied tone as if he were looking forward to his treat and then had finally received it. She gathered up her skirts and ran frantically looking for Horse in every direction. "Horse!" She shouted as his satisfied knickers greeted her shouts. Finally, she stumbled upon a small clearing where Horse, digging into a bucket of grain, was tied up to a hitching post. He turned his head toward her with sheepish eyes almost knowing he was in a bucket load of trouble.

"You mischievous creature! I've been looking all over for you! I would have been stranded in the wilderness all night if I hadn't just found you!" She stopped a few steps away from him, fumes of anger slowly oozing out. Then she laughed and couldn't stop laughing at the ridiculous turn of events. After finally managing to contain her laughter, she had forgotten that behind the hitching post was a log cabin with a lighted chimney, smoke unfurling from its top. It was modest. There was a small corral to the side with a shelter for another horse enjoying a mound of hay. Next to the corral was a wagon to which the horse could be hitched.

She rubbed Horse's nose and asked, "Who found you?"

"I did," a low male voice sounded behind her.

She jumped and turned around to find a man of medium height and hefty build. He was the perfect picture of a lumberjack except for his face. The bridge of his nose was wide, his lips were large and full. His skin had a bronze-reddish tinge. His hair was long, straight, and raven black, pulled back in a ponytail. His chequered red and black shirt was distinctly Western, in contrast to his native roots. He had an axe hanging over his shoulder. His biceps strained against the confines of his sleeves even after he had rolled them up. He was altogether frightening and interesting to look at.

She endeavoured to put on her smoothest smile. She had never come across an Indian. There were many stories of their savagery and stories of their helpfulness. This one seemed tame enough. She stuck out her hand and introduced herself.

He took a look at her hand then back at her, then at Horse before he grabbed her hand in one swift movement and shook it hard. Her hand felt as if it were going to be crushed in his grasp.

"I'm Waawaashkeshi, but you can call me Wally. Welcome."

Three may keep a secret, if two of them are dead.
Benjamin Franklin
July 1735

Chapter 19

Rose looked to Horse, saw that he had been well taken care of, and decided to trust Wally. "Thank you for having taken care of Horse, uh, my horse so well." She dug into her pocket and produced a few coins. "Here's for your trouble and the grain you've given him."

Wally's face was strangely impassive before a low deep chuckle rumbled out of his mouth.

The sudden noise startled Rose. Unsure yet wary of offending him, she slowly joined in his laughter. She cleared her throat. "What's so amusing?"

Wally sobered and closed her open palm with his large hand. "Money isn't everything in this life. Your horse provided my horse with some company for an hour. Stew's on the stove top. Want some?"

The man seemed harmless enough. At the mention of stew, her stomach grumbled and demanded to be satiated. "One bowl, then I must be on my way. Thank you for your kind offer."

He nodded and motioned for her to follow him. She threw one last glance at Horse who still licked his feed pail despite the fact all the grain was long gone.

As she entered the cabin, all the stress in her body washed away. It was a one room cabin, not anything she was used to in terms of size. The myriad of wool blankets and native patterns on the bed and other seating made the setting cozy and warm. She could see how she could live with so little and be happy.

He poured the stew into two bowls and gestured to the giant wood slab and chairs surrounding it in the immediate corner to the right as one entered the cabin.

Wally didn't talk much. From what she had heard, she was impressed with his command of the English language. Also, his logger's clothing spoke of his ease with the Western culture around him. His home was the one indication that he knew his true roots, despite having strayed in some forms of living. Could it be his work was a factor for this dual lifestyle?

The stew was better than she expected from a bachelor living in the middle of the woods. "This is very good, thank you." She didn't even receive an answering glance. "What do you do, Wally?"

"I provide lumber to a company up in Barkerville. Right now I'm alone up here, but come first day of the week, my men come up and we work hard, that we do."

"May I ask how you even came into this business given your…native status?"

He jutted his spoon toward her and said, "Good question! I translated for the white man when he first came to this land seeking gold. Then I went into the logging business and started my own company so I could give my people opportunities to work. I still have very good ties with my people. Some of them work for me."

"Who are your people?"

"The T'exelcemc. Most of them left when the gold rush started."

Suddenly, she realized he might know a lot about the area. He might know where those two streams met.

How do I ask without giving away too much?

"You must know the layout of the land around these parts quite well since it's your people's land. I was looking for a particular area. Perhaps you could help me find it?"

He took one last bite, grabbed his bowl and put it in the wash basin. He sat back down and tented his hands. "I do," he replied slowly. "Why do you want to know?"

Rose's hands started to sweat. Was he after the legendary treasure, as well? Did he have some sort of reason to believe it would be in this area? Would he harm her if he suspected she now knew the direct location? "You see, I'm trying to find something my friend buried a few years ago. She hid a large stash of money. She's been taken advantage of...by someone within her family. No one will believe her. She can't stay at home any longer. She needs the money to leave and build a new life somewhere else, somewhere safe. Will you help?"

He nodded. "What do you want to know?"

"Thank you," she forced some brimming tears to come to her eyes. "An hour's walk from here, I think it's northeast, there's a mountain ridge. At the bottom of this ridge is a stream. I'm supposed to follow this stream until it joins with another into one larger stream. I'm then to follow the larger stream down to where the money is hidden."

His brows knit together. "You said it was a couple of years ago."

"Yes, I was just there earlier this morning. I followed the stream, but instead of it meeting another stream, it was feeding into a lake."

"That's the reason why."

"I beg your pardon, I don't understand."

He smiled and shook his head. "A couple of years ago, that lake was a stream."

Still confused, she asked, "How can that be?"

"Beaver dammed it up."

"Ah," Rose now felt very foolish. She had just been there, beneath the very mountain housing her father's wealth. She had to go back. Because if she found it...it was one step closer to ridding herself from Shaw's grasp, to perhaps having the chance to have a life here in the beauty she had come to love. She finished eating the last of her stew. "Thank you again for everything. I must be on my way."

He clapped a hand upon her shoulder. "I'm sorry to say the money is probably below the lake. I hope your friend finds a way to make it out all right."

Her lips turned down as her insides churned at the blatant lie she had told. "What do I do now?" she muttered to herself.

Horse perked his ears as soon as she rejoined him.

"I'm not letting you loose again. You'll just come right back here and leave me stranded. It's all because of your greediness that we lost precious time."

She cantered the entire way back to the beginning of the stream. This time she tied Horse to a low branch, loose enough that he was able to arch his neck down to graze.

She stood by the stream feeding into the lake and gazed at the mountain whose base was adorned by the marker her father had pointed out. She looked at her bare hands and realized she was poorly equipped to climb the mountain before her. She was still in her skirts, which would not help even with an easy climb. But climb she would. Her fingers itched to grasp the gravelly rocks.

After what seemed an age of arduous climbing, she viewed what lay below her and before her and believed she was a quarter of the way up. A crack of thunder boomed. The sudden change in weather caused the backs of her hairs to stand on end. There was no lightning in sight, no feel of a rain torrent on her bent back. She looked up to see roiling clouds slipping up and over each other, the blue sky having turned into a charcoal grey as if God had dipped his brush in soot and swooped it across his canvas.

I must hurry before I'm soaked and catch a cold.

She doubled her speed, sprinting up, her breath growing ragged. She grasped onto a large rock, and it rolled down scraping the palm of her hand as it did. She hissed from the pain and pressed on.

All the frustrations of the last few months scrambled all over each other in a fight to win her attentions. Every advance in her climb increased the fervour of her exploding emotions and drove her toward the final destination of the seemingly inescapable nightmare. Her father's neglect,

Shaw's overtures, Dave's heartrending betrayal, and her own foolishness—yes, this was her greatest burden, her own regretful actions. So heavily did it now weigh on her heart that she suddenly stopped her climb, beat her closed fists upon the mountain, and cried out in anguish. Her body heaved from the exertion. She stretched her fingertips and dug them into the sloped side. Large splatters of raindrops cooled her scratched up hands. So unprepared, so blind to her own inadequacies— these stumbling blocks couldn't hold the upper hand too long. She continued her efforts, her clothing weighing her down. No matter, she would endure until she would find the opening of the end. She shook the matted hair from her face and wiped the water from her eyes to no avail. Through the heavy showers, she looked around to find a rock shelter a little ways higher from the spot where she was.

She launched herself forward with the remaining strength in her arms, buckling after the effort. A small wind had picked up, chilling her through her soaked habits. She bit her lip to keep her lips from chattering.

After a few stumbles, she reached the opening in the side of the mountain. She was thankful the wind didn't blow in. The remaining light from outside revealed bat and deer droppings scattered around the floor. The wall opposite the opening was really not a wall at all but more like a pile of rubble. She sat upon a large boulder. Once the storm passed, she would continue her search if sundown wasn't close at hand. If that were the case, she would just have to find another excuse to return. Or perhaps, she would have to tell all to Joe and Jack. She hugged her knees and laid her chin upon her forearms whilst looking at the ground in front of her. As the rain continued to pour, tiny rivulets ran toward the rubble wall. The passage of nature lulled her to sleep. She awoke several hours later, the storm having passed. Those tiny rivulets were still at play.

"It can't be," she breathed. She opened her eyes wider, a pool of water impossible to find.

For if that rubble wall were really a wall, there would be a pool of water by now. Instead it moves downward toward the rubble. Wait...

197

She inclined her ear toward the cave "wall"—drips of water rang in a hollow space. She scrambled to stand. "Ah, you clever man!" She moved the rubble to the side. Some pieces were mere stones that fit within the palm of her hand. Others were too large for her to carry, making it necessary to go around them and push them away from the pile with her legs. She began from the top working her way down to the bottom. After much effort, a small opening enticed her to continue the search. The voice of reason inside her insisted on leaving this place and coming back, but the whispers of gold seeming to emanate from the small opening stayed her feet and bid her hands continue the work. She removed enough of the rubble so that she could wriggle inside. She went inside head first and reached out with her arms, trying to feel some ground. When she realized she couldn't, she slipped into the abyss and landed on her shoulder. Her legs followed, tumbling over her head and kicking a metal object. She looked toward the darkness and realized the only source of available light came from the opening she had just made.

Of course, I didn't think to bring a lantern.

A metal box was illuminated in the rim of light. She reached for it and found it to be a matchbox.

That thing I kicked....

Biting her lips, hoping for some good fortune, she scrambled in the dark. A clacking noise…into the light….

Ah, now I can light this…there…oh….

Her mouth agape, she stood, trembling, as she took in the sight. Before her was a natural cave system, the tunnel winding further down into the mountain, out of reach from her lantern's grasping light. She took a few steps forward and turned around in a circle. The reach of her lantern illuminated the walls, glimmers of gold scintillating in their discovery. They had slumbered until now. She padded toward a nugget, the size of her fist, imbedded within the wall. She understood the magnitude of such a find, how a find this size deserved its own myth and whispers of legend. With tears silently falling upon the tunnel floor, she knew why the target had been placed on her father's back, why it was now on hers. The curse and wretchedness of gold—she scoffed, sat against the wall, and marvelled at how many nuggets presented themselves around her, teasing her with their promises of riches.

Her hands pushed back the hair from her eyes. She pondered what the next step would be, how she could possibly evade Daniel's grasp. A deep conviction settled within her heart that she should never reveal to him this place of light. His dark intents would snuff it out, making it a slave to his own greed and desires. Nothing good could come from his finding this place.

She sat there for many minutes, trying to figure out how she could pass through this trial unscathed. Too late…she was already scathed

She got up and decided to leave, for the sun's waning light would soon be entirely diminished. Before she blew out her light, a tucked piece of paper in a crevice near the opening, caught her attention.

Dearest Rose,   *April 7, 1871*

You have discovered the hiding place of my treasure. I wish I could congratulate you, but this place, this treasure has corrupted my heart, or I've allowed it to. I was convinced that it was the greatest possession I have. I now realize the falsity of its lie. You are my greatest earthly treasure, and now I think it's too late. I'm sure your heart has turned stone cold against me. For that I must pay.

Do not let the same fever spread to your body and mind. Remember there are greater treasures than this. Remember the lessons I taught you from an early age of a love that will never fail, of family who must always be cherished. I failed to be your example. Look to the One who never did fail.

I never wanted anyone to find this place. Yet I told myself that if anyone should, it should be you. I fear you're in grave danger to have sought this out and gone on this journey. My original intent was for you to leave and go far, far away, as you well know. What could have incited you to do this…. No matter, we must think of your safety first and foremost. I have formulated a plan should you have found this place. I want you to have all of it so that you need not be dependent on your loving relations. I believe you would prefer this, for you have that independent spirit I always loved about your mother.

Claim this spot as yours. Then go and book passage to England. Stay out of sight as much as you can. I fear for your life.

Once you arrive in England, go to Mr. Donaldson. Ask your Aunt Ingrid. She will know of whom I speak. When you meet with him, he will help you settle your affairs. The danger which tails you in Canada will have certainly disappeared when you arrive in Britain.

After all the business affairs are completed, you'll never want. Live your life to the fullest, whatever you deem it to be. I'm very sorry I couldn't have seen it. Darling girl, do what I could not do.

Your regretful father,

Harland

Oh, Father, please forgive me.

She folded the note and tucked it into her bodice. Taking one last look at her inheritance, she sighed and snuffed out the lantern. She pulled herself back into the dying light and commenced covering the hole from which she had come.

She ran down the mountain and was extremely relieved to find Horse still tied to his branch. She got on and galloped as far as she could. By the time she arrived home, the stars scintillated the sky, and the moon shone bright.

She settled Horse for bed and made her way to the house. She'd have to do a lot of explaining. As soon as she entered, she saw Jack biting his lips anxiously and Joe crossing his arms over his chest with a storm-brewing gaze her way. She tread lightly, afraid to deepen the dark atmosphere. She settled across from Joe.

Joe rumbled, "Where did you go?"

Jack cut in, "Ah, Joe, let the girl get some sleep and a bath."

Rose put out a hand toward Jack, "No, Jack, it's all right. I'll answer the question. I've been tiptoeing around Joe for too long. It's not fair, no more. Joe, I was searching for the treasure."

He got up and began pacing—such strange behaviour for Joe! He paced for no one, hardly shared his true feelings with those closest to him. He began in his deepest voice, "I thought I had lost you, thought some wild animal got you, thought…don't you ever leave without telling me where you're going!" This last part was a roar.

Rose was stunned. She knew this was his most vulnerable, and this one time she would take advantage. "Why?"

"Because…" His eyes darted. "you're like a daughter to me."

The cracks she had worn into his heart now shattered, completely opening his heart for all to see. His pain-wracked eyes turned to hers as he said, "I have a son."

She knew those words encompassed a story of pain, of regret. Perhaps that's why she and Joe had been fused from the very beginning. They were the piece to each other that they had been missing their entire lives. The tapestry of her relationships stretched before her, and she marvelled at the beauty in every single moment.

He has a son.

Rose knew he would tell the story, maybe not now; but he would.

Joe finally sat down and asked, "Did you find it? Are you safe?"

Despite having found the treasure, she didn't feel happy or joyful because of its discovery. So, it wasn't hard to turn her face into a frown and say, "No, I didn't. I thought…I had followed the instructions thoroughly, and yet nothing to show for it."

Whatever ears or eyes were outside her window, she would deceive them with her show.

"I'm very tired and aching. Goodnight, I love you Joe, you too, Jack."

Ah Love! could thou and I with Fate conspire
To grasp this sorry Scheme of Things entire,
Would not we shatter it to bits—and then
Re-mould it nearer to the Heart's Desire!
Edward Fitzgerald

Chapter 20

Rose awoke from the sound of crinkling paper. She rubbed her fingers together and felt the source of the sound lodged between them. She lifted herself up on her elbow. It was folded so neatly, its edges were slightly browned. This sender was entirely unexpected.

Tomorrow evening before the sun sets, go to our spot. Meet me there. I need to see you.

Dave

Her breath caught as she read his name. It was insanity to even consider such a proposition, to meet with the man who must have killed her father. Yet she needed to go to Barkerville anyway to file her claim in secret.

What does he want after all this time? Does he really think I could be stupid enough to believe he still cares for me?

Determined to not think of the encounter until it was fully necessary, until the moment she would actually see his face, she got dressed and prepared herself to tell Joe that she would need to go right away.

She arrived at the dining room table to find an apple with eggs and bacon on the side. Joe sat at the head, and Jack was nowhere to be found.

She cast a furtive glance Joe's way, "Where's Jack?"

He didn't look at her. "Excused himself, sayin' he wanted to eat outside before it turned too cold."

This time, they didn't pray out loud together, but instead did so in the quietness of their own hearts. Rose took her first bite and said, "You have a son."

Joe's fork clattered to his plate. He stretched his hand, picked it up and took a bite of breakfast. After having fully chewed his bite, he put his fork down. "It was many years ago when I met Emily."

Miss Craig? That explains their connection when she arrived a month ago.

Rose bit her tongue and nodded.

"I was…well…the way I am. She talked to me, wanted to know me better. I don't know how it happened, but we started courting. Not three months in and…she made me feel…she made me feel like a real man. One night, I brought her home from one of our outings around town. She wanted to show me the first horse her father had ever bought her. As we walked toward the barn, all I could think about was how beautiful she was. I kissed her. Then it just happened…and she got pregnant. I didn't want the baby. I wasn't ready for that kind of responsibility."

He proceeded to tell all that he had told Emily when she had shown up on the 108 Mile House doorstep.

"I regret it, not having been there for my son, for my Emily. It could have been so much more different." He finally turned to look at her. "You're my second chance. I never expected to think of you like a daughter. I hope you…I hope that doesn't bother you."

Rose shook her tears free. "Never, you are not being presumptuous in the least. I've thought of you as a father for a while now. I don't know what to say—I'm so happy that you feel the same as I. I'm sure it must have been very hard for you to tell me all this just now. Thank you." She covered his hand with his.

He grunted. "Now don't think I'll be less hard on you for all your tomfooleries."

Rose smiled. "I don't doubt it. Now the part where I must confess something. I need to go out of town for a couple of days on a matter of business."

"What kind of business?"

"Business that only the owner of this mile house must know. Please Joe, I need to go. You can't go with me, not this time. Anyway, I need you to help Jack run the place. I'll only be a few days, and I'll be back, I promise. If I'm not, you send the cavalry after me."

He rested his mouth on his fist. "All right, send me a telegram when you arrive and when you leave."

"I will with pleasure." She gave him a kiss on the cheek, finished her breakfast, and packed for the ride within the hour.

***

The whizz of an arrow sounded a foot away; it was immediately followed by the stab of flesh—the sound of a hundred fifty pound deer collapsing to the ground.

The sound of crunching leaves under polished black boots—those boots visible with a sideways glance. "Bulls eye! Do you see the skill my archer has?"

One look at the deer and the arrow in its eye spoke very well of the archer's skill. Convicted fear grew at the atrocious sight. The deer had been running at its fastest speed; yet still it had come to an end.

"One wrong move and you'll meet the same fate."

***

Rose was at the edge of the meadow, the edge bordering the town. Her boots were wet from the evening dew. Thick fog encroached all around her, making it difficult to see a few feet ahead. The closer her feet moved toward their meeting place, the more her heart jumped within its cage. How could he ask to meet after all he had done? Did he not know how she would be affected by his request? Of course, he knew. There lay the cruelty of it all. She couldn't fathom why she was even here, close to breathing the same air as the murderer...the man who had helped her form the wings to fly.

Then...there he was. Not at all how she had pictured she would find him, arms crossed, triumphing in his sarcastic drawl, with his smirk perked way high. He looked straight at her, his eyes...those eyes through which she had seen into his soul, those windows...she had seen all manner of emotions in those eyes—all she saw were the depths of sorrow. She moved closer, again feeling the draw from him to her. She couldn't deny it. She believed her heart to beat in time with his. How could it be?

He didn't speak, neither did she until she stood several feet away. "Dave?"

He kept looking at her with those heartbreaking eyes, his lips unmoving.

A twang of frustration reverberated through her body. "Why have you asked me to come?"

Again silence.

"Why will you not speak to me?" Her voice was now edged.

This time, he cast his eyes downward.

Rose knew she shouldn't let her anger get the better of her, but he had induced her to come out and meet. Now, he wouldn't look at her?

Coward.

She stomped forward until she was only a foot away. "Don't you dare! You asked me to come, and now you...I don't understand! Why do you want to torment me? Look at me!"

Still there was no movement on his part.

She lowered herself to look into his eyes. "Look at me!" she shouted and slapped his bearded cheek hard.

He raised his head only an inch and finally looked at her.

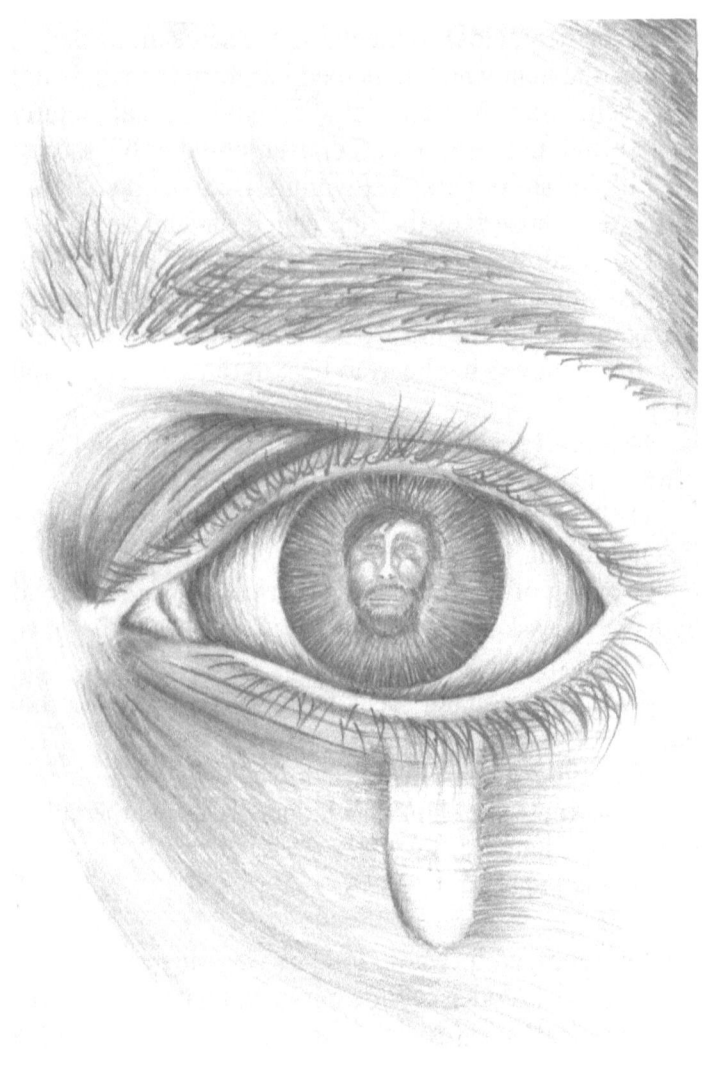

"Why did you kill my father? He did nothing to you!" She looked away, her self-composure completely dissipated. "I've thought a lot of what I would say to you if I ever saw you again. All those times...I confided in you, poured out my heart to you. The whole time...you knew...you were there. You must have quite the stomach to relish the kill and then hear the sob story of the loved one."

He blinked, a mask of struggle on his face.

She took a step closer, the pull too strong to fight, and whispered, her breath mingling with his, "Please, help me understand." Her tears came fast and hard. "I...just need to hear your voice. I need you to tell me that this is all a bad dream, please."

She thought she felt him shift forward an inch. The soothing touch of his thumb wiping away her tears never came. Blinded by her continuous tears, she backed up a few steps. Never had she felt such acute despair as in this moment. She pounded the ground with her fists and cried out. She could still see his boots when she lifted her head an inch.

She couldn't tell how long she cried, how long she waited for him to gather her in his arms. It was the last hope she held onto, that this might all be a terrible mistake. The comfort never came, solidifying in her mind the cold fact that this whole thing was a taunt.

Finally, when her eyes had dried and her whole body ached, she raised her head to tell him that he would never have a place in her head again. However, he was gone, vanished.

There was no sign of Dave, no pull from his traitorous heart. She gathered her skirts, heavy with dampness. After one last look around, she turned her back, vowing never to look this way again whether in her memories or face to face.

A little still she strove, and much repented,
And whispering 'I will ne'er consent'—consented.
Lord Byron
st.117

Chapter 21

Rose, unable to hold her head high, so stripped was she of any confidence, of any self-preservation, shuffled along the path toward town. She wrapped her arms around her torso to hold in the fountains of grief she could until she could break the dam and let it spill in the solitude of her room.

A hand at the small of her back—she turned to look. Daniel Shaw. Oh, she had hoped he wouldn't notice. She had hoped she could slip in and out of Barkerville without being seen. She should have been more careful.

He rubbed her back in a soothing manner. Every rub burned with a touch of fire. "My dear Rose, what has you so cast down? Come with me, and I'll help you forget."

Her dalliance with the devil had come with so many costs, and she'd have to pay another tonight. "No, I…"

Say no, and he will show no mercy.

"I mean yes, that would be lovely, a good bite to eat would do me good. After, I must sleep, I'm very tired."

"Of course, I'll escort you back to your room."

She forced a bright smile. "My room?"

"You should change." He cocked his head. "Follow me."

He held her hand. Her hand kept slipping, so stressed was she from the encounter with Dave and the time she would have to spend with the madman. He went round the back of her hotel and slipped through the back door. A maid saw the two of them with a horrified look on her face. He sidled up to the maid and from his pocket pulled out several bills which he tucked into the front of the maid's uniform. He put a single finger to her lips and nodded. She nodded in return.

Do all the women fall for his charm or do some of them play the game like me so he can't ruin them and their livelihoods?

He continued guiding her until they arrived at her room. He indicated his chin toward the door. Rose opened it and was about to close the door on him when he pushed through and locked it behind him.

"What are you doing? I need to dress."

"I'll watch."

She swallowed hard, "You will?"

He nodded and strode toward her suitcase. He threw it open and rifled through its contents as if they belonged to him.

The bile rising in Rose's throat—oh, she longed to put him in his place; but feistiness would not help her now.

He found a dress that suited his fancy and placed it along her figure. "Perfect," he murmured. He settled himself on the chair and tented his fingers. "Now, dress."

Rose struggled to keep the fear from her eyes and smiled shakily, hoping it would pass for modesty. She unbuttoned. Out of the corner of her eye, she saw his tongue pass over his lips as a wolf licking his chops before the kill. She drew off her sleeve and turned her back to him, hoping to retain what little integrity she had left.

"Turn."

She thanked the Lord above she was wearing undergarments although she didn't know what good those did at that moment. She shimmied her dress off, clutched the dress he had chosen, and began to quickly put it on, not caring that he wasn't receiving the show of his life. As soon as she buttoned the last button, she breathed through her nose in and out, not believing that she had just been subjected to this kind of treatment. "I'm ready. Shall we?"

The look in Daniel's eyes, black as they were— everything had been exposed whether she liked it or not, whether she wore undergarments or not. Oh, he cared for her, cared to satisfy his own sinful appetite, not taking to thought her own respect and dignity. How did she not see this at the beginning?

He strode over and led her to the mirror where he placed strands of hair as he saw fit, as if she were a doll he could toy with, finger in his hands until he was fulfilled. Once he was done with the way she looked, he brushed her hair from her neck and planted his smooth lips upon the slope of her neck, involuntarily making her lean into his firm chest and succumb to the erotic sensations he bestowed upon her.

She stepped away slowly. She dared not be abrupt for fear he would do far worse—her greatest fear, that she wouldn't want to stop him, that she would only give in to assuage her own lust.

As they left the hotel, she barely assessed the surroundings at hand. He led her to a back room of the saloon where there was set the most romantic table setting she could fathom. Steady flames from two tall candles, just lit, set the corner booth in a state of euphoria and elegance. The gleaming silverware and cold, brittle china were the very best she had ever seen. The final touch were the red rose petals scattered over the tablecloth, the booth's seats, and the floor around them, plunging this private corner into a land where her name reigned. Despite the initial beauty of the scene, all of it was tainted with a black tarnish she could not, with any mental scrubbing, remedy. The sole of her shoe squashing a petal, the petals on the bench pressed down by the weight of her body— they screamed in their death and expelled their scent. Rose was sick to the stomach.

Daniel settled across from her with a wicked smile, the smile which had first captivated her heart. "You like it." A statement, as if nothing else could be truth.

"It's lovely…" She bit her lip. "However, I'm not feeling well at all."

"We'll get you a bite to eat, then to bed."

"Thank you."

The waiter came around with glasses of champagne. Daniel ordered for them both. Rose was completely preoccupied with how she would survive the evening without ruining her cover.

Once the waiter had left, Daniel's hand touched the thin sleeve covering her shoulder and slid it down, exposing it to his gaze. Then he moved to the other and did the same. "There, much better."

Eager to pass the time in as pleasant a manner as possible, Rose said, "How is business faring?"

Daniel smirked in return, "I could ask you the same question."

The food came quickly. Although it looked extremely appetizing, Rose couldn't bring herself to enjoy it in his company.

"Do you still think of him?"

Rose's head snapped up. She replied in as firm a voice as possible, "No, I don't think of those who betray me and those I love."

"Good, you know, I've always been clear with you about my intentions, my needs…my wants. Your finding out I'm behind your drive for the treasure—it was a delightful game we played wasn't it?"

Be strong. Don't let your disgust show.

She purred, "I like games."

He stroked her shoulder. "I have many games in mind we can play."

She put on her own wicked smile. "Perhaps, once the treasure is found, we can play as a celebration of our efforts."

He chuckled, "Oh, you read my mind well."

Keep up the angst and mystery. As soon as he gets what he wants, he'll be done with you.

Once he was done his plate, he asked, "Speaking of business, how is the hunt for the treasure?"

She picked at her meal, most of it uneaten. "I'm close,
I know it. Give me a little more time. I won't fail you."

"Exactly what I wanted to hear."

Daniel again escorted Rose back to her room through
the back entrance where not a soul this time was sighted,
where shadows hid their scandalous entrance. Once again, he
entered her room and closed the door behind him.

"Daniel, I need to sleep now. I'm very tired and not
feeling…"

He put his finger to his lips, shed his outer coat, and
whispered, "Shh, I know, darling girl. No games tonight, well
perhaps one." He began to unbutton the top of her dress.

"What are you doing?" Rose whispered, a little
breathless. An ache for his touch spread throughout her body.
Immediately, she scolded herself for feeling so flustered.

He lifted his head to look at her a second before
resuming his task, "This time I will undress you. I was just
going to watch one last time, but I this would please me more.
You must allow me this leisure."

His eyes bored through hers, serious in his demand,
else he would take measures much farther than she could bear.

She nodded.

He continued. He flicked open her buttons with keen
dexterity. How many women had he undressed with those
nimble fingers? As he removed her top, his thumb brushed the
top of her breast, and he pressed his lips against the same spot.

Rose bit her lip and tapped her foot to ease some of her
pent-up energy. This was torture. Every quivering touch, every
hot kiss, made her feel unclean, smeared with lust. Then her
skirt came off, down to her undergarments. He led her toward
the bed, and he sat. His sure fingers danced down her back,
inciting her body to press against him. His hands sailed every
curve as his lips connected with the light clothing covering her
stomach.

As he took advantage of her in this fashion, Rose
realized with ultimate shame that though she could barely look
at him, stomach who he was, she, her body, was still attracted
to him in the most sensual of ways. Somehow he knew. She

involuntarily shivered as his physicality increased. She needed to end this now.

She murmured, "Daniel, I need to sleep."

His last kiss and touch slowed to a stop. He rose and bit her bottom lip, begged her mouth to open. She did as asked. Her body and mind were at war within those moments. She could almost rationalize needing this pleasure after being completely shattered that evening in the meadow. She thought how it could be a balm to the hurt, how she could forget in this forest fire. Her body began to gain ground, pressing closer and wrapping her hands around his neck.

If you do this now, there's no turning back. You will have lost the game.

Her hands moved down his arms and put a light pressure upon them to still his roaming. She huskily said, "Remember we're to play this game when the treasure is found."

He sighed, "You wicked girl. As soon as you find the treasure, send word so we can finish what we started." He picked up his coat, swung it over his shoulder, and left.

That was close, too close. Shame and guilt spread throughout her body as one side of her regretted the fact he had just left. One side of her almost ran to her door to pull him back through and finish what they had started.

She splashed water all over her face, hands, and chest. Suddenly, a coldness seeped into her. She turned off the lights and went under the covers, unable to recognize the girl of a few moments ago.

The attractiveness of sin, the strength of the fire—how the devil did know she could stumble.

In skating over thin ice, our safety is in our speed.
Ralph Waldo Emerson
vii. Prudence

Chapter 22

Last night can't happen again. I need to leave the country. Finish business and leave without looking back. He can't...this can't happen again.

These were Rose's first thoughts as soon as she woke up. She needed to be more careful. She would leave as soon as she was done her secret affairs in town. Back on her horse, fleeing down the road home, then back to Britain.

She put on her trousers and man's shirt. She pinned her hair up and covered her head with a hat. She was determined to pass off as an authentic man so that no one could point and ponder the oddity of such a getup on a woman. Before setting foot out the door, she practiced lumbering like a man in front of her mirror several times. When she was satisfied, she left her room to go to the claims office.

She had to wait in line. Every second that passed without moving or doing something— she felt as if every miner's eyes were on her, as if deep down they knew her secret. She kept her head down and stuffed her hands in her pockets so no one would see their smallness. She focused on relaxing her stiff muscles and calmed her breathing.

The last miner before her concluded his business and bumped into her on his way out. She grunted and cleared her throat before approaching the claim's desk. She said in her lowest voice, "Are you Priscilla's father, John Brown?"

He looked up from his folded hands and said with a broad smile, "Why, yes! Hope she hasn't gotten into any trouble."

Rose turned to see the office empty and lifted her face fully before answering, "My name is Rose. I'm here on urgent business, one of a secretive nature. She said I can trust you. I do so because she has my utmost trust."

His face elongated in small wonder and placed his chin in the cup of his hand. "You sure believe I can. It's such a pleasure to finally meet you." He shook hands with her.

She looked behind her, relieved to see the claim's office was still empty. It wouldn't be for long. "May you please close the office until our business is concluded?"

John looked at the clock above the door and nodded. "I can take an early lunch break." He walked to the door to turn the sign from *Open* to *Close* when another miner was about to enter. "I'm sorry we're closing for an early lunch break."

The man whined, "There's someone in there!"

John replied, "Last customer, sorry, come back in an hour." He locked the door and strode back toward the desk. "All right, Rose, what can I do for you?"

"I need to make a claim."

"Really? How did you come across this claim?"

She looked at him, afraid to say the words.

"Ah, I see. It's your father's fortune, isn't it? There's been a lot of men hunting for it. I'm sure many wouldn't mind killing for it. Is it really all they say it is?"

She nodded.

John exhaled deeply, "You can depend on me for keeping your secret safe."

She bored her eyes into his. "My security, my life is in your hands. You cannot breathe a word of this to anyone, not even Priscilla. Her safety is most important. Please, I want no other eyes on this document until the week's end when I leave the country. Can you make that happen?"

His face became grave. "No one will see it until the week's end. After that, my supervisor will want to see it, maybe even before but...I'll hide it if that's what it takes."

"Thank you."

He began in a hushed tone, "What's the general area where you found it?"

"About fifty miles northeast of the 108 Mile House."

"Okay," he ducked beneath the counter and pulled out a large map of the pointed area.

She scanned it and tapped the spot on the mountain.

He pulled out a sheet of paper and slammed it on the counter. "Let's get started."

When she lumbered out of the office, a weight lifted off her shoulders. Phase one of her master plan had been enacted. At this point, she couldn't wait to leave the country, to be in comfort and safety. Keeping her man's clothing on, she packed her things in a hurry, straddled her horse, and galloped out of Barkerville without looking back.

***

"How did you know, boss?" Hushed tones filled the room.

The lift of an eyebrow as if the question asked was nonsensical.

A begrudging look. "Well, you were right. She claimed it all right. Saw her at the office today. Tried to avoid detection. Did a right good job, made me look twice."

Drumming fingers on oak grain. "Good job, you'll be handsomely rewarded."

***

By the time Rose reached the mile house, her hair, flying in the wind, flapping around her cheeks, had freed itself completely from its hair pin captors. Joe launched outside to help her with the horse. He grabbed the reins from her and put his hand over hers. "You all right?"

She nodded tiredly, "Yes, I'm in one piece. I could desperately use a hot bath, decent food, and a good night's rest. Tomorrow, I must visit Mr. Nelson."

No fight back, he merely nodded. He helped her down and took Horse into the barn. Yes, she would make sure they were taken care of.

After supper, Rose felt she needed to spend time with Jack. After all, she was to leave in a couple of days and then…who knows if she were to ever see him again. His jovial demeanour and tenor voice would forever be etched on the walls of her heart. She found him washing dishes and joined him in drying them.

"Ya've not been makin' plans to leave me now 'ave ya, miss Rose?"

She looked sidelong. Her throat went dry. "Now, why do you say that, Jack?"

He smirked to himself, "Ya got that skittish look about ya. Canna fool me, girl."

She smiled sadly, "All good things come to an end. Whether it's during this life or being parted by death."

"True, dat. But if you be plannin' on leavin', please tell me before ya go. Ya'd poke a 'ole in my heart if ya didn't."

Rose dried her last dish and put it away. She rested her cold hands on Jack's shoulders. "I promise I'll tell you." She leaned in to give him a hug. As she pulled away, his hand gripped her chin and moved it toward the light.

He looked at her with pity. "What's this?"

Rose surmised she had a blue bruise on the underside of her chin, on the softness of her neck from Daniels' roaming lips. "It's one of the reasons why I need to go."

Jack planted his fists on his sides and shook his head violently. "No, no one's gonna touch ya like dat without ya permission and git away with it."

"Shush, not so loud. There's nothing you can do."

"Did he hurt ya?"

She smiled reassuringly, "No, it didn't go beyond this."

Jack seemed to simmer down.

"Goodnight, Jack. This is not something you have to worry about because it won't happen, ever again."

The next morning, before heading out to visit with Mr. Nelson, she helped Joe oil the tack right outside the barn door. Although the days were cooling slightly, the sun bore down in its full strength, warming her hair to the point that Rose needed to wear her wide-brimmed straw hat.

They both worked in silence. The whirlpool-like motion of rubbing the oil into the leather tack and the smell of Horse and his companion drew Rose into a quiet place within, a place she could steady her fear of the unknown.

Joe already knew. She could tell the way his measured eyes watched her work and the way he kept trying to start small pleasant conversation, which was completely unlike Joe.

"There, did I shine this right?"

His fingers touched hers as he handled the bridle. "Yup."

She stepped back and began to grab Horse's brushes. "I need to visit with Mr. Nelson on a matter of business."

He shot her a speculating glance.

"I'm telling the truth this time. You can make sure with Mr. Nelson by telegram later if you like."

He stopped what he was doing and gave her a great bear hug. "I trust you're tellin' the truth. You only mean well."

Rose's eyes went wide with surprise, and she wrapped her limp arms around his broad back. "Thank you."

Joe cleared his throat. "You brush that horse, and I'll tack him up for you."

"Why you?"

"'Cause you take near a decade to do it!"

"Are you trying to get rid of me?" Rose said with a mock horrified expression on her face.

"Nah, the sooner you go, the sooner you can come back."

Ten minutes later, Rose set off at an easy trot in her desired direction. She was certain Mr. Nelson would accept her offer.

She took off her riding gloves as Horse was being led away by Mr. Nelson's stable boy. The sun had retained its strength the entire ride and her throat was parched. She asked the Chinaman cook if she could refill her canteen somewhere, to which he led her. Then she asked to see Mr. Nelson. Fortunately, he was at his study and not busy in the least. She found a novel in his hands.

"Mr. Nelson, how wonderful to see you have leisure time to do some reading. I have a hard time finding the time to sit down lest it be for looking over the books and other business matters."

"Miss Rose, I run a bigger operation than you do which means I have the means to hire more employees who can do the work for me. I can afford five minutes here or there."

"May I?" She gestured to the empty chair across him.

He jumped up a little. "Oh, yes, please do." Once she did, he asked, "What can I help you with?" He put down the novel after momentarily glancing at the page number (she assumed).

"I'm putting my mile house up for sale, but…before I do, I'd like to strike a bargain with you. Now, before you jump on the bandwagon, I want you to hire and keep in excellent care Joe and Jack. Joe, as you know, is my stableman and handyman, and Jack is my cook who…"

"Done!" Mr. Nelson struck out his hand for a shake.

"We haven't settled on a price yet."

"I know you'll give me a fair price, and I've been needing some extra help these days."

"There's one more thing. Jack is…well…how to put this…I'm not sure how you feel about coloured men."

His eyes took on a hard glint. He chewed on his lips a moment and cocked his head. "You say he's your cook."

"Yes, an excellent one."

Mr. Nelson crossed his arms. "Listen, if he works hard and does the work in good time, I'll have no problems hirin' him. I've never met one before but…he shouldn't be too much different, eh?"

"He's a human being, just as you and I are."

"Yes," Mr. Nelson crossed his arms. "Now, for the price…"

Rose laid her price on the table. Although it was a good and fair one at that, she allowed Mr. Nelson to haggle his way down by ten percent. She would not be picky. She already had a fortune at her fingers which would secure her for life. She was already thinking of how she could conceal her identity and history once she arrived in England for fear of being found out a couple years after settling down in her home country. Home country…funny how she could barely remember details of her childhood home and her aunt's family. She would have to make it home again.

As soon as they settled on a price, they shook hands.

Rose said, "Here is my aunt's residence in England. I'll be there the first few months I arrive. Have your lawyer draw up the contract…who is your lawyer if I may ask?"

"A Mr. Smith, typical English, isn't it?"

"Yes, good, have your lawyer draw up the contract with the terms we discussed. Send it to me. I'll sign it and send it back to you. Joe and Jack will run it for you until it is completely under your control."

"Miss Wood, it's been a pleasure doing business with you. Not every day you do business with a woman in real estate. It's usually the unsavoury sort, you know?"

"You mean prostitution, Mr. Nelson."

"Mm, well, return safely to your home."

Rose surmised it to be around two by the time she left Mr. Nelson's mile house. Another weight had been lifted off her shoulders. Why her father had left his mile house to her and not Mr. Nelson as he had promised eluded her. She pondered on this matter most of the ride home. For the first time in a long time, hope of a stable future was possible.

Joe was just outside the barn as she arrived. She slowed to a walk, the mile house in sight. She hopped off and handed the reins to Joe, who brought Horse in and gave him some grain straight away. Rose took off her riding gloves and placed them in their nook.

As Joe took the saddle off Horse, he said, "We have a guest tonight."

"Good, I suppose you already registered them?"

"Yes, it's a...well...you'll see when you get in."

Rose was very tempted to pry Joe for further information. However, he seemed extremely uncomfortable with this new guest. She crossed from the stable to the house and cautiously opened the door. Joe's anxiety began to take root in her, as well. She looked to the desk. All was in order. She saw a blonde sitting on one of her couches.

"Hello, miss...oh!"

Sitting there, fiddling with her fingers relentlessly, was Emily.

"Miss Craig, how do you do? Would you like some tea and biscuits?"

"No," her voice sounded hollow as if she had seen a ghost. She slowly turned to face Rose. "You've been with my son."

Brows knit and mouth parted in confusion, Rose choked out, "Pardon me?"

Emily's face was blanched, her lips were trembling. "I saw you in Barkerville with my long-lost son."

A little neglect may breed mischief...for want of a nail,
the shoe was lost; for want of a shoe
the horse was lost; and for want of a horse
the rider was lost.
Benjamin Franklin
Poor Richard's Almanac (1758)

Chapter 23

Time seemed to halt as soon as Emily's last words were uttered. In that frozen frame of time, Rose felt as if she were being pulled under a current. She fought to breathe a small gulp of air before completely relinquishing all control.

No, it can't be...surely it's impossible....

Rose gingerly sat next to Emily. "Miss Craig, what do you mean? How can you be sure?"

Emily's hands gripped her forearm. "Rose, it's as if I saw a younger version of my father...what's he like?"

Rose gently displaced Emily's hands from her arm. "Where did you see me with your son?"

Trying to remember an eluding detail, her eyes roved toward the ceiling. "Oh, now, you were both walking down main street in Barkerville. His hand was on the small of your back, and he seemed to speak so delicately with you. You see now, don't you?"

The Miss Craig she knew would have given her a sound warning of having strange men touch one's body in such intimate places in public. She was clearly not herself.

Rose needed more. "Describe him to me."

"Oh, just like my father, he's handsome as the devil with black hair, about six feet."

Daniel Shaw. The poor woman—knowing the truth about her son will break her heart.

"You're saying Mr. Shaw is your son."

"Yes," Emily said vehemently, "I cannot deny it. Is he courting you? Please tell me all about him."

Rose fully turned her body away from Emily's prying eyes. How could she handle this in all grace and truth?

"Mr. Shaw..." Emily played with the name. "Sounds very distinguished. Is he...distinguished?"

This was a question Rose could answer with no shame tainting her voice. "Yes, he is. He's one of the most up and coming lawyers, perhaps, even one of the most flourishing in his profession."

"How do you know him?"

Keep it to a minimum.

"He executed my father's will."

"Is that it? The way he looked at you, how familiar he was with you...surely there must be more."

"Surely Miss Craig you don't expect me to reveal details of my private life, whether these insinuations are true or not."

"Just...no...you're right. Mm, be careful. I won't remind you what I think of such impropriety even if it is with my own son. Men are, well...."

"Yes, I know...or I at least have an understanding." Rose took a deep breath. Emily became silent. Rose would take this opportunity to slip away without being asked more uncomfortable questions. "I'm glad you've found your son after all these years."

Just as soon as Rose was about to step out of the room, Emily piped, "You can take me to see him."

"Don't you think a reunion such as this, a delicate matter…would be better if it were only you and he bonding? He is well known and can be easily found."

Emily came to stand by her and grabbed her hand. "I don't think I could do it on my own."

"Let me think about it. Stay here. Why don't I fetch Jack to get you a cup of tea?"

Emily nodded and returned to the sofa.

As soon as Jack tended to Emily's tea, Rose stole away into the stable to seek out Joe. She saw him immediately. He was oiling the last of the tack by the light of his lantern. She had noticed that he did this when he needed settling.

She didn't say anything for a while and neither did he. They waited in comfortable silence until Joe asked, "Emily told you, didn't she?"

Rose sat on a bale of hay. "Yes, I…my thoughts are all a muddle. It begs so many questions to be asked, and yet I could see how many questions could be answered. I'm lost."

Joe huffed, "I knew someday my sins would catch up to me. All my life…it feels like a lifetime ago. Now…it feels as if it happened yesterday. I have a son."

"You know who he is, don't you?"

The lathering of oil halted abruptly. "No…Ach! I left her in the house before she could give me a name. I needed to…"

"You needed to stall the inevitable."

He nodded.

Rose bit her lips, wondering whether she should be the one to tell him who his son was. Then again, she couldn't hide the truth if he asked. He knew her too well. He'd be able to weather the revelation. Couldn't he?

"You know who he is," Joe asked in a husky voice.

"Miss Craig saw me walking down the street with him in Barkerville."

He kept on oiling in smooth motions. It was his way of asking without words. Rose felt the intensity of his question in the air.

Rose breathed, "It's Daniel Shaw."

Joe's eyebrows drew together—so hardened were they—and his lips pursed. Rose had never seen so many emotions on his usual stoic face. As he was breaking, she could also feel the tears rip through her heart. "How can *he* be my son?"

Rose placed her hand upon his bent back. "What do you mean?"

Joe stopped his oiling. "I know all about his women on the side. I've seen the way he looks at you, like you're his. He looks at you like you're a piece of meat."

"You know?"

"Maybe not as much as you want me to. I'm not blind. I see his character. Now…it's all my fault. It could have been different, so…different."

Rose's first instinct was to rebut his remark. However, she, too, was familiar with the serenade of "what if," its tendrils of guilt, or of lost potential wrapping around its all too willing victims. Once trapped inside the cage of an alternate yesterday, there was no saving from the outside but only from within. She held her tongue and wandered outside to view the stars in all their nightly glory.

She wondered if she would have been the way she was even if her father had kept her by his side. Would she still have had those urges to rebel, to push the boundaries? Would Daniel Shaw have still been a womanizer if he had, had a good man to look up to, like Joe? What was the man who raised him like? How much did their parents' actions affect their own? Could she have made better decisions even though her father dumped her at boarding school?

Emily and Joe would have to navigate these uncharted territories without her help. She slipped past Emily, sipping on her tea, while Jack told her stories of the South. Once everyone was fast asleep, she would ride to her claim and grab some more gold for her trip. It would be the last time she would see the accursed place, the place that had caused so much misery for her and her father. She slipped some trousers on and quietly moved about her room preparing for her night caper.

What do you not drive human hearts into,
cursed craving for gold!
Virgil
iii.56

Chapter 24

She packed a lantern, a canteen of water, a miner's pick, and a pack to store the gold. She stole away around two in the morning to be extra sure everyone was asleep. Tomorrow, she'd leave her mile house, travel to Victoria, and board a boat homebound for Britain. So much to do, so little time to say her goodbyes.

A full moon lit her path. Horse's hooves thudded upon the grass a little ways from the road. Eyes fluttering, Rose was ached for sleep. She coiled one hand around the pommel of her saddle and the other around Horse's mane.

As she reached the edge of the forest flanking the mountains, she slowed to a trot and wove through the trees. She followed the stream until she met the lake. She reached it and tied up Horse. She nuzzled Horse's side and relayed soothing tones. A branch snapped, and Rose spun around to face the direction of origin. She didn't see or hear any stirring of movement. Regardless of spectres, being near her large claim of gold, she was nervous, restless.

"I'll be back soon. You stay here and stay out of trouble." She took a swig of water, and grabbed her pack, pick, and lantern. She moved to a moonlit area and lit her lantern. Instantly, she felt more secure. She moved upward, toward her goal. She hadn't thought of how holding the lantern and the pick would affect her climbing. At least she wasn't wearing a dress that she could trip over.

The hike to her secret gold mine seemed faster this time around. Every occasional *hoot* from an owl or branch snapping from a woodland creature sent shivers down her spine, the same shivers she experienced the night she and Dave dug out the *Nevermore* grave in Barkerville. The wind lightly rustled the leaves in the trees which helped soothe her despite the abrupt sounds.

She beheld the entrance to the mine. How cleverly it was hidden! With renewed vigour she marched up to the overhang of stone. She began to move the boulders covering the mouth of her cave.

***

"Keep this pistol cocked on him at all times. When you hear the signal, he…" the man behind them was pointed to, "will take over. After that, you know what to do."

A nod. Nimble fingers loading the pistol, ready to be fired. The pistol pointed at the prisoner's head.

A muffled moan escaped the prisoner's lips.

***

Once Rose had made a slightly larger opening than the first time she had been there, she crouched inside. From now on, she wouldn't have to cover the opening for fear someone would find the gold. She and the claim would be long gone from this land's soil. In Britain, she had plans to change her name, her identity in whatever possible way she could.

The walls of the mine glimmered as they had the last time she was here. Again she felt the pull, the calling of its fire, promising to give whatever she wanted. She fingered the grainy touch of the walls, the many facets of the nuggets, and for a second, believed that she could be happy with only this.

For she would never be in want or need. Whatever pleasures she should choose to indulge in, she could have whenever and wherever. It was a life that everyone dreamed of, to not have a care when it came to material goods. And it was all hers. This gold could buy her anything.

She began to swing her pick at one of the larger nuggets. As soon as she rescued it from its imprisonment, she began her work on the next, and the next, and the next until her bag was overflowing with nuggets. She picked it up with both arms and brought it close for inspection. The gleaming gold—she could get lost in its fancy, give up everything.... She abruptly dropped the bag and let out a small yelp. She slowly backed away in fear. She had easily succumbed to its clinging grasp. A taste of disgust coated her mouth. She should leave. Now. She had already spent too much time here. In about an hour and a half's time, dawn would arise. She had to be in bed asleep and pretend as if she hadn't gone anywhere.

She shook out the gold nuggets she had slaved for and only put four large ones inside her pack. It would be more than enough for her journey and her stay in Britain for many months. She grabbed her lantern and put one foot through the opening as she turned to face the Beast one last time. Suddenly, a hand yanked her arm forward. There stood Daniel Shaw. His black beady eyes bore into her. The fear pummelling from inside her gut was the greatest she had ever felt. For the first time, he was unpredictable. How would he react knowing she hadn't told him of her find? That his pet had turned her back on him? His grip on her arm was the only sign of the magnitude of his anger.

She had no words. She couldn't make up some outrageous lie. He had caught her red-handed.

He knew she was speechless. And so…"Darling Rose, I've been enjoying watching you this whole time. The way you've been gloating over this gold…I know you and I aren't that different. We both want the same thing. That's why you're mine." His other hand reached up to touch her cheek. "Come, show me this little empire you've found."

Rose didn't move but looked behind him wondering if she could dodge this bullet by sheer speed and desire.

"It's not going to work."

Although Daniel wanted her for himself, somehow she knew he wouldn't hesitate to kill if he believed his pleasure would be sated by the action. The gold fever in his eyes intimated *it* was far more valuable than she. Silent, head down, tired of the game, she moved back into the mine. This was the end. Daniel had his poker face on, not giving any tells as to how he envisioned this game to end.

He went over to the walls and ran his hand over them while still keeping a very firm grasp on Rose with his other. He stopped and rakishly smiled, "Your father...how the devil did he keep this a secret is beyond me! I have to give him due credit. He was very shrewd, something I see you've got from him. You hiding this from me...very clever."

"How did you find out?" Rose asked.

"One of my many secrets which you're not entitled to yet. Soon, all in good time." He scanned the area and nodded. "It's perfect. Now, let's move outside. We have some things to discuss."

They moved a few steps away from the overhang. Daniel stared down the mountain and whistled a strange bird-like call.

"Daniel, please let me go. You can have the treasure. Just let me go back to Britain, let me leave this place. My father never intended..."

"I know all about your father's past intentions. No, he never intended to pass the mile house to you. The original will is sitting in a drawer of my desk. I drew up the fake and planted it for you to find, for you to follow as a pawn of my grand scheme."

"Judge Begbie's signature, how did you manage that?"

"I'm an excellent forger. To finish all loose ends, I sent Percy ahead of my party to tell Mr. Nelson that business would be closed at the 108 Mile House for a while.

"You want to leave? I'll never let you go. From that moment you knocked on my door on the steamboat, I knew...you only could suffice."

Rose's cheeks coloured in shame. She should never have put herself in so many of the situations she had put herself in.

He continued, "We have a game to finish, remember? That night in your room, you whispered promises while your open mouth took in mine. Before we revel in pleasures spoken of, we need to deal with the remaining business, this treasure of ours."

Ours. He cannot mean to ask...

His hands drew her close and pressed her waist right against the planes of his body. "You and I will wed. Then this treasure can be ours. I saw the way you hungered after it, the same way I do. I can give you *everything* you want."

This was the end, the point of no return. There was no value in pretending she'd give him what he desired. She wouldn't sell her body any longer so she could live a few moments longer. This was no longer living anyway.

"No, I will not marry you. You can have my treasure, but you won't have me."

He purred, "That's a shame. I could ruin your good character. No man would ever have you. I will be the one with open arms, ready to fulfill those deepest needs that..."

She pushed away, "I don't care what you do anymore. I will not wed you, knowing what kind of a man you are, knowing how far you'll go to get your way, how many people you'll destroy just so you can be fulfilled. I don't want a man who wants my body but not my heart. I don't want a man who when he is done with me will go a whoring with many women until he is unsatisfied only to return to me to fulfill his blood lust. No."

He took a step closer. "You want to know how I knew you betrayed me. That night in Barkerville, the way you let me toy with you without a single retort, the way you let me fondle you without even restraining my roaming hands...you were playing a game, too. You played it well, just not enough."

"Be that as it may, we're here now, aren't we? I won't be your wife."

He put a finger to his lips and nodded, deep in thought. "If that is your final choice..."

"It is." Rose said, in a commanding voice.

"Then there's no choice but to kill you."

"Why? Why must you have blood on your hands?"

He snarled, "If I can't have you, no one will. No one ever takes what belongs to me." An irritated expression crossed his face. "Ah, good, there you are."

"Step aside and let go of her hand."

Rose's blood chilled instantly. She would know that voice anywhere. Priscilla.

The danger chiefly lies in acting well;
No crime's so great as daring to excel.
Charles Churchill
An Epistle to William Hogarth, 1.51

Chapter 25

Priscilla was there! Had she been taken prisoner, as well? Rose broke out in sweat for fear for her dearest friend on earth. She said in a low voice while keeping her eyes on Daniel lest he try to snatch her friend, "Priscilla, you need to run, now. He might have others here working for him. Please!"

"Ha!" Priscilla mocked. "You really didn't fill her in, did you?"

Confusion clouding all present judgment, Rose turned to face Priscilla. Just as her eyes locked with Priscilla's, the tip of an arrow met her forehead. Priscilla held her bow taught, the release to kill. Priscilla's curled fingers touched her porcelain cheek. What Rose found most terrifying was the one sided smirk. Pricilla's blue eyes were poisonous darts. The creature before her looked nothing like the mild-mannered princess she had so often looked up to.

"Priscilla, what…what's the meaning of this?"

Priscilla exhaled and lowered the bow, her eyes crystalline fire. "I'm truly sorry it has come to all this."

Rose dared not speak. The magnitude of this moment stifled her words.

"Won't even give me puppy eyes will you? Rose, ever the strong one, the determined one, the adventurous one, the one who receives all the attention I ever…"

"Silence," Daniel's voice rang beside Rose.

Rose stepped back so that she could see both Priscilla and Daniel together. She looked from one to the other, how easy they were in each other's presence, how Priscilla looked at Daniel, the way Daniel looked at her. The hazy glass this scene had been set in—the glass now crashing down all around her so she could see in perfect perspective the fullness of the game she had been pulled into, perhaps, not even from this past late spring but from years and years ago.

Both Daniel and Priscilla tried to read what her reaction would be next.

Rose looked to Priscilla, "It was you, wasn't it? At the cemetery when Dave…when Dave and I were digging up that grave?"

Priscilla's eyes glinted with mischief.

Rose continued, "You didn't miss."

The sweet smile Rose had only ever known was now the source of betrayal and pride. "I never miss," Priscilla purred.

Rose took a step back.

"Don't move another inch." In one swift move, Priscilla lifted the bow and drew back her arrow. "I'll put this through your foot. How will you ever attempt to escape?"

Despite Pricilla's betrayal, an impenetrable exoskeleton had formed around her heart, making her immune to further heartbreak, albeit her "friend's" taunt. Anger rushed through her veins.

She swung her gaze to Daniel while pointing at Priscilla. "That's how you knew I had found my father's gold. Her father at the claims office, well, he's not even her father!…it was a set up, wasn't it?"

"You're a smart girl, just not smart enough to outplay me." Daniel took a step toward Rose and reached for her hand.

Out of the corner of her eye, she could see Priscilla's arm trembling.

Daniel asked, "Have you reconsidered my offer?"

Rose stood firm, "This revelation changes nothing."

"Well, in that case…" Daniel bowed toward Priscilla and indicated toward Rose with his hand.

Priscilla's arm tightened even more, one more second, the arrow would be loosed…

Rose shouted, "Wait! At least let me die with the dignity of having all my questions answered."

Daniel's face saddened, "I'd rather spare you the details, dear Rose, for you might not die by the arrow but by a broken heart."

"My heart's been beaten around too many times to be hurt anymore." Rose saw Priscilla loosen her grip.

Priscilla gritted out. "You asked for it."

Daniel began his tale: "This story begins even before you met Prissy. The first time I saw her was…. When I first came to British Columbia, I began to frequent a certain madam's house. The drink was always ready, and the girls were excellent. One day, I noticed that a very young girl began entertaining men like myself at the establishment. She was the madam's niece or so this madam claimed. After a buxom girl from San Francisco finished her evening with me, I moved down the hall to exit the upstairs' rooms. Suddenly, I heard a struggle in one of the bedrooms. It sounded like crashing furniture. I broke through the door thinking the poor girl inside had become a victim to men who like to inflict torture rather than play. The man was cowering near the headboard. Then I saw her…" he pointed to Priscilla. "She was half undressed, a knife in her hand, ready to throw it at the man. And she did, knifed his ear to the board. This the madam's niece."

Rose tried to remain stalwart throughout this story. Everything she knew, had loved, had been a lie. She couldn't look at either of them, so disgusted was she.

Daniel continued, "I saw potential in Prissy. She was beautiful and deadly. I knew I had to have her in my arsenal. I bought her from her aunt for a handsome price. She's been mine to do my bidding ever since."

"What does this have to do with me?" Rose raised her voice.

"Ah, of course, this is where you come in. When Harland Wood began his business here, rumours began to float around about his having found a glorious treasure. I began my master plan. I'm a patient man. It's taken many years to come to fruition, but here we are. I then heard Harland Wood had brought a daughter with him and put her in finishing school. This is where Prissy was to infiltrate, your head and your heart. She did it. You never suspected a thing, did you?"

Rose shook her head.

"You see, Prissy is the ultimate con woman. She can get anything out of anybody. She can appeal to the innocent and the guilty alike. Before I put her in school, I trained her in knife-fighting, guns, anything I could think of except her specialty. One day, we were trading with some Indians who had a bow and arrow. My Prissy picked it up and pinned my hat to the tree I was standing beside."

Rose picked up from where Daniel had left off. "You put her in school. She became my friend. What about her family? Her brother who died?"

Priscilla laughed, "I pulled the hood over your eyes before you could even blink. I have no family except Daniel."

Daniel resumed, "You see, Rose, how you never had a choice in this matter. I pre-planned everything. You can thank Prissy for the sweet death notes and threats she left for you in your home. Also, enjoyed stealing some lead ropes and other small supplies just to keep the frustrations ever brimming at the surface. She was the only one who could have pulled it off."

Not the only one.

"What I didn't count on, dearest Rose…" Daniel stood before her.

"I can't get a clean shot," Priscilla shouted.

"Was falling for you, wanting you until you made me utterly mad." He kissed her savagely. "I have consolation that you're leaving this earth under my own hands."

Tears began to run down Rose's cheeks as she smiled and shook her head. "That's what you'll never understand. My life is my own. These are my terms. And my life belongs to those who truly love me and to God Almighty Himself." She looked to Priscilla. "It was you who killed my father."

Priscilla pouted, "I did you a favour. You hated him with every fibre inside you. He cried like a baby, crying out for mercy…"

"Stop!" Rose shouted.

"…for his only daughter!" Pricilla spit with venom.

"Enough!" Rose turned her head away, fighting to breathe. "Dave had nothing to do with it. He was…is innocent. You!" She jabbed her finger into Daniel's sternum.

He wrapped his hands around her arms and squeezed them until she cried out. He seethed, "I couldn't have you with him. I needed you to myself. I just had to place the seed of doubt for you to destroy the man who loved you. You're the one who's so distrusting of everyone."

She looked around flabbergasted at her foolishness, at her own loss all over again. "You're right."

"I was never lying. He's my cousin though not by blood."

Yes, now I could see how that could be.

Rose demanded, "Where is he? What have you done with him?"

"I've been his jailor for the last little while," Priscilla murmured. "I've been treating him real fine. He's been getting the best entertainment in town."

"You little bi…"

"He has been beaten up a few times by that horrendous Percy."

Rose ground out, "Well, that doesn't surprise me one bit that he's working with the two of you."

Daniel laughed, "You should thank me that he hasn't touched you after the last time in the alley, upon penalty of his life. At least, you've had the best."

Rose smiled sweetly, "Yes, I've had the best, but it wasn't you."

Daniel's eyes became black slits.

Rose continued, "You'll never have won because you never had my heart. Only Dave ever had that. What little you did have cannot compare."

Daniel shouted, "Prissy, aim well, and you'll have me all to yourself tonight."

"With pleasure," she drew her bow.

"Before you do, I have information that you don't have."

Daniel stomped around and barked, "What is it?"

Rose leaned on her toes, "I'll not tell you unless you let me go. I know who your true parents are, where you came from."

A wretched look of pain overcame his face. He steeled it seconds later. "I don't care where I came from, who my parents are. You're veering from this game and I'll not have…"

Just then, two gunshots rang out. Priscilla loosed her bow, the arrow whistled past Rose's cheek. Instinctively, Rose fell down and huddled. Checking for blood, her hands roamed over her body. She heard scuffling in all directions, men grunting. Her eyes were shut tight for fear someone could see through her imaginary cocoon. When no hands touched her to kill her, she put her hands to the ground and looked up to see the commotion before her. There was Joe and the Mountie on one side grappling with Daniel's arms and legs. Surprisingly under all his airs, he was remarkably strong, fending off both men with fortitude. To the other side, she found Dave straddling Priscilla, pinning her hands behind her back and tying them with an expert knot.

Priscilla laughed and said under her breath, "Changed positions have we, Dave?" Then she winked at Rose.

Rose's anger skyrocketed as she glared at the traitor. Her anger immediately diminished as soon as she heard…

"Rose." Dave called out.

True to Priscilla's words, his face was the picture of bad bruising. He had a black eye, his lid heavy. Multiple scabs littered his cheek as if nails had slashed across. He had a fresh bloody lip. Despite all his scars, the relief flooding through Rose's body was overwhelming. She was frozen in place, basking in his gaze, hoping he could forgive her for her lack of faith in him.

He slowly walked to her, one leg a little stiff. He stopped five feet away and looked at her. A small smile crept upon his features. With that smile, all the hope in the world swept her in its embrace.

Joe suddenly became the focal point of her vision. "Miss, are you all right?"

Her lingering gaze behind his shoulder finally turned toward him. "Yes, I'm so grateful you came. How...?"

"You'll get the whole story once you've gotten some good sleep in ya, all right?"

Her body aching for a downy mattress, she wouldn't argue.

Joe edged her toward the Mountie, "Are you okay to walk down with him? He'll be wantin' to ask you some questions."

"Of course."

"He's taking Mr. Shaw and Percy straight away to Perth with the other lawmen. You're safe now."

"I know." She turned toward the Mountie. "Sir, you wish to speak with me?"

***

A few of the Mountie's men grabbed Daniel and hauled him down the mountainside. As the Mountie and Rose made their way down the mountain, Joe turned to Dave who was giving Priscilla to another lawman. "Young man, I gotta thank you for all you've done. I'm ashamed to say that I never thought much of you. I see now it's because I never thought anyone could be good enough for my...Miss Rose, you see.

You've proven yourself to be reliable and faithful." Joe shot out his hand to shake Dave's.

Dave took it and returned the gesture. "I know you were just protecting her. I really…um…"

"I know you love her. It's written all over your face. That was my face a really long time ago. Say, you want to stay at the mile house? You could use the rest and Rose will want you there."

"I will, thanks."

Joe and Dave started down the hill, leaving Priscilla behind with the young lawman. Suddenly, they heard a shout and a groan. They looked up to see the lawman flat on the ground with Priscilla nowhere in sight. They ran to the man to see a small knife sticking out of his gut.

Joe growled, "Where is she?"

The man's head lolled to the side. "I…I don't…" He passed out from shock.

Joe pushed Dave to his feet. "Go find her."

Dave looked into the surrounding forest. "She's long gone. Her survival skills are stunning to say the least. Her fighting skills are supreme."

Joe hardened his gaze. "I told Rose she's safe."

Dave replied, "I guess it's a necessity I stay with you, isn't it?"

"I could use your help. We'll tell her about that witch once she's rested."

"I agree."

Once they reached the bottom of the mountain, they found all the Mountie's men on their horses. Hands bound, Daniel was already tied to the pommel of his saddle. The Mountie was about to help Rose mount her horse.

"Sir, let me ride with her. She's tired from what's happened." Dave said, as he swung up.

The Mountie replied, "All right, boy. Make sure she doesn't fall off."

Dave wrapped his arms around her and smelled her hair as he said, "I won't let her go." He eased Horse forward, aware she might not want to start at a fast pace too soon. He followed the men through the woods, weaving this way and that.

***

Remembering the planes of his body against hers, feeling at home with him, Rose lay her head against his chest. She was able to murmur a *thank you* before sleep claimed her. She didn't even feel Horse break into a canter at the edge of the forest.

So tired was she, she barely registered when they arrived at the mile house. Still asleep, she felt Dave pick her up and cradle her to his chest where she could breathe him in. He stripped off her jacket and slipped off her boots before pulling the covers over her. Before he left, he kissed her forehead, both cheeks, and tentatively, her lips before leaving the room.

Wou'd you gain the tender creature?
Softly, gently, kindly treat her,
Suff'ring is the lover's part.
Beauty by constraint, possessing,
You enjoy but half the blessing,
Lifeless charms, without the heart.
John Gay

Chapter 26

She uncurled her fingers from clutching her blanket and slowly wiggled them. A stretch slithered through her body. She opened her eyes to see the wall opposite her window. The shadow of her lace curtains played along the wall. The gentle breeze kissed the baby hairs on the back of her neck.

She turned to see what time of day it was, to fully embrace the newness of the day or night. She found Dave sitting in a chair next to her bed a few feet away. He wasn't awake. Rather, he had dozed off, his chin resting in the spot between his sternum and shoulder.

She was a little surprised to see him at her side and chided herself. The way he had held her on Horse last night spoke volumes of how he had not held anything against her for the way she had treated him. Messy tears ran down her cheeks, so sorry was she for everything he had endured because of her. Unlike her, he never let go.

Her sniffles made him stir. She attempted to stop immediately so he could sleep.

He opened his eyes and found her in distress. He leaned forward in his chair and wiped away her tears. His thumb moved so lightly. "I'm here," he whispered.

She nodded and propped herself up on her elbow. She began to finger the fringe on her quilt. "Dave…" She looked up to find him staring at her with such care unlike the lusty looks she had endured from Daniel. "I've wronged you at every turn, from the start to the end of this journey. I'm sorry more than I could say. Could you ever forgive me?"

The twinkle in his eyes brightened, "That's the thing. This isn't the end of our story. You have a lifetime to repay me."

Her eyes darkened in mischief, "You gloating, self-conceited…"

"Really…" He took her hand in his. "Even if you never did *repay* me in the way I think I need it, I know your heart, your intentions. You never meant to hurt me."

"Do you?" she whispered intently. "I must admit I was too concerned with what I wanted to pay much attention to how it would affect you."

Dave replied, "You changed."

Rose's hand moved to his face and carefully touched each bruise, each hurt. She came to the slice of scratches and questioned him with her eyes.

He acknowledged her question with a nod and exhaled, "That was a special set of torture under your friend Priscilla's hand."

"Tell me," Rose breathed. "I need to know what she did to you."

"What she almost did to me—she was my jailor most of the time. Percy took over occasionally when she had an important errand to run. After our meeting in the meadow, she brought me back to the cabin where they were holding me. That night she offered to shave my beard. I didn't say no. It was getting really scruffy and long. She was sweet about it, making sure she didn't scratch me anywhere. I thought, 'Maybe Daniel's got some kind of hold on her, and she has to do his bidding.' Made sense. She'd been subdued and quiet all the previous times I had seen her. Once she was done, she washed out the bowl and walked toward me. I was strapped to the chair with my hands tied behind my back, my feet tied to the legs. She began to unbutton my shirt until it was completely open. I asked her what she was doing. Then she stroked my thighs and began to unbutton my pants. I leaned back as much as I could and demanded what she was doing. She said she wanted a little fun. I couldn't bear for her to touch me. I flipped the chair so that I landed sideways. That's what this bruise is from." He ran his finger alongside his right cheekbone.

"Then she scratched you."

"No, not then. Then she said if I wouldn't play with her that I'd have to watch the entertainment and not physically enjoy it. She began to unbutton her clothing. Right away, I closed my eyes. I could hear the clothing slipping to the floor, but I kept my eyes shut tight and asked God to keep me strong, to not let this perverted woman continue. Once she was done, she walked over to me and demanded I look at her. I kept my eyes shut. She started yelling, going on about the hold you have on men and that I needed to look at her. I didn't. That's when she couldn't take it. She scratched me and spit in my face. I would take that any day compared to her toying with me the way she wanted."

"I can't believe…it turned out like this, that she was a completely different person than who I believed her to be."

"Daniel was right. She was his weapon. She could charm her way through anyone, almost." He grabbed the glass on her bedside table. "Would you like a drink?"

Rose nodded and drank from the proffered glass.

Once she set it down, he said, "Daniel not wanting you to be with me wasn't the only reason why they captured me. When you introduced me to Priscilla, I had this nagging feeling that I'd seen her before, somewhere. All the while we were dancing, it was in the back of my mind, but I couldn't figure it out. When you left with Daniel, I decided I'd ask her myself. She said she was sure she hadn't seen me before. As she said that, she had this specific look on her face that made me remember where I had seen her.

"It was a night I was going to Daniel's office. I found them kissing. She turned to look at me over her shoulder just as Daniel pulled a heavy hood over her head. I told her I'd seen her and told her where. She lured me to the back door saying she had information about who was behind all of the threats. She said she was scared. I really believed her. When we went through the door, there were four men who knocked me out. Next thing I knew I was in the cabin, my head all fuzzy."

Rose exclaimed, "I looked for you all over that night! Daniel led me to believe that you were in cahoots with him and that you had killed my father. When I couldn't find you, I felt it was proof of my assumptions. I was completely wrong." Seconds passed before Rose asked, "The meadow! How did you escape?"

Dave looked down at their intertwined hands. "I didn't. It was...a *kindness* my cousin allowed me before he would kill me. Turns out it was the hardest moment of my life, more than all the battles I faced, more than all the men I've killed. Not being able to be there for you, to tell you everything...to watch you in agony, it killed me. I couldn't move, couldn't tell you a thing.   "Before you arrived, I was introduced to Priscilla's sharp eye with the bow. There was a deer running at full speed, and she shot it down with one arrow through the eye. That was my warning. I wasn't to speak or even lean forward. She would pierce me through the head. That's why I did nothing, could say nothing."

Rose lay her head back down, pondering over every word. It all made sense.

Dave moved a stray strand of hair from her face and softly stroked her cheek. He swallowed hard. "Did he ever hurt you? Did he ever touch you?"

Of course, he'd want to know. I wanted to know everything.

In hushed tones, she recounted her encounter with Daniel in his office the night of the dance. Her encounter with him in Barkerville, after meeting Dave in the meadow—this is where shame was written all over her face. Every detail she relayed, she imagined his regard for her shrinking until it was null. When she had finished her shameful account, she said, "You must not think of me the same, do you? I've done things, felt things…"

He put his finger to her lips and leaned so close his forehead was touching hers. "Don't say that. Nothing has changed the way I think about you. You were stuck with a mad man. You did what you thought was best. And how you felt…I think I can understand. Never doubt what I think about you."

What are your thoughts of me?

Rose closed her eyes. She was amazed that despite everything that had happened, they had found their way back to each other. She laid her head back on the pillow and closed her eyes. A restful smile graced her visage.

"I've been waiting a lifetime to see you smile like that. Speaking of which, I should leave you to sleep." He rose from his chair.

She groped until she grazed his pants to find his fingers again. "Please don't. Please don't leave." She opened her eyes to see him scooting his chair a little closer until his knees touched the side of her bed. He laid his head down beside her resting form. One hand grasped his while her other hand swept through his unkempt hair. In a few moments, she fell asleep.

Later, a knock at the door woke her up. It was Joe. Her hands could still be found where they had originally settled.

He whispered as low as he could, "Supper's ready. Jack's insistin' you come down and eat. Did you sleep enough?"

"Yes, I have. We'll be down in a few minutes."

"All right. I'll tell Jack." Joe closed the door.

Rose rubbed Dave's shoulder until he grumbled, "What?"

"Time to eat, sleepyhead."

He lifted his head and smiled. "You slept more than I did."

She sat up. "And how is that?"

"I stayed awake until…I felt for sure you were safe."

Rose drew her covers. "I am safe, am I not?"

Dave bit his lip. "I won't keep this from you, but let's go downstairs for now. Let's eat. You'll know the whole story then." He got up from his perch and started toward the door. "I'll wait out here."

Once the door was closed, she slipped out from underneath the covers, changed from her trousers to a comfortable day dress. All the while, she racked her brain and tried to think of how she couldn't be safe. They had caught Daniel and Priscilla. What other dangers lurked now?

She opened the door and found him waiting with his hands behind his back. He gave her his arm. She took it, and they headed downstairs.

For, those that fly, may fight again,
Which he can never do that's slain.
Samuel Butler
c.3, 1.243

Chapter 27

As soon as Rose entered the dining room, her loved ones, holding glasses of champagne, stood up and cheered for her recovery and wellbeing. She glanced at each face and found one particular one missing. The brutal truth of Priscilla's betrayal was a hammer poised to strike her heart should she relinquish any control of emotion.

Miss Craig came forward with two glasses, one for her and one for Dave. Emily's eyes were red-rimmed and puffy. Joe must have told her everything while Rose slept peacefully all day.

Rose looked to Joe and mouthed a *thank you*. He nodded in return. There had been too many burdens on her shoulders. There was no possibility of carrying more for another.

Dave put his hand upon the small of her back. Instead of recoiling from his touch, she leaned into it. He led her to her chair and took a seat next to her.

From the smells floating from the kitchen, Rose knew Jack had gone all out. She turned to find him entering with a large pan of roast beef, already pre-sliced. Emily helped bring in a plate of roasted potatoes and a dish of carrots and peas.

Rose breathed, "What a feast! Jack, you've outdone yourself."

"It's all for ya, dear girl. Ya've returned alive. Dat's all I was hopin' for."

Joe remarked, "You probably have a lot of questions. Let's eat first. Then we'll go to the living room and talk, hm?"

"I can wait, especially with all this delicious food sitting in front of me." Rose agreed.

Dinner was quiet, not for lack of celebration but for the enjoyment its recipients savoured. They all had a trying day, this their time of rest and fulfilment. There was no lack of fondest looks being passed around, of silent, loving communication. Many times Rose felt Dave's hand wandering underneath the table to grasp her own, to sweep his fingers against hers.

Once everyone had finished what was on their plates (many of them had seconds), Jack began to clear the table with Emily as his helper. Rose could hear him putting on the tea kettle and preparing the spread of dessert and tea. Dave wiped his mouth with his napkin and placed it upon the table before helping Rose to the living room.

Everyone helped themselves to tea and dessert before Rose uttered her first question, the one that had been gnawing at the back of her mind during their pleasant supper. "Am I safe? I need to know."

Joe and Dave looked at each other before Joe answered, "Priscilla escaped."

Rose covered her mouth with her hand. "How did it happen?"

Dave covered her free hand with his. "The man responsible for her—he was behind us. Next thing we knew, he was flat on the ground with a knife in his gut. By the time we got there, it was too late."

"She can still come for you," Joe announced.

"Nothing is going to happen to Rose, not while I'm here." Dave stated.

Joe added, "One of the Mountie's top men is here. He'll guard the house until we find Priscilla."

Rose turned to Emily, "Miss Craig, I'm so sorry for…the knowledge of your son. There are no words for how unfortunate…"

"No," Emily's hand was outstretched. "I'm sorry for all my son has done to you, for the man he's become. I know I had a hand in that. The choices I made never amounted to raising a child well." She began to whimper, her tears spilled.

Joe reached for her hand, "The choices *we* made."

Emily reached for her handkerchief. "I thought I was doing the right thing by him, being willing to give him to well to-do people who would have the means to take care of him. I don't know what kind of people they were…"

Dave butt in, "I do. It's true I'm Daniel's cousin but not by blood. I met him once when my aunt, my mother's sister, came to visit us down South. She was a hard woman, couldn't feel a flicker of love from her. She cast my mother to the side for marrying beneath her station. I remember Daniel being there when she visited. I could tell he was afraid of her. He must have been about twelve. Can't imagine what it must have been like to have her as a mother. The father, well…my ma could barely say a word about him. All she did was shudder. That told me everything I needed to know.

"Years later I decided to come this way and find him. He was the only blood relative I had left from what I knew. Don't know what happened to his parents. Apparently they died, and he inherited everything. There were no other children. My aunt was barren.

"He told me he had been sent to the best law school back east and was given every single penny. He had never been in want or need. He asked if I wanted to be a part of his company of men digging for gold. That's exactly what I came up here for so I said yes. We drew up a contract and that's that. I knew he had his vices, but I never thought…that it would all come to this."

"More tea, anyone?" Jack asked.

Everyone said yes. Their cups were refilled.

After drinking a few sips, Rose smiled and asked, "I must know. Joe, how did you…? You were at the mountain and…"

Joe's gaze became hard as he replied, "I knew somethin' was goin'. You didn't have to tell me. This time…it seemed as if this was your last goodbye, like it was the end. My gut feelin' was to send a telegram to the Mountie. That same night, I met him and his company a mile away from the house. Mountie Doug and I have been good friends for a long time. He owed me a favour. A little before midnight we set off for the mountain."

Rose sputtered, "How did you know where to find it?"

"I snuck into your bedroom while you were in Barkerville. Looked under the bed and found the box with the map inside. Back when you figured out the puzzle the first time, Jack told me how you had to light up the map from behind. I was pretty sure I could figure where the gold was so we went. I assumed the second creek was now the lake. We went up the mountain a quarter of the way and sat quietly, waitin' for you to come.

"I thought you'd be there earlier. Mountie Doug was startin' to think I was wrong. I was doubtin' myself, too, thinkin' I was goin' loony. Finally, we heard you. Then we saw you light your lantern and go into a small cave. Almost as soon as you went in, we saw Shaw, Priscilla, and another man. I whispered to Doug to tell his men to get 'im, but Doug told me to be patient, that it would only be lawful to catch him in the act. Shaw went up first. As soon as you and Shaw came out of the cave, Priscilla handed Dave over to the man. A few moments later, the other man was down and Dave was makin' his way up. I grabbed him from behind a tree and told him of our plan. On Doug's signal…"

"How could he signal you in the dark?" Emily asked.

Joe answered, "Owl hoot. As close to the real one as you can get. We all moved up and bided our time. Doug heard everythin'. When he saw Priscilla was about to make her move he signalled his men to shoot Shaw in the leg. Priscilla…we shot near where she was. That gave Dave enough time to tackle her before she recovered. I figured she hadn't been shot."

Rose added, "That explains why she escaped so easily. How did you escape Percy, Dave?"

He shrugged and smirked, "That was easy. Percy's a drunk. He turned around a few moments after Priscilla left to take a swig of whiskey from his canteen. That was all I needed to clobber him over the head. Then I found a knife on his belt. I cut the rope and started making my way up. That's when Joe filled me in."

Rose sipped the last of her tea and shook her head. "I'm amazed at how blessed I am to have all of you in my life, yes, even you Miss Craig. I remembered all your lessons when I finally decided this past summer I was ready to grow up."

"There's one more story you haven't heard, Miss Rose." Jack spoke up.

"What's that?"

"Joe told me about his gut feelin'."

Here Joe groaned.

"He thought he might be goin' crazy, might not 'ave acted on it if I hadn't pushed 'im." Jack gloated.

Rose chuckled and everyone joined in.

Jack slapped his thighs and declared, "I think we should all getta bed. Whad 'y a say?"

Everyone mumbled their agreements and rose from their seats. Emily went to her room. Jack and Joe marched into theirs. Dave waited until Rose got up from the sofa to escort her to her room. Rose's hand wavered on the banister.

Wearing a concerned frown, Dave closed the distance between them. "What's wrong?"

She smiled and said, "I feel completely happy. I know Priscilla's out there somewhere. Maybe with Daniel out of the picture, she'll take this as a second chance, begin her life elsewhere."

He stroked her cheek.

"I think I'm going to stay downstairs and read for a while."

"Do you want me to stay?" he murmured.

"We have a lawman outside guarding the place. I think you can be off duty for one night." She giggled. "Go ahead and sleep."

As she turned, he snatched her hand. "Don't go tripping over me in the dark. You might end up on the floor again."

"Mm, I well remember." She picked a novel from one of her father's shelves and settled in the large armchair across the view of the entrance door. It had been so long since she had enjoyed a simple pleasure without a fretting thought troubling her. She never got past the first few pages. Her heavy lids slumped.

A cold hand on Rose's cheek—Rose's arms flailed as she awoke to find Priscilla's face inches from hers. Rose gasped, "Priscilla, what are you doing here?" She sunk into the back of her seat.

Priscilla retreated to a kneeling position at Rose's feet, her tear-stained face looking into Rose's. "Dear Rose, I had to come to you as soon as I could. I had to see you were well and…" Her mouth twisted in pain. "I have to ask for your forgiveness. After the mad rush at the mountain, I…asked myself what now? What have I gained from all this conniving and deceit?" She threw her hands in the air. "I've gained nothing! All those horrible, selfish acts, and for what? Thank you."

Could Rose deny these sentiments echoing of second chances, of repentance? For not too long ago, she had done the same, and not many would have believed she could turn around, be reborn.

Rose asked quietly, "Why are you thanking me?"

"For being the example I needed to see," she smiled meekly. "Thank you for listening to me now and not calling for the cavalry."

Rose breathed, "I don't know what to believe anymore."

"My escape…it's my second chance to live a better life. I can do anything I put my mind to, can't I? I just…needed to make my peace with you before I go. I promise you'll never see me again."

Rose couldn't decide whether she could trust her or not. If she truly wanted to change, could she deny her forgiveness when she had been forgiven?

Priscilla stood and wiped her tear-streaked face with the dirty sleeve of her dress. "Oh Rose, can you ever forgive me?" She placed her hands behind her back and stared at the floor in shame.

During this time, unawares to Rose, so captivated was she in seeing Priscilla and hearing Priscilla's plea, Dave had stealthily traveled down the stairs. As Priscilla asked for Rose's forgiveness, Rose saw him behind Priscilla pointing a gun at her head.

Her first instinct was to warn Priscilla, but she shut it down. She trusted Dave knew best somehow or other. He wouldn't shoot without provocation.

A foot away, he said, "Let go of the knife right now or I'll blow your brains out." The butt of his gun dug into Priscilla's head.

Priscilla didn't move her hands to the front.

Dave looked at her intertwined hands and the knife cradled between them. "If you do, I'll get my shot in before you can do Rose any harm."

Priscilla moved her hands to the front after Dave snatched the knife and threw it across the floor.

"Now put your hands behind your back."

Face clouded in anger, Priscilla did as she was told.

Dave turned to Rose. "Get some rope."

While Rose did so, Priscilla tried to get free by jutting her foot backward into Dave's leg.

"Ah, I don't think so." He ground her wrists together and countered her attack with his own legs.

Rose returned with some rope which Dave expertly wrapped around her wrists.

As Priscilla struggled against his grip, Rose said, "Priscilla, how I wish that whole spectacle were true! Your game is up. Why?" She looked to the knife on the floor.

"You had everything I couldn't. You had a father who loved you. You were just too stupid to see it. Everyone wanted to be you. Then you stole the one thing I love most. You managed to have Daniel besotted with you. I've wanted him for so long, wanted him to look at me the way he does you. I've been intimate with him more than I can count but it never went beyond a way to fulfill his physical needs. And when we were together, I know…he was thinking of you. You had his heart in your grasp. Now I'll never have him. You took away the most important thing in my life. So I was going to take your life."

Dave tied her up to a wooden backed chair. He pushed the gun into Rose's hand.

"I…can't."

He wrapped his arms around her and positioned her arms into a gun-ready stance. He whispered in her ear, his hot breath caressing the spot behind her ear. "You can just for a minute." He went outside to find out what had happened to the lawman. Minutes later, they entered together. The lawman's head was cut, and blood seeped from the wound.

Dave inspected it. "It looks worse than it really is. Come, man, let's get you cleaned up. Rose, can you send a telegram to the Mountie in Perth? Tell him it's urgent."

She nodded and sent it straightaway while Dave took a cloth and water and dabbed the man's head and kept watch on Priscilla who was tied and gagged to the chair.

As Rose send the telegram, she heard Dave ask, "What happened?"

The man shakily responded. "I don't know. I was on patrol, didn't hear a thing. Next thing I know I'm out."

Dave muttered, "She probably took you down with a rock."

Rose returned, "It's been sent. We should expect him in the morning with a few of his men."

"Do you have any spare bedrooms? This man needs some rest."

"Of course, come follow me." Once she had shown the man his room, she went back downstairs to check on Dave.

He walked out of the kitchen yet stayed in sight of where Priscilla sat. "You need to get some rest." He put his hand on her arm. "You're safe now. I won't let her get away. I won't…"

She put her finger to his lips. "I trust you. That's why I didn't say anything when I saw you with the gun in your hand."

He grabbed her hand and put it to his lips, kissing it lightly all the way up to her elbow. "Get some rest."

"Let me stay with you."

"I want you as far away from her as possible, please."

"You'll have to settle with my lying on the couch."

He smirked, "With you so near, I don't know if I can properly station my post."

"All right, I'll go upstairs. Please take care."

"I'll not sleep a wink, I promise."

True to his word, he didn't. He pulled up a chair across from Priscilla's, albeit a good distance away and watched her all night.

She, knowing it was her end, didn't stir at all.

Victory at all costs, victory in spite of all terror,
victory however long and hard the road may be;
for without victory there is no survival.
Winston Churchill

Chapter 28

The following morning, Mountie Doug with three other men arrived late morning to escort the prisoner to Barkerville where the case would see its day in court.

Once he hauled Priscilla into the saddle, he turned to Rose and said, "Miss, we'll be needin' your presence in Barkerville during the trial. Another group of men are already escorting Mr. Shaw to Barkerville, where both prisoners will be charged."

"I've already booked my passage to England which will be leaving in the next few days. I don't see how…"

His steely eyes didn't flinch. "Miss, if we want to convict both prisoners, we need you there."

"All right, you can assure me the proceedings will be swift?"

"This is a high-profile case. Judge is already waiting in Barkerville. All other smaller cases have been put on hold so that we can get a quick judgment."

She nodded, "I'll leave first thing after lunch." She watched the Mountie move to Dave to say something and mount his horse afterward. The Mountie's company trotted off. Priscilla glowered; her eyes darkened from sky blue to ocean waters roiling under a storm's hand.

Dave strolled over with his hands in his pockets. "Looks like you'll have to settle for my company on another trip to Barkerville."

Rose lifted an eyebrow. "Will I?" She smirked. "It might not be so bad."

Dave swung his hat off his head. "Well, I never would have thought I'd see the day you would ever stoop so low."

Rose snatched his hat and hid it behind her back.

"Oh, no, you don't." Dave grinned and fought to reach the hat behind her back. He finally did—his fingers touching hers, his arms pinning hers. He breathed in the air shared betwixt them. "You'll gladly travel with me?"

She stared into his eyes, so close were those orbs of chocolate. "Mm, hm, although I believe Joe should accompany us."

He swallowed hard. "I think that's very wise."

Rose and Dave relayed to Joe the new travel arrangements. Before Joe could say anything, Emily bustled in and declared herself their official chaperone. She had to tie up loose ends in Barkerville before returning to Victoria for the new school term.

After lunch, the women headed to their rooms to pack while Dave, not having had anything to bring with him, took a long bath. Believing he was close in size to her late father, Rose had given him some of her father's clothes beforehand.

Around two in the afternoon, they saddled up and headed down the road toward Barkerville. They made a quick stop in Perth where Dave inquired into Daniel's move to Barkerville for his trial.

Once they arrived at their desired destination, they went straight to the hotel to rest a little before their dinner. Dave made sure the ladies were settled in their rooms before going off to visit with the reverend in town.

Rose awoke from her small nap and headed toward the church where she knew Dave had gone visiting. Just as she opened the door to enter, the reverend was walking out.

"Ah, miss, you're looking for Dave, aren't you?"

"Yes, he said he'd be here with you."

"He was for the last little while. You just missed him. He left about five minutes ago to collect whatever belongings are still at Shaw's camp. He told me everything, poor man. I knew something wasn't quite right when you came looking for him a while back the first time."

She smiled politely. Her guilty conscience rammed into the walls she had constructed around it, reminding her of the way she had treated the reverend, the way she had ridiculed him. "I wanted to ask for your forgiveness, reverend."

"Child, what for?"

She looked him straight in the eyes and willed her pride to back down. "For the way I spoke to you when I first met you, for…the way I have silently ridiculed you."

He smiled warmly. "I forgive you."

"Thank you."

He looked out toward the crowd. "You're Dave's girl aren't you?"

She looked out in the same direction. A peace settled over her soul. "We haven't put a name to it yet; but yes, you could say that."

"You take good care of him. He deserves a decent girl with a heart of gold."

"I don't know if I could call myself decent or say I have a heart of gold."

"No, not on your own merit, you couldn't. I have a feeling you know that."

She looked to him. "Very true. I do."

He nodded. "You go find him. I think he said he'd meet you at the hotel."

She put a hand to his arm. "Thank you, reverend, for everything." She walked back to the hotel where Dave stood waiting in the hall.

"Emily will just be a minute."

"I went looking for you at the church. Spoke with the reverend for a bit."

"And?" The smile he gave churned warm buttery feelings.

"We might have talked about you."

His face became serious suddenly. "Oh."

"He said you deserved the best. And you got it."

"Aren't we cocky tonight?" he drawled.

She placed her hand in the crook of his arm and said, "Let's enjoy a fine meal tonight before tomorrow's business."

***

Rose and Dave entered the court room, that is to say one of the larger log cabins found in Barkerville. All the spectators hushed as soon as she entered the temporary rustic domain of justice. Men sat on the one side, women on the other, and so divided were their opinions on Shaw's incarceration. One of the three circuit judges available at that time, exempting Judge Begbie, sat at the head of the room, languidly looking around the room. Rose secretly wished that Judge Begbie would have presided over the case, however, he was currently judging another high profile case featuring one of the roughest gangs in the territory.

Rose and Dave, the accusers, had been given a lawyer. They almost entered this case without one, due to the lack of skilled lawyers in the territory. However, one had shown up at the hotel this morning, saying he had been gifted to her. She had frowned in suspicion and wondered who would have pulled the appropriate strings. She had also tried to pry the information from him. He wouldn't divulge the secret. She settled on the very possibility that it could have been Mr. Nelson, for it was in his best interest that she would tie up all loose ends here to head home and sell him the 108 mile house. She had sent him a telegram with the basics of Shaw's reason of arrest and her need to close up shop for the next few days. She noted she would have to profusely thank him for the arrangement.

She and Dave had briefed the lawyer earlier that morning, and he was ready to jump in when the proceedings were to begin.

As Rose sat down, she observed Shaw's defending lawyer. Of course, he could call in a favour and whip up a lawyer who would know the in and out's of British statutes. Looking as impeccable as ever, Shaw entered and sat beside his lawyer. Every person in the crowd was as a statue, cursed to be a stone witness to the proceedings before him.

The trial began with Daniel being sworn in to testify to the truth, with his one hand on the Bible. He turned to wink at Rose once he swore his oath.

Rose muttered, "He's too confident. Do you think there's a chance he'll have an acquittal?"

Dave replied, "I hope to God he doesn't."

The case began with Rose's lawyer posing questions to Daniel about his involvement in the threats against Rose. He smoothly denied each of the claims and insisted he was present in each circumstance because of wrong timing and placement.

Then, Rose was called to the stand. She was surprised that her hands didn't shake. She had been sure they would. She took methodical steps to the stand and swore her oath. She vowed to herself she would speak the whole truth, no matter how much it hurt her character, to put Shaw away.

The defending lawyer arose and asked, "When did you first meet Daniel Shaw?"

"I met him officially on my way to my father's home at the 108 Mile House."

"Please expound on the term 'officially.'"

"I first bumped into Mr. Shaw on his way out of an office in downtown Victoria. We then eyed each other when I was walking in the public gardens with my class a couple of weeks later."

The lawyer's eyebrow lifted. "Class? Which school did you attend?"

"Angela College."

"Why were you out of class that day when you first bumped into Shaw?"

Her lawyer stood up. "Your honour, the question doesn't pertain to the case."

In the corner of her view, she could see Daniel bolting forward in his chair and glaring daggers at her lawyer. She turned to see her lawyer swallow a large gulp.

The judge lifted a placating hand. "I'll allow it. Go on."

The first stab.

Rose lifted her eyes from their view of the floor. "I ran away for a few hours for my own amusement."

The lawyer's eyes alighted and his mouth opened. "So, by your own admission, you're a rebel, a trouble causer. Who says you're not causing this trouble for Mr. Shaw now?"

Again her lawyer stood and called out to the judge. A rumble of voices slithered amongst the spectators.

Rose spoke. "I have to agree I was. I was young and didn't know what I wanted, except a father's love which was denied me. Over the summer, I learned many lessons. I am not the same girl." She looked to Dave for some kind of assurance.

He dipped his chin imperceptibly.

The lawyer continued with his questioning. "How did the nature of your relationship with Daniel Shaw progress?"

"We started seeing each other more often. He paid me his attentions. I willingly took them. However, that all changed when…I went to see him for some business matters. He took advantage of me against my wishes. That's when the threatening behaviour started."

"How do you expect a man to read your mind when you hint otherwise?" The lawyer turned to the crowd. "Women can be so unpredictable! One moment they want something, the next something else."

The men in the room chuckled. Already Rose was under the harsh glare of the women present. They now viewed her as a…

"Temptress! It seems to me as if she was the one manipulating the circumstances Shaw finds himself in now."

The rabble's noise now arose to such a pitch that the judge was forced to wield his gavel to silence them. Her lawyer cradled his head in his hands, shaking his head. The judge prodded her with his stare to defend herself .

"Yes, I was a foolish girl! I only realized the gravity of my actions once I saw where they were quickly heading."

The smug defendant lawyer slapped his desk and said, "No more questions, your honour."

Daniel's burning eyes made her own anger simmer. This was another game for him. He could not win again.

Her lawyer stood and asked her questions finally relevant to putting Shaw away. He did a marvellous job of quietly turning the audience, the jury, and the judge's attention to Shaw's probable guilt. However, Rose could see that the nature of her character had already been damaged, and it would be weighed heavily amongst the jury.

Dave was called to the stand next. His obvious relationship to Rose was questioned against the validity of his statements against Daniel Shaw. Daniel's lawyer ridiculed him and turned his statements into a circus show. Daniel had chosen his lawyer very well. Rose wouldn't be surprised if he knew without a doubt his client's true guilt.

The accusing lawyer again held up his side with unwavering fortitude and intelligence. The expressions flitting amongst the jury were disbelieving to believing the next when each side relayed their positions.

The Mountie and several of his head men were called to the witness stand, and each relayed an accurate account of what went down at Rose's claim a few nights ago. Once they were done, Rose peeked toward the jury. Their faces hardly relayed what side they would choose. Daniel could not walk, and yet his lawyer was doing an excellent job of portraying him as the victim of being framed because of his position and reputation.

"I have one more witness to call up, your honour." Her lawyer turned around to the back of the room and nodded in the direction of a man in the shadows, who stood up and made his way to the front. As soon as he crossed in front of her, Rose jumped in surprise because Percy was taking the oath. What a gamble! Who wasn't to say that he would botch the whole proceeding and secure Daniel's freedom?

Rose sat in amazement the whole time as her lawyer questioned Percy, and Percy replied in truth, painting his employer as the true criminal he was. He even brought up other unknowns that further solidified their accusatory stance.

Once he was done, the defending lawyer was asked if he had further questions, to which he shook his head. Daniel had his poker face on, but Rose knew he hadn't expected such a witness.

The jury left the room along with the judge. Shaw and his lawyer also left. The audience spread outside slowly leaving Rose, Dave, Percy, and their lawyer in the room. Percy and Dave's eyes met for a good long moment before Percy stomped out of the room. Rose's lawyer shook her hand, for he truly believed they would win the case after all.

When he left, Rose turned to Dave and breathed, "Can you believe it? How was he found? How was he even convinced to testify against Da...Mr. Shaw?"

Dave smiled, his eyes twinkling.

Rose's mouth opened. "It was you! How did you...?" She lowered her shout to a whisper. "How did you do it?"

"I paid his bail. Once he got out, I tracked him down to where I told him he would testify or be forced to leave the country. Percy's a coward, and he loves the possibility of his gold too much. I didn't even have to threaten him.

"He started whining about Shaw ruining him if he did testify in our favour. I pointed out that if he testified, he too, would be out of Shaw's grasp. Shaw would hang. I knew we had the witness we needed."

"I'm sorry for my part in all of this. I know my past behaviour wasn't conducive to putting him away on my own testimony."

Dave put his hands on her shoulders. "Don't. That's in the past. You were a girl, now you're a woman. Don't keep regretting past mistakes. You can move forward." Drinking in their moment of near victory, he circled his arms around her.

While the jury deliberated, Dave and Rose walked to their spot. They didn't need to speak. They sat side by side, one of Dave's arms around her shoulders. Rose's head rested in the crook between his neck and shoulder. So peaceful was the sound of the twittering birds, the branches creaking, and the Dave's breathing beside her that Rose fell asleep.

A slight shaking of her shoulders told her it was time to hear the jury's final say. The courtroom was filling up. No one spoke, the slow shuffling of feet was the only sound. Dave and Rose took their seat next to their layer. A few moments later, the judge appeared, and everyone stood in respect. Then the jury filed in one by one, their faces were stony and unreadable.

Rose began to play with a part of her dress, pinching it this way and that, afraid Daniel would be let go and that she would never be able to escape him.

The judge's voice rang out, "Member of the jury, what is your verdict?"

The chosen member of the jury stood up and said in a clear voice, "We, members of the jury, find Daniel Shaw to be guilty, guilty of being an accomplice to murder, threatening to kill a young woman, and guilty of kidnapping."

The judge's gavel came down to ring out judgment. Her ears rang, muffling the gasps in the crowd, the judge's instructions to the guilty party, even Dave's questions of her well-being. She had thought she would have felt an overwhelming sense of pleasure, of freedom. Instead, she was hit with the gravity of his sentence, twenty years imprisonment. The greatest feeling she now felt was pity, pity for the monster that had made her life miserable.

But I say to you, love your enemies,
bless those who curse you, do good to those
who hate you, and pray for those who spitefully
use you and persecute you...
Matthew 5:44

Chapter 29

The next day was Priscilla's hearing in court. Again, Rose and Dave were called on as witnesses. At Daniel's hearing, the courtroom had been packed so tightly that the stench of unwashed bodies had been close to overwhelming and the leg room had been sparse. This day, the number of the audience had dwindled considerably. Not even half of the chairs were filled. A welcome breeze bristled through the halfway open windows.

There were no women pressing upon each other to get a glimpse of the guilty party. Only a few half-interested men came out. One had already fallen asleep.

Priscilla was brought out, her golden hair was tied simply in a bun. Her hands were in shackles. Rose could see the same lawyer sitting beside her as the one who sat beside Shaw the day before.

Daniel's last gift to her.

Priscilla didn't even look at her or Dave as she came out and sat down. First, Priscilla was called to the stand to give her oath and to be questioned by Rose's lawyer.

266

Rose had to give her an outstanding ovation for the act she put on, crying so pitifully, saying she did all those things because her life was in danger, because she had no one to turn to. The lies, the tall tales made Rose feel sick. She was happy there wasn't much of an audience that Priscilla could sway.

Rose was called to the stand to give her account. Afterward, Dave gave his testimony and was cross-examined by the defence. Priscilla's lawyer had the same bulldog's tenacity he had shown the day before.

Both Rose and Dave were made to be seen as troublemakers, ones who were in cahoots to give their version of the story. He played his part perfectly of aiding a damsel in distress.

Once again Percy was Priscilla's downfall. Unbeknownst to Daniel or Priscilla, he was never supposed to have known of her involvement. Yet, one evening when Daniel and Priscilla were in confidence, he had eavesdropped and heard the entire plan of killing off Harland Wood, how Priscilla would be the one to do it. His incriminating statement of "She would do anything for Mr. Shaw 'cause she followed him with puppy eyes everywhere, even if 'e used her," mete out the final blow. She was found guilty, and her sentence was hanging by the neck until she was dead. The hanging would be on the morrow's afternoon.

Priscilla was taken out with a wailing of "It wasn't supposed to be like this! He promised!"

Rose put a hand to Dave's arm. "I don't want to be in town when she…um…Could we leave as soon as it's dawn?"

He nodded, and they headed back to the hotel. They heard Emily weeping in her room on and off the whole evening.

"You've been quiet all evening. Because of Priscilla?" Dave asked Rose at dinner.

"Strangely, no," she replied quietly. "It's Daniel."

Dave stopped eating and stared at her.

"I've been thinking about it all evening. I…I need to see him one last time. And…I don't expect you to understand…"

Dave's face fell ragged, and he clutched her hand. "Why? You don't have to see him. You don't owe him anything!"

"It's not that!" Her voice rose. A few faces turned to look their way. Somewhat unsure of where this was going, she looked to her plate of food. "I feel I need a few more moments of closure, that's all."

Pain clouded his eyes. "Don't do it, please."

"I can't explain it, I just have to."

Eyes averted, he whispered, "You still have feelings for him, don't you?"

"Not the kind you're thinking of. Now that I know his true history, the circumstances of his life, I can't but help think that he could have been a completely different person, with different dreams and ambitions…"

"You can't help him, you can't fix him."

She squeezed his fingers. "I know. I want to plant the seed of the idea and then let go." She got up and laid her napkin on her plate. She went over and kissed Dave on the head before leaving.

He held on as long as he could until her fingertips slipped from his.

People still milled about the main street. The town was thriving under some "good" publicity. She entered the jail and strode over to the Mountie's desk. Out of the corner of her eye, she saw Daniel lift his head and eye her lasciviously.

"Mountie."

"Miss Wood, what can I do for ya?"

"I would like a moment with the prisoner, please."

He lifted his brows in concern, "I don't think that's such a…"

"I'm asking for five minutes. You can be right outside. I promise to scream if anything goes amiss."

He rolled his eyes. "All right, five minutes, then I'm comin' in." He hooked his thumbs over his belt and strolled out.

She turned to face Daniel and walked toward him.

His onyx eyes drew her toward him as she pulled up a stool and sat a few feet away.

He rested his elbows on this thighs and straightened out his back. "You can't live without me, can you?"

She smiled, "I can and I will. This is my goodbye."

He purred, "Did you finally guess?"

"Guess?"

"Who did you think sent him?"

Her mouth open in astonishment, she took a step forward. "It was you? Why would you pay for me to have a more than proficient lawyer?"

He sighed, "I had hoped you would know…" It was the first time he was at a loss for words. Could it be that in some deranged, malformed way he loved her? His mischievous eyes returned. "I thought our last stand off before our union should be fair."

She looked at the ceiling and shook her head. "Fair? He wasn't to legally reprimand your lawyer in court when your lawyer decided to defame me. I hardly call it fair. I'm glad he had the decency to disobey your orders."

He rubbed his hands excitedly. "You are quite the vixen. At least I didn't leave you at a total disadvantage."

"I thank you for levelling the playing field a tad during the trial. It was quite thoughtful."

"Drop the charges. Don't you see? You and I, we can be unstoppable!"

"No, Daniel."

He stared intensely. "Why are you here?"

"I want to say I'm not angry with you. Instead, I pity you. I know the history of your circumstances which you never will, for you said you don't care to know. I want to let you know I forgive you for all that you've put me through. I needed to tell you that."

He got up and strolled to the bars. "Because you love me."

She took a step forward and smiled. "Perhaps I do, but not the way you think or want."

"You feline, teasing me with riddles."

A strange calm fell over her. "I am called to love my enemies, to bless those who persecute me. This is my parting blessing to you."

All the sexual nature of his glances and speech disappeared. Rose prayed he would understand the true nature of her statements. Could this be it?

A look bordering on wonderment and insanity appeared, lending him a boyish appearance. "I believe you."

She took his hand, the hand that had touched her in the most intimate of ways when she had prayed it would stop. She held his hand of sin with no resentment, no flinching and said, "Remember this moment as I will, goodbye." She turned and never looked back.

A woman's friendship ever ends in love.
John Gay
IV.vi

Chapter 30

The corded rope where Priscilla's neck was to be placed swayed ominously in the wind, The sound of the creaking boards of the gallows ushered in the new day. The dawn's rays stretched over the instrument of death as Rose, Dave, and Emily rode away from the grim sight. Rose truly believed she would wretch if she had to watch today's judgment. Little in the town stirred. It reeked of a ghost town.

Rose looked sideways at Dave, a grim expression plastered over his face. When she had returned at the hotel the night before, he hadn't been there, waiting in a seat for her. She had only seen him an hour ago when he came knocking on her door to let her know the horses were saddled and ready to depart. He had averted his eyes the whole time.

Her twitching arms desired to reach for his hand. She could only imagine what he had been thinking last night when she said she wanted to see Daniel Shaw one last time, the man who had been his rival for her heart. Truth be told, she hadn't known what exactly she wanted to say to him, only that she strongly felt she had to. Before she had revealed to Daniel the true nature of her visit—well, she had only known what to say the second before she said it. Then it was done.

She sidled Horse closer to Dave. She reached out to touch his arm, solid and unbending. "Can I talk to you?"

He said nothing but kept staring straight ahead.

Emily noticed Rose's gesture and the frigidity between them. She trotted on before them until they were two specks behind her.

"Dave?"

He savagely stopped his horse and abruptly said, "Do you love him?"

"Not the way you think I do."

"What is that? What am I supposed to think?"

She said calmly, "You think I love him in the romantic sense of the word. I don't."

Dave snorted.

She reiterated what she had relayed to Daniel the night before and stated how she didn't understand why she had to visit until the reason became crystal clear the second she needed it to be.

He spurred his horse into a walk and remained silent. His face was an impassive mask of contemplation rather than jealous anger. Minutes later, he pointed to a lone tree to the side of the road. "Race you?"

"Is this payback? You know I won't say no, you also know I can't win. I'll go along with it just to help you feel better."

They grinned at each other and set off at a gallop.

The next evening, after having arrived and having caught up with the bookkeeping, Rose lounged on the sofa and curled up her feet.

Dave came from behind and laid a hand on her shoulder, giving it a light squeeze. He walked around her chair and sat on the sofa beside her. Emily, Joe, and Jack came next. She yawned and said, "I have some important news I need to tell you." She turned to the chairs where Joe and Jack sat. "Joe, Jack, I've sold the Mile House to Mr. Nelson. It was my father's original intention until Mr. Shaw put together the imposter will. I've sold it to him for a good price. He's promised to keep you on at a more than fair wage. He's been needing some extra help recently. The agreement was in both of our favours."

Joe nodded.

Jack was flabbergasted. "You thought to take care of me, miss? I'm honoured. Thank you. I promise to make de best dishes for Mr. Nelson."

Rose exhaled and looked to each one of them. "Lastly, I'll be leaving the country in a few days. I'll leave here tomorrow, for I must catch my ship in Victoria in proper time."

Dave blurted, "Ship to where?"

"I have some business in England I need to take care of. Originally, the most imperative reason for my going was to escape Daniel's clutches. Now, that's not…however, I've written ahead to my aunt and cousins and to my father's previous banker. They're all expecting me to make speedy and safe travel to England. I was supposed to have left sooner, but I had to stay for the court case."

Everyone looked to each other, the news to sinking in. Their time together was at an end. Dave was the only one whose head hung low, his eyes not meeting anybody else's.

Rose whispered, "It's not my intention to leave any of you for years on end. I will come back. I just wanted to make sure you were taken care of. This is my home. I don't know what my plans are when I return, but I hope that each of you of you will be a part of my future."

Joe and Jack both got up and gave her a hug.

Jack's face was covered in tears. "God knew I needed you in my life when you found me in Quesnel. I promise ta be a good cook ta Mr. Nelson."

Rose gave him a kiss on his cheek. "Oh, I know you will."

Joe lightly grabbed her arm, "You've got to come back, ya hear?"

"That's what I wish. England used to be my home…I've found a new one with you." She whispered in his ear, "You make sure no one mistreats Jack on account of his colour."

Joe nodded firmly.

Hands in his pockets, Dave stepped toward her. "I'm bringing you back to Victoria."

Rose coloured, "Do I have no choice in the matter?"

He smirked, "No."

Emily interrupted, "Could I travel with the two of you? I must head back to Victoria for the school term. It's perfect timing."

Everyone began to climb the stairs in order to ready themselves for bed. Dave held Rose's hand at the bottom of the stairs until the last person disappeared from view.

He pulled her close. His hand slowly rose to meet her cheek. "Why are you doing this?"

"I don't want to leave this place, everyone, you… but I have to."

"Give it to me straight, Rose, no beating around the bush."

"All the aforementioned reasons still hold. There's another I must pursue. It's time I knew about my mother, who she was, what she was like, where she came from. The answers lie in England with my relatives and the people who knew her there."

His hand moved to her shoulder, "Then you won't be back soon."

She bit her lip. "I don't know how long. But, no, I won't be back soon. I don't expect to find you here waiting for me. I know everything is going to change and…"

"Then we'll change together. I'll always be there for you."

"Can you truly promise such a thing?"

He screwed his mouth tight.

"What if you move down South? What if you've found yourself someone to settle down with? What if?"

He barked a soft laugh. "You really think, knowing me so well, that a nice girl is going to be able to put up with me the way you do?"

"Yes," she said as the fear of losing him to another overwhelmed her. She buried her head in his chest and sobbed.

he arrived for dinner. All their talk steered clear of tomorrow's event, her departure.

As soon as Rose awoke the next morning, she rechecked all her luggage to make sure everything was in order. She made sure her boarding pass was secure. She put on her travel dress and pinned up her hair so that she could place the matching hat atop and secure it with her hat pin. She had never sailed across seas and an ocean on her own. It was entirely a new adventure, a thrill and fear snaking through her body.

She wished she could have Dave by her side. It was too much to ask. There had never been any spoken words of love between them. Could she equate words of love with the actions and other affectionate words they had lavished upon each other? She couldn't say. She never had any example to follow, only ones where the idea of love had been twisted to make only one of the individuals satisfied and happy.

Dave came knocking on her door and led her out, his hand on the small of her back. It was a brisk windy day as they drove the buggy toward the harbour. They arrived and saw the whole area was surrounded by newcomers from inbound ships. She went to the counter and showed her boarding pass. Dave tied the appropriate tags to her trunks and passed them to the stewards of the ship in charge of carrying the luggage.

Amongst the crowd of jostling men and shouts of direction, Rose and Dave stood together. The whole scene faded away—the deafening chaos of the occasional stranger bumping into them, the cries of the seagulls, and horns blasting

Dave wrapped his arms around her waist and intently stared into her eyes.

Unable to move, Rose shivered not knowing what to say or do except stare back. "I don't know if I have the strength to leave."

His eyes glowed fiercely and mischief spread across his whole face.

"What do you have up your sleeve now?" Rose tried to step back but couldn't because of his strong grip.

He looked around him and said, "I didn't know if I could do this now, if I could do this ever—I didn't know for sure until now." His hands moved to hers. Then in an instant he was down on one knee. "Rose, I fell in love with you the day I found you in the alley. It wasn't because you were a damsel in distress, and I was able to rescue you. I knew I needed to be a gentleman and help whatever poor girl was there. But then you opened your smart mouth and let me have it…I knew I could spend the rest of my life discovering who you really were.

"We've been on a journey together, and I don't want it to end. I want our whole lives to be one long journey that only ends until one of us dies." He looked up expectantly into her face, surprised to see her long face and sad eyes. He stood up and cradled her face in his hands. "What's wrong? If you don't love me, tell me."

She shook her head, the words wobbling, "It's not that. I can't make you wait."

"It's my decision."

"It would be unfair to you. You could be living your life and moving on."

"You don't get it, do you?" He laughed. "I only want to live my life with you. If I have to wait, so be it. I'm going to stay here, buy some land and build a house for us. I'm going to earn enough to be ready for when you come back. We'll write to each other, I promise."

Rose just looked at him, amazed. He had this all planned out. How long had he been thinking of this moment?

He inched his head closer. "Do you love me? I've already told you I do."

She whispered, "I do."

He inched his lips closer and grazed them over her ear and whispered, "I didn't hear you."

"There's no doubt about it, I love you."

"Those are the words I've been waiting to say and waiting to hear for a very long time." His lips moved from her ear to just above her lips where they hovered, waiting for an invitation.

Rose opened hers slightly to invite them in.

With the sea of men hooting and calling for others to watch the show, Dave and Rose were lost in a fire all their own. He pressed her against himself until he felt they had melded as one. Her arms wrapped fiercely around his neck, and her fingers dug into his hair—she had waited so long for this moment. She hadn't realized it until now. Their kiss was so intense she had to break it so she could take a breath of air. Before she could continue, a thought came to her mind.

She pushed away and said, "What about the ring?" Before he could respond, she giggled.

He laughed so hard as he put his fingers in his pocket and produced one before her eyes.

"This was the errand you ran yesterday?"

"Yup." He slid it upon her finger.

"I thought you said you weren't sure you were going to ask until a few moments ago."

"True, if I hadn't, I would have waited for you anyway and asked you when you returned. It was never an option to move on without you."

She fingered a lock of his hair. "I know that now, how true you are, that you won't abandon me. Now there's no choice for me to come back is there?"

He feigned shock. "You wouldn't have come back if I hadn't asked?"

She pouted, "I'm so pitiful. I would have come back even if you had moved on with someone else just to see with my very eyes that my chance with you was gone."

The horn of the ship blew, a five minute warning for all passengers to board and take their place on deck.

"I need to go. You just made it harder for me to leave," Rose whined.

Dave put his hands in her hair and kissed her again slowly, savouring every movement her lips made. "Write to me. When you come back, we'll be married and resume our adventures together." He walked her to the gangplank and watched her ascend.

As the ship pulled away from harbour and its horn blew on and on, she only saw one face, her fiancé's. She hadn't even had really good look at the ring, despite her insistence on one, because there was only one treasure that deserved her attention at this moment. Her eyes never strayed from his until the shoreline was gone. She memorized every feature and patch of stubble on his face. She memorized the twinkle in his eyes and the way his lips curved up in a smile.

She faced the ocean before her and looked down to see the ring he had given her as a sign of his promise, their promise.

Absence is to love what wind is to fire;
it extinguishes the small, it enkindles the great.
Comte De Bussy-Rabutin
pt.II

EPILOGUE

A year and a half later...

"Senorita, es tiempo de ir!" The sailor shouted as he
turned around to speak with the guide.
Time to go already?
"Un momento mas, por favor." Rose shouted over her
shoulder before gazing upon the Argentine skies, the skies that
had witnessed her mother's birth, her mother's days of play
and hard work, the day her mother met Harland Wood.

Her feet were upon the brink of the salt desert, its
crusty settlement making this whole experience surreal. The
snowy white sprites drifting above her made her raise her eyes
heavenward to watch their dance. The sparse tufts of rough
folia scattered throughout was the land's only embellishment.

She tightened her shawl closer around her neck, the
alpaca fur a soothing touch to the beauteous savageness of the
land. These last few days at the port of Ushuaia in the
legendary land of Tierra del Fuego had been some of the most
eye-opening in her life.

She was thankful she had taken those Spanish lessons
those last few weeks in England. She seemed to have an

affinity toward it, for she spoke it with much ease with those on board her ship. She would have to remember to write to Lord Faversham and thank him most generously for his time and help.

With an eager mind, she had soaked in the entire culture culminating in this land, the ever-present emphasis on family, the contentment she saw in their faces day by day though by her standards they lacked much. The sailor's gentle manners in guiding her through the streets and markets were to be remembered always.

In a few hours, she had come to love these people, her mother's people. Being here, she could feel a piece of her mother although she had never really known her. Yet she had come to know more of her mother's character through the special acquaintances she had made during her stay in England.

Her heart soared with the turkey vulture above her. She would forever keep this place in her heart.

"Senorita, ahora, por favor!" The sailor waved her over with a smile.

"Si!" She followed their tried and true steps back to the port where they were to sail soon back to her home, back to Dave. Thoughts of him were enough to stir her heart in a flurry. Would he be waiting for her on the docks? It had been a while since she had received a letter from him. At first, letters had flown between them as fast as they could fly a continent and an ocean away. They gradually slowed down and then…there hadn't been word for three months.

She was going home.

ACKNOWLEDGMENTS

Jesus, I wish to desire You more than anyone or anything in this world. May You be the treasure I seek above all.

To James, thank you for always being so supportive of my passions and gifts. I love you with all my heart.

To Felicity, thank you for being such a sweet daughter. You are a beautiful encourager.

To Edward, thank you for always being so affectionate.

To Elena, thank you for always putting a smile on my face. You're a natural comedian.

To Titus, thank you for filling my life with such joy.

To Veronika, thank you for being such a great beta reader and giving me clear constructive criticism.

To Cathy, you've saved the day again. If it weren't for you, I'd still be browsing endless forums on how to format my book. Maybe one day. the info will all sink in, I'll be just as good as you (there's hoping).

To Alexis, thank you for delivering an amazing cover photo again. You're always so keen on bringing my vision to life. It turned out better than I imagined.

To my brother Aaron, thank you for your enthusiasm to illustrate some of the scenes in this novel and delivering some great complimentary art.

To Saraih, thank you for being such a sport in getting dirt all of over your face for the cover. You delivered a stellar performance on both the shoot of the cover and the book trailer.

To Leidy, thank you styling Saraih's hair perfectly for the cover and book trailer.

To Anika, thank you for being the best on-set book trailer assistant ever! You were a huge help.

To my parents and Joash, thank you for sticking by me at the beginning of this incredible journey and being excited for every new project.

To Phil, thank you for all your prayers for my success and well-being. God bless you. Thank you for being my mentor.

To my book club ladies, thank you for being my core group of reading buddies and for supporting all my writing endeavours.

To my readers, both old and new, thank you for all your support, interest, and excitement. I hope you've enjoyed this latest instalment in the Canadian Reminiscence Series.

AUTHOR'S NOTE

I had such a blast writing this book. I was really going for a different feel from my first novel *Redeemed From the Ashes*. I couldn't help inserting a murder mystery into the tail-end of the Cariboo Goldrush. I'd like to shed some light on some of the entertaining highlights of writing this book.

Daniel's character really threw me for a loop when he started demanding I give him the profession of being a lawyer. At first, I didn't see how it suited my needs in developing him as a villain. I argued back and forth with this character for at least twenty minutes before I finally acquiesced and trusted my character knew better. Turns out he did (I promise I'm not crazy).

I came across the story of Judge Begbie dumping the contents of his chamber pot on a couple of men plotting to take his life while I was doing research on the Cariboo Goldrush and the Canadian West. I thought the story was too colourful not to weave into my novel. And so I did with great delight.

I struggled quite a bit with the idea of putting the real name of the headmistress who was running Angela College at the time of Rose's enrolment into the novel. I did quite a bit of research to find that particular fact. In the end, I thought it prudent and tactful to change the last name of the headmistress at the time and make her completely fictional since I have no idea what the real headmistress's personality and character were like.

Pretty Little Liars (particularly the Ravenswood scenes) and Edgar Allan Poe were heavy influencers for the beginning/middle chapters.

It was important for me to find the right mountain that housed Harland Wood's gold. I researched the topography of the area surrounding the 108 Mile House, keeping a two hundred mile radius. I looked for the mountain that would best fit the description I gave in my story. The mountain I found was none other than Eureka Mountain. Go figure!

Every step of writing this novel was exhilarating and a daring new experience for me.

As you may have guessed, Rose and Dave's story isn't over yet. Keep your eye out for their next adventure within the coming year.

Sign up for my newsletter

@

www.leahlindeman.com

You can also find me on

Twitter

Facebook

Instagram

www.ingramcontent.com/pod-product-compliance
Lightning Source LLC
Chambersburg PA
CBHW020957120726
47905CB00009B/2733